HER IMPULSIVE MARRIAGE TO THE HANDSOME STRANGER PROMISED TO BE A REFUGE FOR CAMILLA—UNTIL SHE LEARNED THE TRUTH ABOUT HER HUSBAND . . . AND THE SECRET THAT THREATENED TO DESTROY THEM BOTH. . . .

Marry In Haste

Jane Aiken Hodge

A FAWCETT CREST BOOK
Fawcett Publications, Inc., Greenwich, Conn.

MARRY IN HASTE

A Fawcett Crest Book reprinted by arrangement with
Doubleday & Company, Inc.

Library of Congress Catalog Card Number: 72-89109

Selection of the Young Adults Division of the
Literary Guild of America, February 1970

Printed in the United States of America

Marry In Haste

CHAPTER 1

Catkins shivered in the cold spring wind that blew bitter gusts round Camilla Forest's ankles. Shivering too, she pulled her light shawl more closely round her and wished for the warm pelisse that lay in her box. She had packed in such hurry and despair that there had been no time to think of the discomforts of a journey by the mail coach. Mrs. Cummerton, hysterical, reproachful, and then hysterical all over again, had insisted that she catch today's coach to London. What with her pupil's lamentations at her going, her employer's reproaches, and Gerald's insulting apologies, there had been no time for thought.

And now, at the lonely crossroads, she was beginning to wonder if she could have missed the coach after all. Mrs. Cummerton's coachman, who had deposited her here, had assured her with rough, unspoken sympathy that the mail coach from Bath would stop somewhere between half-past four and five. "Allays does, miss, allays has, allays will, for all I know. Has to pick up Lord Leominster's mail, see, him being a bigwig, as you might say, and own cousin to the Duke of Portland. So rest you here, miss, and wait for it," he had concluded, "and you'll be in London by morning sure as eggs."

And for a while she had been happy enough, after the day's alarms, to sit quietly on her box in the country road, listening to the evensong of starlings and trying not to think about what was past—and what to come. Memory of Mrs. Cummerton's insults was, she found, rather less unpleasant than expectation of what her father would say. He had told her this project would never do and he had been, odiously and, for once in his life, right. Best not think about it. She rose to her feet and took a brisk turn down the road to the corner from which the coach should come. The air was colder now, the shadows long, the starlings almost silent. It would be night soon, and where was the coach?

As if in answer to her question, she heard, far off, the rumbling of wheels and soon a carriage clattered into view. At first hearing it, she had hurried back to stand by her box, but as it came nearer, her heart sank. This was not the mail coach, with its sweating job horses, its coachman and uniformed guard, but a gentleman's carriage, drawn by four elegant bays. As it passed her, she heard an order shouted from within, the coachman reined in his horses, and when it stopped a little further down the road the groom jumped down from his perch and came back to speak to her.

"Excusing me, miss," he said, removing his livery cap, "but would you be waiting for the mail coach?"

"Yes." She looked at him doubtfully in the gathering twilight.

"Because if you are, master said to tell you it's met with an accident." Suddenly he became human. "We passed it not three miles back, as deep as you please in the mud, one wheel gone and splinter bar broke, coachman swearing hisself hoarse, passengers moaning and guard in fits on account of he'd lost the key to the mail-box as he fell. Only good thing is, it happened not five minutes' walk from the King's Head ... Anyways, miss, you won't see no coach before morning, if then, and so master said I had best warn you."

"It was kind of him to think of it. But what am I to do?" The question was addressed more to herself than to him, but he took it seriously enough.

"Why, what but go back where you come from and wait for tomorrow's coach. Master said as how I was to help you with your box, if so be you needed it."

"It is very good of him," she said again, almost automatically. Her mind was in a whirl. No coach tonight. What should she do? To return to Mrs. Cummerton's, after what had passed, was impossible. And yet, what else could she do? She turned again to the man. "Is there an inn at the village where I could spend the night?"

"Well, miss, I dunno," he was beginning doubtfully, when an imperious voice summoned him back to the carriage. With an awkward apology he turned and left her at a trot. With him went hope. It had grown darker as they talked and she observed that the coachman had spent his time in lighting the carriage's lanterns. A fine rain was now blowing in the wind and she felt its icy fingers begin to find their way through her shawl. Soon she would be wet through. Should she run after the man and put her plight to his unknown master? Surely no one would be so callous as to leave her benighted here. But it was already too late. The man had jumped back to the box and the carriage had begun to move. She watched with sinking heart, then felt her hopes revive as the coachman took his horses in a wide turn on the grass verge and drove rapidly back towards her. Again the groom leapt from his box, but this time it was to open the carriage door and let down the steps. A tall man in a many-caped travelling coat emerged, removed his beaver to reveal close-cropped dark hair, and approached her with a bow that would have won the approval of Brummel himself.

"I fear you are like to find yourself benighted here." His voice was low, pleasant, almost diffident. "Perhaps I may have the honour of driving you back to your friends' house. My man has informed you, I think, that the mail coach does not run tonight. But allow me to present myself: Leominster, at your service."

"And I am Camilla Forest, and much beholden to you for your kindness. If you would but be so good as to give me conveyance to the nearest inn ... " She stammered to a halt, painfully aware of how strange a request this must seem, how odd, indeed, her whole plight. And of all people it must be Lord Leominster who had discovered her—the haughty earl, Mrs. Cummerton called him, too high in the instep to take notice of his untitled neighbours.

"To the inn, Miss Forest?" He could not quite keep the question out of his voice, but turned, nevertheless, to tell his servants to take up her box, and then, taking her arm, helped her up the steps into the carriage. "But you are wet through." He settled her in a corner and wrapped a fur rug warmly round her. "This has been an ill-managed business on someone's part. You will pardon me if I ask what your parents are thinking of to let you be wandering about the countryside like this."

She gave a little laugh, half amusement, half bitterness. "I fear I owe you an apology for trespassing on your good nature under what I fear you may think false pretences. I am not a young lady, sir, but a governess."

His reaction to this tragic pronouncement, was, surprisingly, a laugh. "You are a very young one, then," he said, "or your voice belies you. And you must allow me the privilege of protecting you just the same. I have yet to learn that it is impossible to be a governess and a young lady at the same time."

This came near the bone and she found it, for a moment, impossible to reply. He was looking at her thoughtfully, and she was grateful for the near darkness of the carriage that hid her blush. At last he seemed to come to a conclusion.

"I have no possible right, of course," he said, "to question you about the predicament in which you find yourself, but surely there must be somewhere more suitable than the village inn for you to spend the night. It is not at all, I feel sure, what you are used to. And besides—forgive me—even a governess has a reputation to consider."

"Particularly a governess," she said, with some bitterness. "But needs must, Lord Leominster, and I shall rely on your goodness not to mention tonight's happenings."

"Oh, as to that, it is a matter of course." He sounded mildly affronted, then returned to the attack. "And I am to abandon you, then, to the tender mercies of Tom Marston at the Blue Boar and his slattern of a wife? Surely, Miss Forest, it would be better to return to your previous place, however terrible the umbrage in which you left."

She laughed, again with that mixture of bitterness. "I fear you mistake the matter somewhat, my lord. The boot is on the other foot. I have been turned off, in disgrace. I cannot possibly go back."

His laugh, in the darkness, echoed hers. "I see. And what heinous crime, I wonder, have you committed. No, no; a moment; let me guess. I do not for a moment believe that you have been making free with your employer's diamonds—or her port. But, let me see, she has an older son, perhaps, your charges' brother—indeed, I believe I could name him. You are come, I take it, from Mrs. Cummerton's house."

She gasped. "How in the world did you guess?"

"Easily enough. You must not think, because I am known as the arrogant earl, that I am not passably well informed as to what goes on in the district. I have a housekeeper who considers it her duty to keep me *au courant* with the local gossip. So naturally I know that Mrs. Cummerton recently engaged a French governess for her children and was thought to be giving herself considerable airs in doing so. And equally

I know of Gerald Cummerton—who does not? I can only
wonder at his mother's idiotism in engaging you in the first
place. But then, I always understood her to be a fool. The
only thing, I confess, that does surprise me is that you should
be French. You do not sound it."

"Thank you." Eagerly. "I do not wish to."

"No?" He considered it. "I remember about you now.
Mrs. Lefeu—my housekeeper—said you would never do at
Mrs. Cummerton's because—forgive me—you were so much
better born than your mistress. You are Mademoiselle de
Forêt, are you not, daughter of the Comte de Forêt."

"No!" Almost angrily. "I am Miss Forest, if you please,
English bred, if not English born. I ask you, sir, what is the
use of clinging to an empty title? For a year or two,
perhaps, it did well enough. One was always going back
tomorrow, or at least next week. But it is seventeen years
now, since we fled from France, and I have not found a title
much substitute for a competence. Nor does it seem likely
that we shall be returning in the near future."

"No," he said thoughtfully, "you are right there. Bonaparte
is well in the saddle and I do not suppose you would find it in
your heart to compound with him."

"I should think not indeed." She flared out at him. "You
do not understand, sir. My only memories of France are of
the Terror and our escape; of blood and tumult which killed
my mother—and my brother, too, for all I know to the
contrary. Do you think I wish to go back there, on any
terms? The only kindness I have known—and I have known
much—has been in England. I am as English as you, sir,
perhaps more so, because I know how lucky I am."

He laughed. "I am glad you think so. I would not, myself,
have considered it the height of good fortune to be waiting,
in the rain, for a coach that did not come. Nor, indeed,
would working, in any capacity, for Mrs. Cummerton be my
ideal of worldly bliss."

It was her turn to laugh. "Nor mine, I assure you, sir,
though in all fairness I should say that it was tolerable
enough until Gerald came home from Oxford. One of the
advantages of being a governess is that you see so little of
your employers."

"Indeed." He sounded amused. "It seems a barren enough
recommendation. But, tell me, what possessed your friends to
let you go as a governess in the first place?"

"What else could I do?" The bitterness was back in her voice. "One cannot go on, forever, depending on the bounty of strangers. Oh, they were kindness itself at Devonshire House, but ... " She paused. The less she said about life at Devonshire House since the Duchess's death, the better.

But he had turned away to look out of the carriage window into the darkness. "Here we are at the Blue Boar." The carriage had slowed to a halt and the groom now opened the door and let down the steps. Camilla made as if to rise, but Leominster remained seated between her and the carriage door, looking doubtfully into the darkness.

"I am sure I do not know how to thank you, sir," she began, but he interrupted her.

"No." Abruptly. "It will not do. You cannot possibly spend the night here, Miss Forest. It will be far better to risk your reputation at my house than your health here. And, for the matter of that, though I have no doubt you have heard me described as the proud earl, that, I think, must have been the worst of the slanders against me. Besides, I have an excessively respectable housekeeper in Mrs. Lefeu, who is also, as she frequently reminds me, my seventh cousin six times removed. I think you had much best pass the night at Haverford Hall."

Without allowing her time to answer, he gave the necessary orders and then settled back, with a sigh of relief, in his corner of the coach. "How I dislike making decisions. But you were speaking of Devonshire House. Were you indeed brought up in that *galère*?"

"Yes. My mother made great friends with the Duchess when she visited Paris in 1789." And then, returning to the matter in hand: "It is very good of you, Lord Leominster, but truly I do not know whether I should accept your kind invitation."

He gave an angry and, to her, unfamiliar exclamation, then continued on a milder though still formidable note. "You quite mistake the matter," he said; "you have not been invited so much as abducted. I am not the arrogant earl for nothing and I intend you shall spend the night at Haverford Hall. If it makes you feel any happier about it, I am probably old enough to be your father and have yet to meet the woman for whom I would trouble myself so much as to miss a day's hunting. You will be safe enough with me, a good deal safer than in the hands of the rascally landlord of the

Blue Boar, about whom I know nothing good. So, come, let us say no more about it and do you tell me, instead, what you think of Lady Elizabeth Foster."

"She has always been kindness itself to me." Her voice was dry.

"And therefore you found it necessary, on the death of your original patroness, to find yourself a situation." Again there was a note of laughter in his voice. "But it is not fair to tease you, Miss Forest, and you are right to refuse to gossip about her, and equally right not to remain at Devonshire House under such ambiguous circumstances. It is bad enough for the Duke's own children ... but I will not gossip either. Tell me, instead, what possessed you to think Mrs. Cummerton a possible employer."

"Have you ever tried to find a position for a governess?" she asked.

"Why, no, since you ask me, I do not believe I have. But what is that to the purpose?"

"Because if you had, you would not ask such foolish questions." She was amazed at her own temerity, but, once in, went boldly on. "There is not such a demand for governesses, specially ones educated at Devonshire House, that I found myself in a position to be particular. I was grateful to Mrs. Cummerton for sinking the gossip in the snob and engaging me."

"And what will you do now?" he asked.

It was what she had been wondering herself, but she contrived a confident enough answer. "Oh, visit my father for a little and redeploy my forces."

"Your father? Oh yes, of course, the Comte de Forêt. I have met him, I think. Where can it have been?"

"At Watier's, I have no doubt, or one of the other gambling clubs. I hope you did not play with him, sir."

She was aware of his eyes, in the near darkness of the carriage, fixed on her with an uncomfortably piercing scrutiny. Then, "I beg your pardon," he said. "I would not have spoken of him if I had remembered the whole in time. But consider, Miss Forest, that it is not given to everyone to shine in adversity. His example makes your behaviour all the more exemplary." He broke off. "I cry your pardon again. It is inexcusable to preach at you so. But here we are at last at Haverford Hall where you are to consider yourself my guest, under whatever protest you wish, until morning. And here, you will doubtless be glad to see, is my Cousin Harriet to greet us."

The carriage door was flung open and Camilla saw a flight of wide stone steps leading up to a lighted doorway in which stood a stolidly middle-aged figure with grey hair under a dowager's turban.

Lord Leominster leapt lightly down, turned to give his hand to Camilla, and led her up the gently sloping steps towards the light.

"Cousin Harriet, you should not be out here in the cold." He shepherded them both indoors as he spoke. "I have brought you a guest, you see. The mail coach has broken down and Miss Forest was like to be benighted, so I have brought her home to you. She is sadly chilled and will be glad, I am sure, to be taken to her room at once." A footman shut the big door behind them as his master made the two women formally known to each other. Most of the qualms Camilla had been feeling at this unorthodox visit vanished at sight of Cousin Harriet's formidable respectability. What Mrs. Lefeu thought about Camilla was another question. She was busy with a speech of warm greeting for Lord Leominster, who had, Camilla gathered, been away for some days on a visit to his grandmother, the Dowager Lady Leominster. As he answered his cousin's questions about this lady's health, Camilla was able, for the first time, to take a good look at her rescuer. She liked what she saw, but realised with a little shock of surprise that something positive about his manner, together with his own remarks about being old enough to be her father, had seriously misled her. She had been treating him as she would an uncle, or (if he had had any) a friend of her father's. Now, looking at him by the warm candlelight of his hall, she decided he could not possibly be more than thirty, which, though a great age when viewed from the standpoint of twenty, is still hardly decrepitude.

More alarming still, he was formidably handsome. His dark hair curled shortly round a high forehead and his large and piercing eyes gave a romantic impression to his face which was somewhat contradicted by a straight nose and small, firm mouth. Looking at him, Camilla was perfectly certain that she should never have agreed, however tacitly, to spend a night in his house.

He, too, while apparently absorbed in talk with his housekeeper, was getting his first real look at his guest. He saw a slight, graceful girl, not beautiful, although there was something appealing about the large brown eyes in the thin face and something else about her that he had recognised even in the dark carriage. Very much the aristocrat himself, he had been aware of breeding in her despite the governess's drab costume and awkward plight. He had known her at once for a lady; now, looking at her, with her soft brown curls escaping from under the unbecoming bonnet, he thought her almost a child, and it was with an adult's impatience that he broke off what he was saying to Mrs. Lefeu to exclaim: "But Miss Forest is soaked to the skin and we keep her standing here. Had you not best take her to your apartments while a fire is lighting in the Blue Room?" Having thus indicated to his housekeeper that this unexpected guest was to be treated as an honoured one and given the best guest chamber, he took a quick leave of Camilla, hoping formally that she would do him the honour of dining with him when she felt more herself.

Camilla, appalled now at what seemed in retrospect her incredible boldness, merely curtsied, too shy to speak, and thus, though she did not know it, did much to win over Mrs. Lefeu, who had so far been regarding her with well-concealed distrust. She had seen too many lures thrown out for her handsome cousin not to be suspicious of this child's story. Now, however, she reserved judgement, confining herself to polite nothings as she led the way up a handsome flight of stairs and down a long corridor to her own apartments, where Camilla, shivering as she removed her sodden shawl in front of the fire, turned to her with an impulsive gesture.

"Dear madam, what *am* I to do? I beg you will advise me. He said he was old enough to be my father and—I believed him. He sounded so—so composed that I thought there could be no harm in spending the night here with him and his—excuse me—his housekeeper. But now I see it will not do at all. What *shall* I do?"

Thus approached, Mrs. Lefeu, who heartily agreed with her as to the impropriety of her visit, found herself in something of a quandary.

"Well, my dear," she temporised, "it is not perhaps an arrangement that would quite satisfy your friends. Can you not send to have them fetch you away? I am only surprised that Lord Leominster did not propose it."

"But that is just the difficulty." And Camilla plunged head-long into the story of her troubles. Mrs. Lefeu, who had begun to purse up her lips when she heard that her cousin's protégée had been brought up at Devonshire House, relaxed a little when Camilla turned to her after describing the death of her patroness the Duchess: "I *loved* her so. And then, when she was gone, Lady Elizabeth just stayed and stayed. 'To look after the poor dear Duke,' she said. And how could I stay then? It was bad enough for the others, but he was their father, they had to. But I—I could not bear it."

"And quite right, too," said Mrs. Lefeu. The gossip about Lady Elizabeth Foster and the Duke of Devonshire had been widespread enough so that there was no need to pretend ignorance. "So what did you do?"

"I went to stay with my father, but I found that would not do either." Camilla coloured. She did not wish to tell anyone how appalled she had been by her father's way of life. It was all very well to meet him, the man about town, sauntering elegantly in the park, but something else again to be let into the sordid secrets of his ménage. "So . . . I could not think what to do for the best. We have no money, you know, Bonaparte has taken our estates. Father says we shall get them back one day, but what is the use of 'one day.' Besides, I do not believe it . . . Anyway, 'one day' is too late. I have to live now. So, altogether, there seemed nothing for it but to go for a governess, and Miss Trimmer—she was the gover-ness at Devonshire House, you know—was so good as to find me a place with Mrs. Cummerton."

"Oh." Mrs. Lefeu was beginning to see.

"Yes. Mrs. Cummerton was only too happy to have some-one recommended from Devonshire House. I do not believe she would have minded it I had been as ignorant as she is herself; all she cared about was to be able to tell her friends that she had me 'from the dear, dear Duchess.' Which was not true, since the Duchess died a year ago. But it went well enough, just the same, and I was fond of little Harry and Lucy. They were just beginning to mind me when Gerald came home from Oxford." She stopped, colouring.

"I have heard about Gerald," said Mrs. Lefeu helpfully.

"So I can imagine. Even the housemaid warned me about him. But what could I do? He was forever making excuses to come to the schoolroom, and how could I give him the setdown he deserved in front of his brother and sister? But to have his mother say that I had encouraged him—" She stopped, scarlet with mortification at the memory of that scene in the shrubbery, where Gerald had come upon her unexpectedly; of the stale smell of wine on his breath as he forced his kisses on her, and the hot moisture of his hands on their rough way down the front of her dress. At first, when his mother irrupted upon them, she had felt nothing but relief, but when she found that it was upon her not Gerald that Mrs. Cummerton's reproaches fell, she had flared up in self-defence. The result had been instantaneous dismissal and that weary vigil at the crossroads where Lord Leominster had found her. And so she was back at her immediate problem. "Dear madam," she said again, "advise me. What must I do?"

"Why, make the best of things, I think, my dear," said Mrs. Lefeu kindly. "And be grateful you have fallen into such good hands. At least you can have nothing to fear from my cousin, who is indeed . . ." She stopped, then made a new start. "For a moment, when he handed you out of the carriage, I hoped . . . " Again she paused. "But what am I thinking of to keep you gossiping here? The fire will be lit in your room by now and you must be changing for dinner. Leominster always dresses, even when he is alone."

"Alone? But dear madam, you will dine with us surely?"

"No, no. Our arrangement was, when I came to live here, that I would dine with him only by invitation. And tonight." Once again she paused. "Tonight I have not been invited."

CHAPTER 2

Camilla found the Blue Room full already of firelight and dancing shadows. Her box had been unpacked and her best muslin laid out for her, but she gratefully declined Mrs. Lefeu's offer of her own woman, Hannah, to help her dress. "I am used to manage for myself," she said with truth, forbearing to add that her shattered nerves cried out for a few minutes alone before the ordeal of dining with Lord Leominster. And yet, when she was at last alone, she could not help a thrill of enjoyment at the unwonted luxury of the room. Life had been like this before, at Devonshire House, and now, as she brushed out her curls in front of the fire, the whole misery of the cold and dreary attic at Mrs. Cummerton's seemed like a dream. This was her world, and she was back in it at last.

But only for one night, she reminded herself, as she turned to the glass to adjust the soft folds of her dress and then, with hands that would not stop shaking, tied her one jewel, the miniature of her mother, on its ribbon round her neck. Ready all too soon, she turned from a last reassuring glance in the glass, then stood for a moment, hesitating, in front of the fire. The sound of a gong, growling somewhere below-stairs, alerted her. She must go down and face her host. And after all, she told herself, what was there to be afraid of? How often, as she ate her meagre supper in the schoolroom at Mrs. Cummerton's, had she longed for one more civilised evening. Now, she was to have one. Why not make the most of it?

Just the same, it was with some trepidation, and a becomingly heightened colour, that she joined her host in the small salon Mrs. Lefeu had pointed out to her, and allowed him to conduct her, as formally as if they were met for a great

18

dinner, across the hall into the dining room. To her relief, this was not so formidable an apartment as she had feared. The mahogany table had been contracted to its smallest extent, and as the room's whole light came from the heavy candelabrum that stood on its centre, it was possible almost to forget the outer reaches, where only firelight flickered. Settled on Lord Leominster's right, Camilla was able, for a moment, to consider him unobserved as he turned to give an order to a footman, and congratulated herself, as she took in his impeccable evening attire, on the trouble she had taken with her own.

The meal was a simple one, but was accompanied, to her slightly shocked surprise, by champagne. Catching her eye as her glass was filled, Leominster smiled at her for the first time. It changed his face entirely, transforming the rather formidable handsomeness into something infinitely more engaging. "My butler thinks I am run quite mad," he said, lifting his glass to hers, "to be drinking champagne with my soup, but I hoped it would be what you would like. Besides," his smile included her in a small conspiracy, "I like it myself. I trust I do not need to reassure you that this is not the prelude to a scene of seduction. Nothing, I promise you, is farther from my thoughts."

Camilla, who had been wondering that very thing, smiled, blushed, disclaimed, and drank to him. If it was not exactly a complimentary speech, it was certainly a reassuring one. "Though indeed," he went on, "I have what you may think a somewhat unusual proposition to make to you—later, when we are a little better acquainted. In the meantime, pray let me help you to some of this pâté which my chef, being a compatriot of yours, makes to perfection. But I beg your pardon, I remember that you did not wish to be considered as French. You have no hankering, then, to return and throw in your lot with Bonaparte?"

"Good God, no. You must understand, sir, that I do not *feel* French. After all, I have lived in England ever since I was three years old. Patriotism, I think, is a plant of later growth."

He seemed pleased with her answer. "Yes, I suppose so. Though I cannot think that your treatment at the hands of the English has been such as to fill you with any great gratitude."

"You are mistaken, sir." She flared up at once in defence

of her friends. "Everything I am and have I owe to the Duchess of Devonshire. You do not understand—how can you?—what it is to be a refugee, to have nothing. If it had not been for her . . . I . . . I do not like to think what might have happened to me."

He smiled at her very kindly. "It becomes you to defend her, but surely to end up as a governess—and in such a house as Mrs. Cummerton's—is hardly the pinnacle of worldly bliss?"

"But that was no one's fault but my own," she said. "I could have stayed at Devonshire House forever, I am sure, if I could have borne it, and I have no doubt, if the Duchess had lived, I should have done so. Everything was different when she was alive. It did not seem to matter then that I was the object of charity, penniless, without a dowry, but when she died, everything changed. You have no idea, sir, how difficult it is to be the victim of benevolence."

He smiled, signalled to the footman to refill their glasses, and changed the conversation to politics. "I collect, since you were brought up at Devonshire House, that you are the fiercest of Whigs," he said, "and think nothing Government does is right."

"Why, not exactly." She considered it for a minute. "Because, you see, we *must* beat Bonaparte, or he will tyrannise over the whole world, and the Whigs do not seem to be sure about that. But what are your politics, sir?"

He smiled at that direct question. "Why, Tory of the deepest dye. In fact, I rather expect to be employed in the new government that is now forming—the Duke of Portland, you must know, is my cousin, and you will, I am sure, have heard that we Tories carry nepotism to the point of scandal."

"Nepotism, sir?" She raised delicate eyebrows at him.

"I cry your pardon. I am lecturing you as if you were a political meeting. Nepotism, Miss Forest, is the gentle art of giving jobs to your relations. You must have heard that we Tories are perfect in it."

"Well," she considered, "the Whigs seem to do pretty well at it too."

"Ah yes, but in their case, of course, it is pure coincidence. Or so they say. But tell me, now we have reached our second glass of champagne, is it possible that you have come out of Devonshire House heart-whole? Are you not secretly wearing the willow for young Hartington? Or one of those noisy Lamb boys who hang about there?"

She coloured—what an extraordinary conversation this was—but answered composedly enough. "Why, as to Hartington," she said, "no one who knows him could help loving him—as a brother—but I am not quite mad, sir. To be Duchess of Devonshire is something above my touch. Besides," she added with transparent candour, "I think I lived too closely with them all to fall in love with any of them."

"So here you are, a full-fledged governess, and, if I am not very far out in my calculations, twenty years old, and without a romantic attachment to bless yourself with?"

She laughed. "You make my condition seem deplorable indeed, but I refuse to despair. We French, you know, are a practical race. I gave up dreaming of a grand romance when I was seventeen and began to understand that all the men I met were quite beyond my mark. Since then, I have had various plans. I should make an admirable wife for a country clergyman, I think; and a governess, you know, has frequent chances of meeting *them*. And, if all else fails, I can always set up as a modiste."

"What a talented young lady you are, to be sure. You will be telling me next that you are skilled in cookery and made that charming dress you are wearing. I cannot, however, think that you know Portuguese."

"Portuguese?" She looked at him in amazement. "What is that to the purpose?"

"Why, perhaps, a great deal, if you are indeed as practical as you suggest. Do you drink port, Miss Forest? No? I thought very likely not; it is hardly a young lady's drink. Marston," he turned to the butler, who had been, for some minutes past, hovering nearby in a faintly threatening manner, "fill up our glasses, set the dessert on the table, and leave us. Miss Forest will take pity on my solitude and drink another glass with me. You see," he turned back to Camilla, "that I am something of a tyrant in my home."

She had been thinking that on the contrary he seemed oddly ill at ease. Throughout the meal she had been aware of a certain tension behind the miscellaneous questions he had fired at her, and this awareness of strain in him had done much to ease her own nervousness. Just the same, now, with the room empty, the candles flickering, and the fire burning low, she found her hands uncontrollably shaking as she helped herself to the cheese Leominster recommended. What could the proposition be that he had spoken of at the beginning of dinner? Why had he asked her so many questions, almost, she thought, as if she were applying for a position? What was the cause of the strange excitement she felt burning beneath his outward calm?

"A glass of wine with you, Miss Forest." His voice interrupted her thoughts. Solemnly they drank, then, his glass empty, he pushed his plate aside and leaned over the table towards her. "Will you bear with me, Miss Forest, while I tell you something about myself?"

"Of course."

"Good. Then to begin with, as I think I told you before, I do not like women. Anyone will tell you that. I do not understand them, I do not appreciate them, I do not want them. Please remember that. I never had a mother; my sister might just as well be my daughter. My cousin Harriet is well enough; she teases me, but not beyond bearing—but as for young ladies—heaven defend me. I know nothing about them, and I do not wish to learn. You will forgive me, I know, for making this plain from the start. You are, you have told me, a practical Frenchwoman; very well, then, I have a practical proposition to put to you. Will you marry me, Miss Forest?"

"Marry you?" She could not believe her ears.

"Yes, marry me. On the strict understanding that it is a marriage of—shall we say—appearance only. You look confounded, Miss Forest, and I do not blame you. I fear I have set about this quite the wrong way. Let me explain. I have a grandmother, the Dowager Lady Leominster, to whom I have just been paying my yearly visit of duty. She is a fierce old lady with a great sense of family pride—and a close hand on the family purse. I have the title, this house, and a pittance with which to support them. My grandmother has millions, which I had always assumed would come to me, in the fullness of time. Yesterday, she told me that unless I marry, she will leave the whole to my cousin. So you see you are not the only one to know what it is to be the victim of benevolence." His voice was bitter. "You, with your spirit, which drove you out into the world as a governess, will perhaps ask why I do not snap my fingers at my grandmother and her money. But I have family pride too. I love this house and cannot bear to see it falling to pieces about my ears. Besides, a title has its responsibilities; there is my cousin Harriet; there are others, whom I feel bound to support. I had hoped, perhaps vainly, that I might find a solution to my difficulties in Government office. Now, I have been offered a place by my cousin—he wishes me to go as special assistant to Lord Strangford, our Minister Plenipotentiary at the Court of Portugal. It is a position of the greatest dignity and difficulty—and one that will cost me infinitely more than it brings in. And as if that was not enough, my grandmother has to tell me that she wishes to see me married before I go. I tell you, Miss Forest, I was in despair when I met you, but since then, I have been beginning to hope. You are everything of which my grandmother would approve, and—forgive me—you are in a position where even the half marriage I offer might be—well, preferable at least to turning modiste. If you were head over ears in love, I would not have ventured this proposition, but you tell me you are heart-whole. Would it amuse you to come to Portugal with me, Miss Forest?"

She had heard him out in amazed silence; now she thought for a moment before speaking. "It is indeed a remarkable proposition, my lord. But have you thought closely enough, I wonder, about what you are doing? Your grandmother, you say, wishes you to marry out of family pride. Surely, if I may speak plainly with you, this means she wants you to marry and get an heir. May you not find, if you venture into the kind of arrangement you have done me the honour of suggesting, that you are saddled with the wife, and still deprived of the fortune for lack of the heir?"

He looked at her with a new respect. "I confess that is an idea that has occurred to me. But my grandmother is a woman of her word; she has not stipulated the heir; she will hold to her side of the bargain. Besides, she is hardly to know on what terms we live—and—she is a very old lady. That is the ground on which she insists on my marrying forthwith. She wishes, she says, to see me established in life before I go to Portugal because she does not expect to live until my return. As a matter of fact, I have no doubt she will live to be a hundred, but there it is; she has delivered her ultimatum and will abide by it. And anyway, if I must marry, there could be worse times. It is bound to be something of a nine days' wonder, and we would be safe away from it, in Portugal. Besides, a wife is always a useful adjunct to a diplomat."

Camilla could not help laughing. "I must say, sir, that your proposal is scarcely a flattering one. 'If you must marry' indeed. What do you expect me to say to that?"

"Why, anything to the purpose." There was a note of impatience in his voice. "I have been at some pains, already, to explain to you that this is anything but a romantic proposal. Flattering, on the other hand, in some ways, I think it is. You are the first young lady I have met with who had enough sense to entertain it for a moment."

"Or enough foolishness." Thoughtfully. "But then, you must remember, sir, that I am only by courtesy a young lady. Do you really think your grandmother will be delighted at the news that you are to marry a governess? Not," she hurried on, "that I have at all decided to agree to your remarkable proposition, but I think we would do well to have all clear between us. And she does not sound to me like the kind of person who will take kindly to a _déclassée_ grand-daughter-in-law."

"What a sensible girl you are," he said with approval. "All your objections are admirable ones. Of course we would have to handle it with care, but I think if we make you known to her first, and tell your story afterwards, we will do well enough. Besides, she will be too delighted at having me marry at all to throw many rubs in our way."

Again she laughed. "More and more flattering. Well, sir, it is an odd enough proposition, but I tell you frankly I find myself so circumstanced that I must at least consider it. Since you have dealt plainly with me (and I am grateful to you for it) I will do as much by you. A year ago, I would not have entertained such a proposal for a moment. I was still full, then, of dreams of romance. Now, I am not so sure. Romance, I begin to see, is something of an expensive commodity and I wonder whether I can afford it. But tell me, when do you need your answer? I would like, if I may, to see my father before I decide. Not, of course, that I would tell him anything about your proposition. I can see that one of the terms of our agreement would have to be most absolute secrecy on both sides. It is not the kind of arrangement one would wish to discuss even with one's dearest friends. Not," she added reflectively, "that I have any very dear friends. Which would make it all the easier. But, frankly, I would like to see if my father has any more eligible suggestion for me. Perhaps—who knows?—he has won a fortune at cards since I saw him last, and I may set up heiress on the proceeds. It is not, I can tell you, likely, but I would like to make sure before I commit myself to—forgive me—so desperate a hazard."

It was his turn to laugh, somewhat wryly, and she found herself thinking with amusement that he liked her plain speaking no better than she had his. But he spoke with his usual grave courtesy. "Of course, Miss Forest, you must have time to decide. That you will even consider my proposal is, to my mind, a great point gained. I must, in any case, go to town tomorrow to discuss the terms of my appointment and begin my preparations. It will hardly be possible for me to set out for Portugal until, at the earliest, the middle of May, and, in my opinion, our marriage, if you agree to it, should take place at the last possible moment."

"Naturally." Again she could not help a little laugh.

"Before then," he went on, "we should, of course, have to pay a visit to my grandmother, and you, too, would have your preparations to make. You will want, I suppose, a trousseau, for which, in the circumstances, I shall consider it my privilege to pay. Altogether, the sooner you make up your mind, the better. Besides, I should be glad to have my anxiety at an end."

"To be put out of your misery," she said kindly. "Yes, and, of course, if I should refuse, you will have to start looking about for another candidate."

"Quite so." He refused to be roused. "So, all things considered, I would suggest that you do me the honour of accompanying me to London. We will take Cousin Harriet too, in deference to the proprieties. If you are to be Lady Leominster, you cannot be jauntering about the countryside alone with me."

"Caesar's betrothed?" she said, teasingly.

"Exactly so. Indeed, I must ask Mrs. Lefeu to look out for a maid for you. And," a new thought struck him, "where are you to stay? I do not imagine that your father's lodgings will be quite the thing for my future wife."

This was suddenly too much. "Not your future wife yet, sir," she said. "You are going a little too fast for me. And naturally I had not the slightest intention of staying with my father. I am quite as well aware of what is suitable as you are, and plan to return to Devonshire House, where I have carte blanche. You would not, I collect, consider it beneath your dignity to take a wife from there."

"I beg your pardon." She was aware of his increasing respect. "No, even my grandmother can hardly quibble at Devonshire House, though your coming from there may give her ground for some anxiety about your politics."

She laughed, in charity with him once more. "So that is why you asked me whether I was a fierce Whig. I can see that would hardly do for the wife of a Tory diplomat, any more than a secret passion for Lord Hartington, or one of those tiresome Lambs. But it is getting late and you do not, I am sure, wish your servants to be gossiping about this any more than is inevitable." She rose. "I shall be most grateful for your escort—and Mrs. Lefeu's—to London. When do you intend to start in the morning?"

"Why, as soon as Mrs. Lefeu can be ready, which will be early enough, if I know her." He too had risen and now escorted her ceremoniously upstairs to Mrs. Lefeu's apartments, where the arrangements for next day's journey were quickly completed, Camilla noticing, not for the first time, how absolutely he was obeyed and how entirely he took such obedience for granted. What kind of a husband, she wondered as she undressed in the luxurious warmth of her bedroom, would he make? Was she not mad even to consider his strange proposal? But on the other hand, what else did the future hold for her? She had spoken truly when she said that she had outgrown her romantic dreams. For some time now she had considered her future with a cold and gloomy realism. In this spring of 1807, Bonaparte remained all powerful in France, and even if she could bring herself to submit to him, the chances of his restoring the family estates were so slight as to be pitiful. She was condemned, so far as she could see, to be a displaced person for life, dependent on her father's slight support and her own resources for a livelihood. Her first experience as a governess had hardly been an encouraging one, and what chance of marriage had she, dowerless as she was? Her hopes along that line had been dashed once and for all when the older of Lady Elizabeth Foster's sons, after showing all the signs of a *tendre* for her, had made it clear that it was very far from being marriage that he intended. If she was not good enough for Augustus Foster, what hope of a respectable establishment had she? No, she told herself, as she began to drift off to sleep, she must think very seriously of Lord Leominster's proposal. After all, to be Lady Leominster ... and besides however odd his proposal, there was no denying his attractiveness. And already, she thought, she had learned something of how to deal with him. He might dislike women (why? she wondered sleepily), but he could be brought to respect one who would not let herself be browbeaten. It might do . . . it might very well do. And she drifted into sleep incorrigibly troubled by romantic dreams.

Waking, she told herself briskly that that would not do at all. If she did decide to marry Lord Leominster, it would be strictly upon his own terms. If it was to work, there must be no romantic nonsense about it, on her part any more than on his. Just the same, she was human enough to take particular pains about her appearance, exchanging the governess's drab in which she had been expelled from Mrs. Cummerton's house for a most becoming travelling dress of dark red sarsenet which had been a present from Harriet Cavendish.

Hurrying downstairs, she saw, in daylight, much that last night's candles had failed to reveal, and began to realise the truth of Lord Leominster's remarks about his straitened circumstances. The red turkey carpet that covered the main stairway was frayed in several places, and the shadows of many years' candle smoke darkened walls and ceilings. In the breakfast room, where she found herself the first, it was the same story; the brocade curtains were faded and the chair seats that matched them had been exquisitely mended in several places. The house might be luxury itself compared to the governess's quarters at Mrs. Cummerton's, but, compared instead with the extravagant elegance she had been used to at Devonshire House, it was scarcely fit to live in.

The rooms, however, were beautifully proportioned, and the window, to which spring sunshine drew her, showed a handsome prospect of beautifully kept lawn and parkland. It was like a man, she thought, to have spent all he could on the grounds and let the furnishings go. She was mentally repapering the breakfast room and hanging it with rose-coloured curtains when she was interrupted by the fluttered appearance of Mrs. Lefeu, who apologised breathlessly for being late, explained that she had been at her packing since six o'clock, offered Camilla a choice of green tea or bohea, exclaimed about Leominster's absence, and then, all in the same breath, greeted him warmly as he appeared from a door at the end of the room. He in his turn greeted Camilla with the automatic courtesy of a host, announced that they had

fifteen minutes before the carriage would come round, and
applied himself to the consumption of devilled kidneys with a
concentration fatal to the romantic visions that had wreathed
themselves among Camilla's dreams. Very well (she helped
herself largely to scrambled eggs), if he could play at detachment, so could she.

It was only later in the carriage that she began to be
aware of the difference between them. However collected an
appearance she contrived to present, behind it her emotions
were in a constant whirl of indecision. Whereas he, having
made his proposition and left her to decide, really seemed to
have forgotten all about it, and was soon deep in a serious
discussion with Mrs. Lefeu as to the comparative urgency of
various repairs and refurbishments of the house which she
had apparently been pressing upon him. After listening for
half an hour to their earnest discussion of the woodworm in
the attic and the dry rot in the cellar, Camilla was in a fair
way to flying into a miff, and had to remind herself that so
far as Mrs. Lefeu was concerned she was merely an object of
casual charity, a poor little governess who had been given a
night's lodging out of kindness. Braced by this thought, she
endured another hour or so of dilapidations and retrench-
ments, merely making a mental note, from time to time, that
if *she* should chance to find herself in charge of the house,
she would go quite otherwise about things. But then, of
course, if she did marry Lord Leominster, his grandmother
would be bound to increase the allowance she made him.
Everything would be different.

Different indeed. But that was not the way to achieve
detachment. She had told herself she would attempt no
decision until she had found out how her father was circumstanced, and now firmly put the problem out of her mind
and turned instead to listen to her companions' talk. Mrs.
Lefeu and Lord Leominster had reached the subject of
the stables by now, and here it was evident that he would
allow of no economy. His guests might suffer some diminu-
tion of luxury; his horses never would. Camilla, who had
noticed with approval the handsome team of matched bays
that drew his carriage, saw nothing out of the way about
this. It would have been equally ridiculous to suggest that
some local tailor might dress him as satisfactorily as the
master hand that had cut the capes of his travelling coat.

Thanks to their heroically early start, they reached London

betimes in the afternoon and Camilla was quite human enough to enjoy being driven up to Devonshire House in an elegant travelling carriage instead of dwindling to the door in a hackney as she had expected. She parted from Mrs. Lefeu and Lord Leominster with many expressions of sincere gratitude, and a little niggling worry at the back of her mind was set at rest when he promised himself the pleasure of calling upon her next day to make sure that she was none the worse for her journey. So he had meant it, last night. He would no doubt expect her answer tomorrow. She must lose no time in getting in touch with her father.

To her relief, she found no one at Devonshire House but Miss Trimmer, who welcomed her with her usual reserved affection and told her that the family were in the country and likely to remain there for some time longer. This suited Camilla admirably, and she sat down at once to write a note to her father, urging him to call upon her that very evening. He arrived with suspicious promptness and greeted her with an enthusiasm that boded no good as his guardian angel, his *"Camille bien aimée."*

Detaching herself as best she might from his port-wine-flavoured embrace, she observed with the still patience of constant repetition that she preferred to be called Camilla and asked him how he did.

"Villainously," he replied, with that faint but unmistakable French accent that had won him so many female hearts, years ago, when French refugees were still a novelty. "I am *au désespoir, Camille*—Camilla, I should say, since you insist. You arrive most happily to be my saviour, *mon ange guardien*—and to make your own fortune, my love, which, no doubt, you will think more to the purpose. I was on the point of writing to you when I received your note."

"Really, Father?" She looked at him with a suspicion based on long experience. "And pray how am I to set about being your saviour—and making this fortune?"

"Why, so easily, my love, that you will hardly believe it possible. But 'tis something of an *histoire*. Shall we not be seated and will you not, perhaps, offer your *vieux père* some refreshment?"

"Of course, Father." She rang and gave the necessary orders, while he prowled about the room with a restless air that made her wonder more and more just how he proposed to make their fortunes. Established with his necessary glass of wine, he raised it at once to drink her health, emptied it, refilled it from the decanter, drank again, and said, "Well, *mon amour*, what do you think of an advantageous marriage?"

"Marriage? For me? Father, you cannot be serious. How can I expect to marry well with no dowry?"

"But that is exactly the point of the whole *affaire*," he said. "The dowry will be provided, the groom is willing, it is but for you to say yes and our troubles are over."

"And who is to be the lucky man?"

"Oh, *ma Camille*, always the cynic, always the sceptic." He burst into one of his fits of exaggerated and unconvincing laughter, while she wondered more and more what was coming. "But I have much to tell you, and first for a piece of news that will make you *folle de joie*. What think you of your brother's being alive all this time?"

"My brother? Charles?" She could not believe her ears.

"Yes, Charles. My son, your brother. Not dead in the Terror as we thought, but alive and well, the adopted son of some good people in Clichy who told him, only the other day, who he really was. Only fancy my heir, the future Comte de Forêt, masquerading all this time as Monsieur Boutet, a butcher's son. And only see how blood will tell, for even as a butcher's son he has achieved distinction."

There was a cold dread now around her heart. "How, Father?" she asked.

"Why, as one might expect, serving his country. It is a trifle embarrassing, I confess, but understandable enough that he should have thrown in his lot with Bonaparte. After all, he was not to know that he was an aristocrat—and besides, let us be a little realistic, *ma petite*. Nothing will shake Bonaparte now; he is master of Europe and will remain so. These bungling fools of Englishmen will be lucky if they can keep their own freedom. Any idea of their invading and freeing the continent is merely laughable—*à faire rire*. All they think of here is their party squabbles; there is not a man among them fit to set up against Bonaparte. And then, only consider that poor exiled king, fit for nothing but the gout stool and water gruel. Who is he to rally the French to his cause? And what has he ever done for us, despite the years of faithful service we have offered him? Now, through your brother, only see what prospects open up before us!"

"You have heard from him, then?"

"But *naturellement*, how else do you think that I know all this? There is a friend of his, even now, in London, who sought me out with the most proper messages of filial regard from Charles."

"A friend of Charles's in London? But you said he was a follower of Bonaparte!"

"And so he is." Not for the first time she recognised embarrassment under her father's joviality. "And so, of course, is his friend, who passes, for the nonce, as M. Mireille, an émigré. In reality, he is here on a secret mission of the greatest consequence."

"You mean, I collect, that he is a spy."

"Oh, *ma Camille*, why must you always take things so awkwardly? I tell you of your brother's friend, and you must talk to me of spies. Do you not think the English have their agents too, in Paris? But when you meet M Mireille, as you will shortly, you will realise how wide you are of the mark, and how greatly things must be changed in France. He is an aristocrat to his fingertips. I will not tell you his title—the less you know, perhaps, the better—but to find such as he serving Bonaparte—*ma foi*, it makes me sure it is time we went home, you and I. This England is well enough for a while, but to tell truth, I am passing weary of their roast mutton and that dishwater they call coffee, and as for their manners! I have stood their condescension long enough. To be treated as an inferior by such *canaille*; it is a wonder I have endured it so long. Why, only the other day, when I was walking down St. James's—"

"But, Father," she cut him short, recognising the beginning of one of his long stories of offended dignity, "what is this to the purpose?"

"Ah ha, *ma petite*, always so practical. You wish to hear about the handsome husband and the dowry, *n'est-ce pas?* Well, so you shall. As for the husband, Mireille is the man and head over ears in love merely from hearing your praises, and, for the fortune, what say you to your share of our own estates, which I am promised on my return to France?"

"And what must we do in exchange?"

"Why, nothing of the slightest importance. Nor indeed would you have to return to France for the moment. Mireille is fixed in London for some time, so you would not be leaving your friends. I know how much the connexion with

Devonshire House has meant to you: I am too good a father to snatch you away from all that."

She saw it all now: "And how much does the connexion with Devonshire House mean to M Mireille?" she asked. "Does he expect me to assist him in his spying?"

"Oh, Camilla." He shrugged despairingly. "We are given a chance to recoup our fortunes, to go home to France, to see once more the brother you adored, and all you do is make difficulties. Well, let me tell you then, which I had hoped to spare you, that if you do not marry Mireille, I am a ruined man."

"Ruined? What do you mean?"

"Why, merely that I owe him more than I can possibly pay. He has it in his power to disgrace me, Camilla, and all you can think of are your British niceties."

Now she was beginning, indeed, to see. "And because he has done this to you," she said, "you wish me to marry him." She rose and took an angry turn about the room, then came back to face him. "Father, you have surpassed yourself. But, tell me, how much, in fact, do you owe this M. Mireille?"

He was extremely reluctant to tell her, but she got it out of him at last. The figure, it seemed, was upwards of five hundred pounds and she knew only too well how impossible he would find the payment of such a sum. She was pacing the room again, in distracted consideration of his plight, when a disapproving footman appeared to announce that "a M. Mireille" was below asking for her.

"Tell him I am not at home," she said at once, and then, when the man had withdrawn, turned on her father, who had made as if to protest. "Really, Father," she said, "this is the outside of enough. I collect you told him to give you the meeting here. Have you so little thought for my position that you would have me entertaining every Tom, Dick, and Harry of your acquaintance, and with the family away, too."

"But, *mon amour*," he protested, "your intended husband? Surely that alters the case? I wish you may not have affronted him by having him sent away. I had best hurry after him, I think, and explain."

"Yes," she said, "perhaps you had. Say to him what you please, but do not tell him I have accepted him. He is no intended husband of mine." And she cut short his further protests and exclamations by ringing for a footman to show him out.

Alone at last, she paced the room in an agony of indecision. So this was the help she had hoped for from her father. Well, she told herself, she should have known him better than to allow herself even to imagine the chance of assistance from him. But what should she do? He was all too evidently on the high road to ruin. Could she save him? Almost, for a moment, she was tempted to sit down and write to Lord Leominster, accepting his offer on the spot and asking his help. Then she thought better of it. That his offer must be accepted, and his help asked, seemed certain, but, from what she had already seen of him, she thought she would do better to leave him tonight in doubt, rather than to seem to fall too easily into his hands.

This decided, she went up to her room and unpacked her box, then joined Miss Trimmer for an evening of handwork and polite conversation. It was, she found, strangely soothing to be exchanging, once more, dry comment on the new ministers, the course of the war, and the new style in sleeves with this calm and reliable friend. Only, at last, alone in her room, did she let herself think of the future. "Well, my Lady Leominster," she told the pale, large-eyed reflection in her glass, "and how, pray, do you do?"

There was, of course, no answer.

CHAPTER 3

The morning had its own terrors. Suppose Lord Leominster should have changed his mind? But she would not even consider that possibility, setting herself instead to decide how to receive him. Theoretically, she certainly should not do so alone, and yet this was obviously essential. After some thought, she decided, inevitably, that the time had come to take Miss Trimmer into her confidence, and did so, telling her, of course, as little as possible of the story, and nothing about the strange nature of Lord Leominster's proposal. Always reliable, Miss Trimmer congratulated her warmly on forming so eligible a connexion and came, with her usual good sense, straight to the point. "And he is calling on you today for your answer, you say? Well, I think I had best play mama to you, my dear, since the family are all away. We will receive him together, if you will be ruled by me, and then I will act the part of a wise parent by leaving you alone with him."

Since this was exactly the reaction Camilla had hoped for, she received it warmly and settled down to learn from Miss Trimmer whatever she knew of her future husband. This was not much, since Lord Leominster, as a Tory, moved in a very different circle from that of the Devonshire House set. But Miss Trimmer had heard enough about his charm and promise to make the time pass very pleasantly for Camilla, who allowed herself, for a little while, to be soothed into the illusion that this was an ordinary marriage she was contemplating. At least, there was something very encouraging about the warmth of Miss Trimmer's congratulations, confirming, as they did, her own belief that a respectable marriage was worth achieving at almost any cost.

But the time passed slowly and when Lord Leominster was

announced at last, it was with a sensation of astonishment that Camilla realised that he had come almost as early as politeness warranted. Nothing else about him betokened the eager lover, and Camilla, watching him exchange polite nothings with Miss Trimmer, could hardly believe that his proposal had ever been made. Only, when he turned to her with a gleam of—what was it? Irony? Solicitude? Or something between the two?—and asked her how she had found her father, did she know that it was all real enough. Suddenly overwhelmed with nerves, she stammered out an incoherent reply and was still further shaken when Miss Trimmer took this as her cue to rise and take her leave.

Alone with her, Leominster wasted no time. "Well," he said, "you do not look, Miss Forest, like a young lady whose father has just won a fortune in the lottery. Nor," he twinkled at her suddenly, "like one who awaits a proposal of marriage. Is it so very bad? Do you wish you had never encountered me?"

Again she found herself at a loss for words. This would never do. With a fierce effort she pulled herself together and contrived to match his lightness of tone. "On the contrary, my lord, I think I may have much cause to bless the day we met. But whether you will do so, I cannot but doubt." And then, with a sudden rush: "Tell me, my lord, have you any money at all? Without recourse to your grandmother, I mean."

He laughed. "Well, that's a frank enough question," he said, "and one, I hope that you feel yourself entitled to ask, for the best of reasons. Yes, I have a few pounds to command at a pinch. Why? Am I to take it that you have found your father not so much fortunate as embarrassed?"

Not for the first time, she blessed him for his quick comprehension. "Precisely so," she said, "and there is worse than that. I think, before there is any more talk of marriage between us, I must tell you the whole. You may well feel, when you have heard it, that as a wife I should prove more of a liability than an asset."

And without stopping for any further doubts, she poured out the whole story, only minimising, as best she might, the sordid part played by her father and, by implication, her brother. At last she paused, looking at him expectantly, rather, he found himself thinking, like a young bird hoping for crumbs. A sudden, unfamiliar wave of feeling swept over him, part anger at her father, part pity for her desolate position in which, instead of being protected, she had herself to play the protector's role. But his voice lost none of its lightness as he replied. "So, I take it, as a bride's present, you would wish your father cleared of debt? Well, with a little contriving, I believe it can be done, and you are right when you think I do not much want a father-in-law in Bonaparte's camp. You say he admits to five hundred pounds of debt? Then, I suppose we had best assume that the total amounts to half as much again. Well, I am afraid Cousin Harriet must say goodbye to her improvements at Haverford Hall." He rose to his feet. "You had best give me your father's direction, Miss Forest, and let me handle this. But, first, have I your permission to announce our engagement in the *Gazette*? It will infinitely strengthen my hand in dealing both with your father and with this M. Mireille, whose pretensions I propose to myself the pleasure of depressing."

"Yes, of course," she said, then hurried on to a point that had been troubling her. "You will not have M. Mireille arrested, will you?"

He laughed. "As an acceptance, it lacks something of enthusiasm, but I thank you, just the same." With a sudden courtly gesture he bent to kiss her hand, then continued, "And I promise I will do my best to make the married state tolerable to you. As for M. Mireille, do not trouble yourself over him. For one thing, he is not worth it; for another, I do not propose to do anything so drastic as having him arrested, which might, just remotely, involve you, but shall merely drop a word in the proper quarters. Once he is known for a spy, he can do little harm and may indeed do us good. But now, for our plans. My grandmother is most happily come to town—she wishes, she says, to see the last of me—and I am sure you will agree with me that we should lose no time in making you known to her. With your permission, I will call on her even before I see your father and ask her leave to bring you to visit her this evening." Again came that irrepressible twinkle. "I think I can promise you that she will be the most surprised dowager in London. It is but three days since she made me her ultimatum, and here I present myself to her as a happily affianced man."

"Yes." Camilla considered it somewhat doubtfully. "Do you think she will really *believe* it?"

"You are not exactly flattering, Miss Forest. Do you find it so impossible that I should be able to woo and win a young lady in three days?"

It was her turn to laugh. "I cry your pardon. I am convinced you could do it in one. And besides your grandmother will doubtless be too charmed at your obedience to look very closely into my motives. But, my lord, I do not know how to thank you—"

He interrupted her. "Then do not try. Or rather tell yourself that I rescue your father merely out of motives of self-interest, which, you must long since have realised, is paramount in my nature. And, Miss Forest, I must beg you to give over calling me 'my lord,' which might, indeed, rouse some justifiable doubts in my grandmother's breast. If you boggle at Maurice—and I should not blame you—my family name, Lavenham, will do well enough until we are better acquainted. And what, pray, am I to call you in return?"

"Camilla, my lord—I beg your pardon, Camilla," she said, colouring deeply as once again the extraordinary nature of this engagement was brought home to her.

"Camilla," he said with approval, "a pretty name, and suits its owner." And with this, the first compliment he had paid her. he took his leave, promising to call for her that evening and conduct her to his grandmother's house in St. James's Square.

He arrived punctually upon his hour and greeted her with a reassuring, "All's well so far," as he handed her into his carriage. "I have seldom had the pleasure of seeing my grandmother so surprised."

"And pleased?" she asked, somewhat wryly. "Is she prepared to sink my past in my future?"

He laughed. "You make marriage with me sound like some kind of barbaric sacrifice," he said. "I will do my possible to make it something less unpleasant. As for my grandmother, to tell truth, she reserves judgement until she has seen you, which, in my opinion, is more than half the battle. My only fear was lest she condemn you unseen, but she is all eagerness for the meeting. It has given her, she says, a new lease of life. And, of course, to see you will be to approve."

She inclined her head gravely. "That is the second compliment you have paid me," she said, "this is better and better . . . "

"It is more, I think, than you deserve, with your hints that I am some kind of modern Minotaur merely because I am no lady's man. But I have more news for you and what, I know, will please you. I have seen your father."

"Already? Oh, that was *kind* of you."

"Not at all. Think rather that I wished to have your mind clear for this important interview with my grandmother. Yes, I am happy to say that I now appear as your suitor approved by your father. No, that is putting it mildly; welcomed, I should say, and indeed kissed, most enthusiastically, on both cheeks."

"Oh dear," she sighed. "I can imagine how you must have enjoyed that. I only hope it is the worst you will have to suffer for my sake. But what of M. Mireille, sir? What has my father's approval cost you?"

"Why, to tell truth, less than I had feared. I have met your other suitor, too, and put him roundly to flight. When I suggested to M. Mireille that a word from me in the proper quarter might put an end to his capacities for wooing for some time to come, he was only too happy to waive his claim to your hand and is now, if I mistake not, busy packing his traps ready for a precipitate return to France."

"And the five hundred pounds?"

"I suggested to him that it would be well worth his while to waive his claim to that, too. Blackmail, Miss Forest, is a game two can play at, and I was in very much the stronger position. No, you will have no more trouble from M. Mireille, and your father is my very dear friend already."

"Dear me," she said, "how"—she hesitated for a word—"how competent of you, my lord."

"Lavenham," he corrected. "I beg you will remember not to go 'my lording' me at my grandmother's. I can see that you are disappointed in me, Camilla—I must get into practice too," he explained in parenthesis. "Does my method of ridding you of your difficulties seem odiously unromantic to you? I suppose it must, but you will, I hope, admit that it has many practical advantages. Mireille dead at my hand—or even in prison—would prove a continuing embarrassment to us. Mireille in France is none. Besides, I have warned you already to expect no romance from me. But here we are. Remember, I beg, that my grandmother is a very old lady indeed and used to say what she pleases."

Camilla laughed. "I am glad to think somebody bullies you."

Lady Leominster's house differed most remarkably from

Haverford Hall. Here were no peeling paint and shabby
curtains. The very smell of the house suggested beeswax, and
everything shone, from the silver candelabra to the footmen's
wigs. They were conducted, at once, to Lady Leominster's
own apartments, where they found her enthroned in an
enormous velvet-hung four-poster bed. She was a little monkey of an old lady, so small, so shrunk, so shrivelled up with
age that it was hard, until one saw her eyes, to imagine her
as a rational being, still less as the powerful tyrant of a whole
family. But her eyes told another story. Large, dark, and
brilliant as Leominster's own, they seemed, to Camilla, to
have an added something that his lacked—was it, perhaps,
wisdom?

She held out a fragile claw to Camilla. "I shall not kiss
you—yet." And then with a laugh, "Very likely you will not
wish to kiss me at all." Both voice and laugh were an
astonishment, deep, resonant, and beautiful. "But I am old
enough to be tyrannical, as Lavenham will doubtless have
told you, and you are young enough, I hope, to learn something from me. As for you, Lavenham, you will be so good
as to leave us. We will get on very much better without you.
Tell Chatteris to give you a glass of whatever you wish. I will
send for you when I am ready." And she held out her tiny
begemmed hand to him in greeting and dismissal.

Alone with Camilla, whom she had imperiously motioned
to a seat by the bed, she looked her up and down for a
moment, then said, with a sigh of satisfaction: "Well, at all
events, you look ladylike enough."

Camilla could not help a little laugh. "Thank you, ma'am."

"Hmmm—and got some spirit, too, have you? Why, this
may do well enough yet. Tell me, then, what makes you wish
to marry my grandson?"

Camilla looked at her thoughtfully for a moment, then,
"Why, his money, ma'am," she said simply.

Once again that amazing laugh rang out. "And a very good
reason, too," said the old lady. "If you had told me some
stuff about love at first sight I would never have trusted you
more. But as it is, we may deal admirably yet, you and I. So
you have been out as a governess, hey?"

"Yes. I told Lord Leominster I thought you would not like
it."

"Not Leominster," snapped the old lady. "Lavenham to
you and me—his first name is too ridiculous for use—

Maurice—pah! But there were Lavenhams at Haverford Hall long before the house of Hanover was thought of—or the Stuarts either, for that matter. You are yourself of good family, I understand, despite the governessing. The Comte de Forêt, is it not? Surely I know something of him?"

"Nothing good, I fear, ma'am," said Camilla calmly. "I come to you with many liabilities." She made it a statement, rather than an apology and it was taken as such.

"Oh, as to that," said the old lady, "you will find that we have enough of our own. To begin with, I must tell you that I hold the purse strings, and shall continue to do so. Since you tell me that you are marrying Lavenham for money, you had best understand at once that it is mine."

"So it is easy to see, ma'am, by the state of this house compared with Haverford Hall," said Camilla dryly.

"*Touché*," again came that swashbuckling laugh. "You have me there, Miss Forest. Is it so very shabby? I have not been there this age."

"Deplorable," said Camilla simply. "It is worse than shabby, ma'am, it is falling to pieces. It will cost a pretty penny to set in order again."

"Well, there is time enough to be thinking of that," said the dowager. "But let us return to you. This Mrs. Cummerton was your first employer, was she not? And until you went to her you had lived at Devonshire House—as one of the family?" she added sharply.

"Yes, ma'am."

"And are now back there?"

"Yes, ma'am."

"And will remain there till your marriage, of course. Will the Duke give you away?"

"I have no doubt he would if I were to ask him. But you forget, ma'am, that I have a father. Whatever may be said against him, I will be given away by no one else. Besides, I do not wish it suggested that I am another of the Devonshire House miscellany."

"That's good." The dark eyes flashed approval. "That's excellent good; the Devonshire House miscellany! No, we'll not have you confused with that. But the Cavendishes will be there to dance at your wedding, I take it? Oh, it might be worse—it might very well be worse."

"Leominster—I mean Lavenham—said you would be too

happy he was marrying at all to make many objections to me," said Camilla, greatly daring.

"Why, to tell truth, child, he was right there. I do not know when I have been more astonished—or more delighted. I only hope you know what you are doing. We want no more scandals in our family: if you marry Lavenham, you are to stick to him, understand?"

"Of course, ma'am. That is my idea of matrimony. But," Camilla hesitated, "you say, 'no *more* scandals'?"

"Ha." It was a grunt almost of satisfaction. "I thought he'd not have told you. Well, you'd best know, since it explains much about Lavenham that might puzzle you else. Besides, if I do not tell you, there will be enough kind friends to do so. Best hear it from me. What has Lavenham told you about his parents?"

"Why, nothing, ma'am. We have not, to tell truth, had much time for conversation."

"No, I suppose not, since you only met—am I right?—the day before yesterday. But it would be years before Lavenham told you, and you had much best know now. Lavenham's father—my son—was killed in a duel defending his wife's honour (as he thought). She watched from her lover's carriage and left England with him afterwards. They are living still, in Italy. Lavenham was a child of ten at the time, his sister a mere baby. He has not, I think, forgotten."

"Oh." There seemed nothing to say, but then, "He ... he told me he did not like women. I could not understand it, but now I begin to see."

The dark eyes snapped. "Told you that, did he? A good sign, a very good sign. This may do yet. But you will have to be patient, child, patient as Job. Do not delude yourself this is a romantic history you are embarked on ... it is something quite other ... Hmmm," she paused for a moment, "told you he did not like women, hey? Did he tell you he's had all the eligible girls in town dangling after him and paid them as much attention as he would a flock of sheep when he's hunting? I tell you, my threat to disinherit him if he did not marry was the throw of despair: I never thought it would work. But now, we must talk business, you and I."

"Business? You mean I have passed?"

"Passed? Why, child, I am thanking heaven for you, on bended knees, or would be if it were not such a confoundedly awkward position. You'll do far better for Lavenham than one of those milk and water society misses who think marriage is just another kind of nursery game. You seem to have some idea of practical living, and I tell you, you'll need it with Lavenham. But now, to business, I shall buy your trousseau and put Haverford Hall in order for you. I shall also deal with Mrs. Cummerton—which should not, I think, be difficult—and launch you in society. If you are to be a diplomat's wife, no one must be able to cast the least slur on your antecedents. You have not, I take it, been presented, or made your appearance at Almack's, or done any of the things a young lady should? Well, it will be difficult, and that will make it interesting. I have not the least doubt in the world but that we shall succeed, if you will keep your head and do as I tell you. I shall also provide your dowry and give you an allowance independent of what I give Lavenham— which I shall, of course, increase. But I think it will be better for you—and for him—if you are in some sense independent of him. I would rather I was your tyrant than he. And, one more thing, when you bear us an heir, your allowance will be doubled. Now, I am tired. Ring, and have Lavenham sent for."

So there was to be no more discussion, and Camilla was relieved. The question of the heir was something she did not feel she could discuss even with her remarkable old grandmother-to-be. Nor, needless to say, did she mention it to Leominster, who was, however, heartily satisfied with what she did tell him of the interview. She had wondered how he would take her separate allowance, but he welcomed it with evident relief. "So you are to be independent of me. Admirable; we shall agree much better so." It was one of those remarks of his that gave her, each time, a strange little pang about the heart, and, each time, she told herself, angrily, not to be a fool. He did not for a minute forget that this was a business arrangement they were embarked on. Well, neither would she.

Lady Leominster had announced, in parting, that she was tired of being, as she put it, "a bedridden old crone" and would be up betimes in the morning to take Camilla shopping for her trousseau. "Clothes come first, always: society must wait." Arriving, Camilla found her dressed in the very height of the fashion of ten years ago and looking more like a performing monkey than ever. This morning, she offered a brown, rouged, and wrinkled cheek for Camilla's kiss saying, as she did so, "I am glad to find you so punctual, child: we have much to do today. Lavenham has been here already this morning. His orders are changed: he must leave for Portugal before the month is out."

"So soon?"

"Yes; they are having some crisis or other over there and apparently his presence is urgently required. He seemed doubtful whether you could be ready in time, but I told him not to trouble himself: we shall do it if it means hiring every mantua maker and milliner in town. He has gone off to arrange for a special licence, and you have but to decide, since it must be done hugger-mugger like this, whether you would liefer be married quietly in town or at Haverford on your way to Falmouth."

Something in the course of this speech had alerted Camilla. "Dear madam," she said, "forgive me, but I must ask. Does Lord Leominster *wish* me to go with him now?"

"Lavenham, child, Lavenham, if you love me," barked the old lady, and then, with her cavalier's laugh, "What a sharp little thing you are, to be sure. I confess it had crossed my mind too that Lavenham was, shall we say, prepared to bear a delay. But I am not; and we'll not discuss it further. In many ways, too, 'tis an admirable arrangement. There will be no question, now, of presentation, or appearing in society. You marry Lavenham, leave for Portugal, and return, at leisure, Lady Leominster full blown. I must look out some dowager's purple: I have ladied it in the title alone for so long I shall hardly know how to conduct myself. But, come up to my room: I have commanded the attendance of all the best modistes in town and we must apply ourselves to tricking you out as every inch the diplomat's wife."

That was the most exhausting week of Camilla's life. She did, between fittings, manage to make an opportunity to speak to Lavenham alone and ask him with a straightforward anxiousness that he found oddly touching, "Do you very much mind having to marry me so soon?"

He laughed. "Surely an odd question from bride to groom? No, of course, I do not mind. The sooner, in many ways, the better."

And with this Camilla had to be satisfied, though she could not help feeling that he sounded uncomfortably like someone swallowing a disagreeable dose of physic, to get it over with. Perhaps it was as well for her that she was too busy for much thought. It was not only her personal trousseau that had to be assembled, but almost the entire furnishings for a house. Her betrothed, who knew Portugal well, assured her that although the houses were handsome enough, she would not find a towel or a pair of sheets fit for an English beggar. They must take with them everything necessary for comfort, let alone luxury. "You see how selfishly wise I have been in getting myself a wife to do all this for me."

After he had left to make one of his long visits to Mr. Canning at the Foreign Office, Camilla nibbled slowly and luxuriously on the crumb of comfort he had offered her. She might, after all, be able to earn her keep as a wife, and perhaps his gratitude, by looking after his comfort in Portugal. She threw herself with a new enthusiasm into the choosing of the household linen for which old Lady Leominster was so lavishly prepared to pay.

After some discussion, it had been decided that the wedding had best take place in the village church at Haverford. Lady Leominster, who normally proclaimed herself far too aged and infirm to travel, was so miraculously rejuvenated by a week of hard labour and constant bullying of tradesmen that she pronounced herself easily fit for the journey. "And besides," she twinkled at Camilla, "it will give me an opportunity to see just what kind of a fortune I have committed myself to spending in setting the house to rights for you."

She and Camilla's father were to be the only witnesses at the wedding. Camilla, on learning this, had raised a problem that had been troubling her. Lavenham had come in, briefly, on his way to the Foreign Office to discuss the arrangements for shipping their household stuff, and he and his grandmother had then turned to the order of the journey down. Learning from this that only her father was expected to go with them, Camilla had ventured to interrupt. "But surely," she said, "will not your sister be accompanying us?" She had wondered several times why no move had been made to make her known to Lavenham's sister, who was, she knew, at a school on the outskirts of town, and now it seemed that Lady Chloe Lavenham was not even to be present at her wedding.

"Chloe?" Lavenham raised an eyebrow. "I confess I had not thought it necessary. What think you, ma'am?" As usual, he referred the point to his grandmother.

"I think she had much best stay at school and try to learn

some conduct," said the old lady roundly. And then, seeing Camilla's amazed expression, she laughed. "I collect Lavenham has told you nothing about his sister. Oh well, unpleasant duties always fall to my share. Go you to your appointment, Lavenham, for which I suspect you are already late, and I will explain to Camilla why Chloe had best not grace your wedding." And then, after Lavenham had taken his leave, "You will think our family cursed with scandal, child, when I tell you that, young though she is, Chloe had already come near to disgracing us all. What think you of her trying to elope, at sixteen, and with the music master? Did you ever hear of anything so Gothic?"

"Well," said Camilla thoughtfully, "I suppose it is not really so much worse than marrying a governess. But, tell me, how far did they get?"

"Not too far, by God's mercy, though far enough in all conscience. Lavenham was in Portugal at the time, so it fell to my lot to rise from a sickbed and pursue them on their very inefficient way to Gretna. Luckily, the young man was a fool of the first water and all their arrangements went awry. By the time I caught up with them I think poor Chloe was positively glad to see me. She has never spoken of him since. That was six months ago, and we told her that a further year at school must be her penance. I think when you return from Portugal will be time enough for you to meet her."

Camilla could not help but be sorry for the motherless girl, who, had had, she suspected, all too little of thought or affection from either her brother or her grandmother, but she had learned that, when Lady Leominster spoke with that touch of finality, it was best to let a subject drop, and therefore did so, only resolving that, if she could not contrive to meet Chloe before she left, she would at least enter into a correspondence with her. She had learned the direction of her school and kept hoping for an opportunity to go there, greatly daring, and visit her without consulting either Lavenham or his grandmother, but the press of work was too great, the day came for their move to Haverford, and the opportunity had still not arisen.

It was an oddly assorted quartet that set forward in two travelling carriages for Haverford Hall. Camilla's father was resplendent in gleaming new buckskins and topcoat that she shrewdly suspected her betrothed had paid for, and was more Gallic than ever in his flowery attentions to her and to Lady

Leominster. In some ways, it was a relief to find she was to drive down with him, while Lavenham escorted his grandmother. At least he would not be troubling them with his airs and graces, but nevertheless, she could not repress an illogical pang of disappointment. It had been absurd to hope that Lavenham would accompany her, but she had done so just the same, and had counted more than she had quite realised on this time alone with him to allay some of the doubts and fears that tormented her. Instead, she had to listen for the intolerable length of the journey to her father's enthusiastic congratulations on her good fortune—and his. In the course of his long and exclamatory monologue it came out that Lavenham had undertaken to make him a small allowance— on condition that he kept away from the gaming tables. Camilla did not know whether to be more touched at this instance of Lavenham's thoughtfulness or amused at the ungrounded optimism that made him believe her father's asseverations that he would never touch another pair of dice. She would as easily believe him if he told her he would never draw another breath. Still, it was clear from a slight bitterness in his tone that the allowance was so tied up that it would be impossible for him to anticipate it. At least it should help to safeguard him from blackguards like M. Mireille, who, she was relieved to learn, had indeed packed up and left at once for France. But here, too, was matter for a slight pang. To have been so nearly in touch with her long-lost, dimly remembered older brother and then to have had nothing come of it was a sad blow. But the fact remained that he was only dimly remembered—and he had thrown in his lot with Bonaparte. Perhaps, after all, it was best this way. If peace ever came, which seemed unlikely, it would be time enough to resume relations with him.

At Haverford Hall, as in London, she was too busy for thought. Lady Leominster, after a volley of horrified exclamations at the state of the house, turned to with a will to plan its renovation. And Camilla must be consulted about everything. If she suspected that this was a device of the old lady's to keep her, as she had done in London, too busy for thought, she was, in the main, grateful. The die was cast. What was the use of thinking? Instead, she must decide which paper should be hung in the dining room, and whether the curtains there should be of green- or rose-coloured brocade. She must decide the colour scheme of her own suite of

apartments, which Lady Leominster intended entirely to re-
model: "We'll have no memories of his mother lingering
there to haunt Lavenham," she explained, when Camilla
protested at the expense. This was a silencer. Impossible to
suggest to the old lady that the chances of Lavenham's ever
visiting these apartments were remote indeed.

As their wedding day drew relentlessly near, he seemed
more and more a courteous stranger. Considering her in
everything, he nevertheless contrived really to talk to her
about nothing. They might, she thought in despairing tears
one night, be the merest of chance acquaintances, not a
couple who were to marry in two days. And, as so often
before, she pulled herself up, dried her tears angrily, turned
over the pillow, and composed herself for sleep with the
thought that they were indeed mere acquaintances, and likely
to remain so. Since this did not, somehow, prove conducive
to slumber, she made herself, instead, catalogue the items of
her trousseau, which despite the speed at which it had been
assembled, overwhelmed her by its richness and variety. But
not even the enumeration of silks and gauzes proved soporific,
and it was with a tear still trembling on one eyelid that she
fell asleep at last—to dream, maddeningly, of Lavenham.

She woke to something like panic. Tomorrow was her
wedding day. They were to be married early in the morning,
then leave at once for the long journey to Falmouth. By
spending one night in Exeter, they would break the journey
and reach Falmouth in time to go aboard their ship the evening before she sailed. It all seemed too near, too soon; in
short, impossible. And yet to retreat was equally impossible;
she was caught, a helpless prisoner in the web of Lady Leominster's kindness. The certainty that this was exactly what
Lady Leominster had intended made no difference. She had
gone too far, now, to turn back; she must go through with her
mad bargain.

But it was with an aching head and a pale face that she
joined the others at breakfast. Lady Leominster looked at her
sharply, said nothing, and presently engaged her grandson to
drive her out to pay a morning call on Mrs. Cummerton. "I
will not go so far as to invite her to your wedding, my love,"
she told Camilla, "but I warrant you I'll silence her effectively enough without."

At last, it seemed, Camilla was to be allowed thinking
time, though whether, at this late date, she really wanted it

was another question. Anyway, the formidable dowager soon took care of her. "Camilla, my love, you look pale this morning. Perhaps you would do me a kindness and yourself a benefit by taking a message to Forbes for me? Your father, I know, will accompany you."

Since Forbes, the bailiff, had a cottage at the farthest end of the estate, this would have entailed a ride of several miles there and back, but soon after Lady Leominster and her grandson had left, Forbes appeared in person and Camilla was able to give him the message. This done, and her father having vanished with scarce concealed relief to the billiard room, where he would, she knew, spend the rest of the morning pushing the balls about and betting left hand against right, Camilla found herself alone indeed. At once she knew that it was the last thing she wanted. She prowled about the house, trying to think of anything but tomorrow, and it was with a sensation of pure relief that she saw a dusty hired carriage turn into the drive and come to an awkward stop at the front door. She had been half-heartedly considering colours for the drawing-room curtains; now she stood and unashamedly watched as an untidy postilion let down the steps. A golden-haired girl in a maroon travelling dress bounced out of the carriage, said something to the man, hurried towards the house, and vanished into the front entrance.

Camilla had hardly time to wonder who she could be, arriving thus unheralded and, it seemed, unaccompanied, when Marston, the butler, appeared, looking even more melancholy than usual. After apologising for disturbing her, he came quickly to the point. "Here is Lady Chloe arrived, Miss Forest, in a hired chaise, and wants the man paid off, and my lord out, and my lady too. I am sure I don't know what to do for the best."

"Why, pay the man of course, as Lady Chloe tells you," said Camilla with an assumption of authority that surprised herself. "And bring her in here to me."

This further instruction, however, proved unnecessary, for Lady Chloe had followed the man and now stood hesitating in the doorway, a look of mixed fright and amusement on her exquisite face. Why, Camilla found herself wondering as she went forward to greet her, had no one thought to tell her that her future sister-in-law was a beauty? The explanation flashed into her mind almost as soon as the question. For

Chloe Lavenham's golden ringlets, exquisite pink and white complexion, and huge blue eyes must proclaim her, for all the world to see, her errant mother's child. The less said about it, perhaps, the better. She was tiny, too, and had to reach up to plant an impulsive kiss on Camilla's cheek.

"I *knew* I should like you," she said. "You are not going to give me a scold, are you?"

Camilla laughed as she returned the kiss and temporised. "That must depend," she said, "on what you have been doing."

"Why, nothing so very dreadful," said Chloe, taking off her bonnet and gloves and throwing them on a chair. "And, besides, it serves Lavenham right for trying to keep me away from his wedding. It was perfectly bone-headed of him to think I would stay virtuously minding my book at such a time. You do not mind my coming, do you?"

"Of course not: I have been longing to meet you." And then, aware that Lavenham and his grandmother might think her sadly lacking in firmness, she changed her tone. "But I trust you have at least your school mistress's permission to come, if not your brother's?"

Chloe threw back her head in a fit of delighted—and delightful—laughter. "Permission," she crowed. "I should just about think I had. I am not only permitted to leave, but most earnestly entreated not to return. I told Lavenham I'd make him regret it if he left me mewed up with those old women much longer. I am seventeen, you know," she confided. "All my friends are being presented, and I must stay muddling over French verbs and the pianoforte. Well, I have taken care of that now: the old cats will not have me back even if Lavenham goes on bended knees to them—which, mark you, he is quite incapable of doing."

"Oh dear." Camilla could see trouble ahead. "Have you done something so very dreadful?"

"Of course not. Do not look so grave: I have been in enough trouble already as I have no doubt they have told you: I do not wish for more. No, no, I took the most particular pains to make it something the old pussies could not forgive—and Lavenham could not mind too much: it was only what he had taught me anyway."

"What was?"

"Why, the composition they gave me to write. It was a punishment, of course, for whispering in church: I was to write about what religion means to me. Well, I told them right enough, just what Lavenham has said to me, all about enlightened self-interest and the church being a bogey to frighten children. No, no, they will not have me back, and I do not see how Lavenham can be so *very* angry." But her voice shook a little, and Camilla, recognising fright, put out an impulsive hand to her. "Never mind," she said, "I will stand your friend, and truly I am glad to have you here for my wedding."

Just the same, it was two visibly frightened girls who greeted Lavenham and Lady Leominster on their return. And the scene that followed amply justified their fears. But it was over at last, and, as Lavenham said, if Chloe had indeed been turned out bag and baggage, there was not much to be done about it. "But, in your mighty contriving," he turned on her with a renewal of anger, "what do you propose to do with yourself after you have graced my wedding? Perhaps you are not aware that I leave for Portugal tomorrow."

"Oh, I did not know." Chloe's face fell.

"Exactly! You did not know. Now, you had best go on bended knees to your grandmother to ask for house room in St. James's Square, for I am most certainly not going to leave you here alone with Cousin Harriet to get into what scrapes you please."

It was clear to Camilla that this proposal was equally unwelcome to both the parties concerned, nor did she wonder at it. Lady Leominster was too old to go much into society and too selfish to change her habits for the sake of a young visitor. And Chloe visibly thought that this would be but to exchange one form of servitude for another. Camilla let the unenthusiastic discussion dwindle towards deadlock before she intervened.

"May I propose another plan?" she said. "Could not Chloe come with us? I am sure I should be glad of her company, Lavenham, when you are away, as you tell me you will often have to be." She felt herself colouring at her own temerity, but was rewarded by a quick kiss from Chloe: "I *knew* you would stand my friend. Oh, Lavenham, do, do let me come. I will behave like an angel and not give you or Camilla a moment's anxiety, I promise it, cross my heart."

Lavenham laughed. "For you to talk about keeping out of trouble, puss, is like a fish planning to live on dry land, but to have your promise that you will try is something, I suppose."

Since Lady Leominster warmly seconded this plan, all obstacles to it were quickly dealt with, and indeed Camilla soon began to suspect that after his first doubts Lavenham himself had come to greet this breaking-up of their tête-à-tête existence with considerable relief. For herself, she was not sure what to think, only that there was nothing else she could have done.

Certainly Chloe's presence added a gaiety that had hitherto been lacking in the wedding preparations, and her warm sympathy carried Camilla through the trying hours, while the extra preparations entailed by her joining the travelling party kept everyone too busy for thought. It was Chloe, of course, who helped Camilla dress for her wedding, exclaiming in dismay at the simple dove-coloured travelling dress she had chosen and then keeping up such a stream of chatter about what *she* would wear when her turn came that Camilla had hardly time to be frightened. Chloe talked all the way to the village church and only paused, at last, to give Camilla a little reassuring pat on the shoulder and say, "You look like an angel." She reached up to pinch Camilla's cheeks in an attempt to bring some colour into them and added, "A rather frightened angel, but there's no need for it. Lavenham's bark is much worse than his bite, I tell you, and I should know."

And with these encouraging words ringing in her ears, Camilla took her father's arm and started up the aisle to meet her husband.

CHAPTER 4

It was over, it seemed, in a flash. Lavenham's cold hand slipped the ring on her finger, the clergyman finished the short service, and she clung grateful and uncontrollably trembling to her husband's arm as they walked down the church through the sparse and curious congregation to the vestry, where, for the last time, she signed as Camilla Forest. Then her father was kissing her enthusiastically, shaking Lavenham warmly by the hand and seizing the chance to press a more than paternal kiss on Chloe's flushed cheek. Glancing up, Camilla saw Lavenham's dark eyes taking this in.

"I should kiss you?" he said.

"It is, I believe, customary." She held up her cold cheek to his still colder kiss. Then they were all outside, grateful for April sun after the winter cold of the church. There was laughter, a scattering of flower petals from the village children, a volley of farewells. The day's journey to Exeter was so long that Lavenham and his grandmother had decided that any delay for a wedding breakfast was impossible. So bride, bridesmaid, and groom were loaded forthwith into Lavenham's travelling carriage, while Camilla's new maid, Frances, took her place with the valet, Jenks, in the second carriage with the luggage.

"Well," said Chloe into the stretching silence as the carriage swung out on to the main road, "that was quick. I shall expect something quite other when my turn comes, and so I warn you, Lavenham."

He laughed shortly. "I doubt if there are bride's cake and champagne at Gretna Green."

"Oh, that." She dismissed her elopement as a youthful folly, long forgotten, then turned with a pretty gesture to Camilla: "You cannot conceive what an encumbrance I feel. To be acting third on a honeymoon party is a most monstrous piece of ill manners. Should I, do you think, ride with Jenks and the maid?"

Camilla, whose gratitude to Chloe for breaking the silence had indeed been mixed with a shade of regret at her presence, began a polite protest, but Lavenham interrupted her, telling his sister not to be more absurd than she could help. "You wished to be of the party; now you will put up with the consequences."

Even Chloe found this something of a silencer and after exchanging a glance of quick sympathy with her new sister-in-law settled down to gaze out of the carriage window. Camilla, too, was silent, sorry that Lavenham had given his sister such a setdown, and yet sympathising with the almost intolerable strain under which she recognised him to be labouring. She longed to make some gesture of sympathy— after all, she was his wife—but restrained the hand that would have gone out towards him. The first advance, if there was to be any, must come from his side, not hers. She remembered Lady Leominster's warning, "You will have to be patient ... patient as Job," and sat back, quiet in her corner. So they travelled across the heart of England all day, almost as silent as if they had been three strangers in the public coach. By the time they reached Exeter, late in the evening, the silence of constraint had given place to that of fatigue, and Camilla observed a crease across Lavenham's brow that she had never seen before. Was he, she wondered, regretting their marriage already?

Chloe brightened up at sight of the outskirts of Exeter with its promise of food and rest. For all her seventeen years and attempted elopement, she was enough of a child still so that the mere passage of time could put her at her ease in any situation. By now, her sense of awkwardness of intruding on her brother's honeymoon was lost in the excitement of the journey. She began to chatter excitedly to Camilla and was soon running from side to side of the carriage in her attempts to see Exeter Cathedral. A lurch of the carriage as it hit the paved road overset her, and she cannoned heavily into her brother, who let out an exclamation of such black rage that Camilla shrank back in her corner.

Chloe did not seem particularly surprised, however, but settled back in her own corner with an apology, and added, "Have you one of your migraine headaches, poor Lee?" Her sympathetic tone and the use of the pet name, which Camilla had not heard before, showed that his start of bad temper had neither surprised nor alarmed her.

He admitted to the headache. "I am afraid I have been vilely bad company all day," he said to Camilla. "You must forgive me, M——" He had almost said, "Miss Forest," but remembered himself in time, coloured deeply, and contrived to turn it into "my dear."

The mild endearment moved Camilla almost to the point of tears, which she however took care to conceal, remarking instead, in her gentlest voice, on the length of the day's journey and enquiring what treatment he found best for the headache.

"Oh, nothing but to endure it," he answered a shade impatiently as the carriage turned into the inn yard, and she could only admire the fortitude with which he endured the bustle of their late arrival. Fortunately, rooms and a meal had been bespoken for them, and a question, which had been troubling Camilla, of whether she and her husband were to share a room, had apparently been settled in advance. They found two large bedrooms with a sitting room between them ready for their occupation. Chloe's presence, of course, had not been provided for, and the obsequious host was soon deep in apologies because he had no other room available that was fit for her occupation. But this was easily settled, "Of course she must sleep with me," said Camilla, and felt herself amply rewarded for the sacrifice of comfort and privacy by her husband's grateful look.

Dinner, the host told them, would be served immediately, and they retired to their rooms at once to repair the ravages of the long day's journey. To Camilla's relief, Chloe did not comment on the odd allocation of bedrooms, being far too busy hanging out of the window and counting the number of gentlemen's carriages in the inn yard below. "If only Lavenham would eat at the ordinary like anybody else," she wailed, "we might see their owners, but he is so mortally high in the instep he would never even think of it. And how am I to find myself a husband if I meet no one?"

Camilla paused with the comb in her hair and looked across the room at Chloe. The time, she felt, had come to be firm. "You must not speak like that of your brother," she said, "and most particularly not to me. As for a husband, there is time enough to be thinking of that when the world has forgotten about your excursion to Gretna," and then, seeing the ready tears in the child's eyes, "Come, that is enough for a first scold, and I promise you we will never speak of Gretna again."

When they joined Lavenham in their sitting room they found him staring pale and gloomily at the table which a man and a boy were engaged in loading with food. Chloe exclaimed with delight at the plenty before her, but it was soon obvious to Camilla that Lavenham ate only by a heroic effort of will. At last, she could bear the sight of his struggles no longer, and as Chloe embarked on her third helping of devilled chicken, asked: "Would you not be very much happier in the quiet of your own room, my dear?" She ventured the endearment he had used. "Chloe and I will do perfectly well without you, and, with your permission, I will come, presently, and see if I cannot massage the pain away. I used to do it for the poor Duchess of Devonshire when she had one of her headaches and she said it was wonderful how it eased her."

He protested, but was obviously glad to leave them. Later, when she knocked timidly on his door and found him stretched fully clothed on his bed in the darkened room, he was obviously in too much pain not to be grateful for any chance of alleviation. He turned over obediently and lay flat on his face while her gentle hands worked their way over the tense muscles at the back of his neck where the dark hair grew close and curling. Gradually, as she sat there in the half dark, she could hear his breathing ease off into sleep and at last, very quietly, she rose to leave him. At the door, his voice stopped her: "Camilla," he said, and then, as she paused, "thank you."

"Good night," she whispered, closing the door softly behind her.

They had another long day's journey before them, and were up early again, but Camilla had already lain for a long time, listening to the noises of the inn yard, and Chloe's quiet breathing, and thinking about her husband and the strange life before her. Later, the first sight of Lavenham was encouraging: he was visibly better, his colour nearly normal and the furrow gone from above his eyebrows. But if she had hoped for any increase in warmth on his part this morning, she was to be disappointed. He was brisk almost to the point of rudeness, both to her and to Chloe, and it was a subdued little party that climbed punctually into the carriage as the cathedral clock struck the hour. Chloe, however, had had enough of silence and, having ascertained that his headache was indeed gone, began to tease him with questions about Portugal. What was he to do there? Where were they to live? Did he like the Portuguese, and was their Queen really mad? And a thousand other questions, which he began by answering monosyllabically enough, but gradually, as the carriage rolled on through fitful sunshine and the sounds of spring, he began to thaw a little and answer her questions, and those that Camilla now dared to raise, more fully. Yes, he told them, Lord Strangford, the Minister Plenipotentiary, had already secured a house for them on the eastern outskirts of Lisbon; they would be able to go there directly from the boat. "I found the dirt and discomfort of my lodgings intolerable when I was last there and insisted that this time I would have a house—fortunately, as it has proved. You will find the Portuguese a good enough kind of people, I think," he was addressing Camilla now, rather than Chloe, "if curiously unaware of dirt or discomfort. But the climate, I am sure, will make up for much, though I hope you neither of you find hot weather oppressive."

They both assured him that it was of all things what they liked best and took advantage of his mellower mood to ply him with more questions, which he was glad enough to answer. "You are to form part, remember, of the diplomatic colony and much may depend on your behaviour." This time, the speech was made very directly to Chloe, who laughed, blushed, stammered a promise of good behaviour, and changed the subject by reiterating an earlier question about the Queen.

"Oh yes," he assured her, "she is as mad as you please, and shut up in her palace of Queluz while her son Dom John governs as Regent—and but a poor business he makes of it, I am afraid, though he is a good enough sort of man."

"Is it true that he and his wife never speak to each other except on state occasions?" put in Chloe.

"True enough, but not the kind of thing upon which you will remark in Portuguese society," was his repressive answer.

She was not to be cowed. "That is all very well, Lavenham, but how are Camilla and I to avoid making gaffes if we do not know these things?"

There was such obvious sense in this that he unbent still

more and proceeded to give them a lively account of Portuguese society, its delights, such as they were, its tedium, and its pitfalls. "And above all," he ended warningly, "you will avoid comment of any kind on their religion, which is, to the Regent certainly, and to many of his people, the most important thing in life. And, equally, you will avoid association of any kind with the French—oh," he remembered, "forgive me, Camilla, but at least you are English now."

She laughed. "And a good thing too, I can see. But do the French maintain an embassy in Lisbon, then? I had not thought of it."

"Of course they do, since Portugal is, officially at least, neutral."

"How do you mean, officially?" asked Chloe.

"Why, merely that, in past years, Portugal has always been our very good friend both at land and sea. Now, Bonaparte is trying to change all that, and is exerting the utmost pressure on Dom John to persuade him to close his ports against us."

"And would that be bad?" asked Camilla.

"Disastrous."

"And you are going to Lisbon to persuade the Prince Regent that he must not give way!" exclaimed Chloe. "What a great man you are, to be sure, Lee."

He laughed. "Well, call it, rather, to assist Lord Strangford in his persuasions. My cousin thought my knowledge of the country might prove of some service. I spent several years there when I was a very young man indeed," he explained to Camilla, "since the rest of Europe was closed to me by this unending war. I hope you will find the countryside and the people to your taste. I have grown to find them good friends, for all their faults."

She could not help laughing at this characteristically reserved commendation. "Do not praise them too high," she begged, teasingly, "or you will rasie expectations quite impossible of fulfilment. But I can see that we will have plenty to do, Chloe and I, in ensuring that we do not handicap you in your negotiations. Tell me, though, in what language will we converse with these paragons of yours, for I must confess that I know no more Portuguese than I do Greek."

"I am afraid that with the ladies you may find yourselves largely reduced to sign language," he said, "for you will find their ideas of female education amazingly behind ours."

Camilla laughed again. "So Chloe and I will find ourselves

miracles of learning," she said. "Well, at all events, it will
make the chances of our offending considerably less if no one
can understand what we say. Do you know any Portuguese,
Chloe?"

"Why, yes," she said surprisingly, "I do a little. I tried to
learn it when Lavenham was there last, but I am afraid I did
not make a great deal of progress: to tell truth, I could not
believe that any human being could make such strange
noises; but perhaps I will recall it when I hear it spoken."

"You never told me that," said Lavenham, with a mixture
of surprise and pleasure that Camilla found most promising
for his relations with his sister.

"You never asked me," said Chloe simply.

The day wore on endlessly. They had left the red Devon
fields behind now and were rattling over the dreary uplands
of Cornwall. The fatigue and tedium of travelling had them
all in its grip and conversation dwindled and died. Chloe
curled up in her corner and fell asleep with the easy abandon
of a child; Lavenham, in his, leaned back with eyes half
closed, brooding—about what? Camilla wondered, and then
warned herself against the vanity of imagining his thoughts
were of her. It was far more likely that he was considering
the difficulties of the mission ahead of him.

She had difficulties enough of her own to face. Impossible
not to like Chloe, but equally impossible not to wonder just
how their curious *ménage à trois* would develop. The prospect of working out some kind of possible life with Lavenham had been frightening enough without the addition of his
lively sister to the party. And yet, she could not regret her
suggestion that Chloe accompany them. It was obvious that
much of her thoughtless behaviour was the direct result of her
forlorn childhood. She had been a baby when her father was
killed and her mother ran away and no one had really
thought about her since. Her grandmother cared nothing for
her; her brother hated women; she had been brought up by
servants, bandied about from this casual relative to that, and
finally deposited at a school in Wimbledon from which she
had been lucky if she escaped once a year. It was really no
wonder, Camilla thought, that she had leapt at the proffered
affection of a music master. After all, no one else had cared
for her. Nor was it surprising that her one idea now was,
apparently, to get herself married as quickly as possible. She

must be suffering from lack of family life and this was the only way she could secure it. Camilla and Lavenham would have to form themselves into a family, however odd a one, for her sake. At least, after his first outburst Lavenham seemed to have resigned himself easily enough to her accompanying them and indeed, considering how little they had seen of each other, brother and sister seemed to be on remarkably easy terms, and Lavenham had been visibly touched by her attempt at learning Portuguese for his sake. Perhaps it would do well enough yet. Perhaps, even, she and Chloe between them might contrive to teach him that women were not so very dreadful after all. And, smiling at this idea, she fell asleep.

In his corner, Lavenham was asking himself if he had, perhaps, gone raving mad. Here he was, at the outset of what he intended to be a successful career in the diplomatic service, burdened with not one, but two of the females he detested. Now that there was time to think—for his wily old grandmother had allowed him quite as little as she had Camilla—he could only decide he was recovering, too late, from a fit of insanity. It would take more than his grandmother's fortune to compensate him for its results. With an impatient sigh, he looked from the corner where Chloe slept, her face flushed, her mouth half open, her curls dishevelled under a lopsided bonnet, to Camilla in her dove-coloured dress, as neat asleep as awake, her face a little pale, as it had been all day, her eyes dark-shadowed, her hands loosely clasped in her lap. His wife. If he was mad, he thought, suddenly sorry for her, so was she to have accepted his terms. There was nothing ahead for either of them but trouble and sorrow. The migraine headache began to flicker once again behind his eyes. Best try not to think about it. He reached into a pocket of the coach, drew out the instructions Mr. Canning had had drawn up for him, and made himself concentrate on them.

The inn at Falmouth was far from luxurious, and it was a weary little party that boarded the packet next morning. Once out at sea, the fresh land breeze seemed to become a hurricane, the little ship tossed and shuddered, and Camilla found it increasingly difficult to endure Chloe's tearing spirits. To Chloe, everything was exciting; even the idea of possible pursuit and capture by a French man-of-war seemed to delight her. She was free at least, the world before her, and nothing could subdue her.

Camilla, on the other hand, was worn out with the events of the past week and it was with a sensation of relief that she finally found herself so overcome by nausea that she had to admit her sickness and hurry below to her cabin. Chloe was all sympathy at once and during the wretched week that followed, Camilla thanked heaven, over and over again, for the lucky chance that had brought her with them. The maid, Frances, who had never even seen the sea before, had retired to her cabin before the boat left harbour; if it had not been for Chloe, Camilla would have been entirely dependent on her husband's ministrations. It was an appalling thought, for it was all too obvious that he found a sick woman even less attractive than a well one. After the first visit of duty he paid her, she begged Chloe to keep him away and Chloe laughed and promised to do her best. "Not that it will be difficult," she added. "Poor Lee never could abide the sight of sickness. I think perhaps it was from seeing our father die," she added as she prepared to bathe Camilla's forehead with lavender water.

"Seeing what?"

"Did you not know? I thought my grandmother would have told you. You know about the duel, I collect?"

"Oh yes, Lady Leominster told me." This was dangerous ground. If only her head did not ache so.

"Oh well, then," Chloe went on cheerfully, "she cannot have told you that when they fought not only was my mother in the other carriage, she had Lee with her. If it came to flight she was going to take him too."

"Good God! But what happened?"

"Why, when my father fell, Lee saw, jumped out of the carriage, and ran to him. They could not drag him away, and the runners found him there when they came up. Of course, my mother was gone by then; they could not afford to stay."

"She left him there alone?"

"Yes, it is no wonder that he cannot abide the sight of blood, or, indeed, of illness of any kind. You can see," she went on, "that in a way I was lucky. My mother never thought of taking me. I would have been far too much trouble. Indeed, I have been nothing but a trouble to everyone ever since," she added with sudden passion.

Camilla reached out to catch her hand. "Not to me,

Chloe," she said. "I cannot think how I would have managed without you."

Chloe pressed her hand fiercely. "I will never be a trouble to you, Camilla."

CHAPTER 5

Life in Portugal proved everything that Lavenham had said. Chloe seemed neither to notice nor to mind the dirt, but Camilla was Frenchwoman enough to be appalled by the condition in which she found their house, and spent the first few weeks of her stay battling—in sign language—with her Portuguese servants in an effort to have it made habitable. They thought her quite mad, but luckily, liked her, and liked blond Chloe, with her smattering of Portuguese, still more. If the crazy *Inglêsas* wanted their floors scrubbed to a fantastic standard of cleanliness, they should have them. Only in the servants' quarters did Camilla have to give up the struggle. There, by an honourable compromise, chaos still reigned, with pigs and poultry happily sharing the apartments with the staff.

Their first few weeks were surprisingly peaceful. When they arrived the Court was at the Caldas da Rainha taking the waters, and, since Lord Strangford was there too, Lavenham felt obliged to join him, leaving his wife and sister to their domestic devices. It would be time enough, he said, for them to make their appearance in society when he—and the Court—returned. They had found British society in Lisbon sadly shrunk since he had been there last. Bonaparte's demands on Dom John, the Prince Regent, had not been limited to the closing of his ports against English ships: he also wanted the thriving British colony banished from Portugal and their possessions expropriated. And the Regent, while trying desperately to please both sides, had strongly advised the English residents to sell up and go while the going was good. The English factory was closed, its staff gone, and until they had made their debut in Portuguese society, Camilla and

Chloe were almost entirely dependent on each other for companionship.

But then, there was so much to do and see and talk about. The weather was just what they had expected, but so far they had not found it too hot, revelling in a warmth and richness of sunshine that made their light muslins practical almost for the first time in their lives. Their house, which stood on a hill at the eastern end of Lisbon, had a broad marble terrace overlooking the harbour, and here, every evening, they sat, alternating between sun and shade as the spirit moved them, Chloe growing browner every day, while even Camilla was gradually losing the sallow tinge that had previously marred her pale complexion. Soon she too was faintly brown, with a glow of health that made Chloe exclaim one evening as they settled themselves with books and work, "Why, you are growing quite a beauty, Camilla. Lavenham will be amazed when he returns."

Camilla laughed. "If he notices," she said. She found Chloe wonderfully easy company these days and was increasingly grateful for the chance that had brought her with them. Though in many ways an adult, Chloe still had a child's easy acceptance of a situation. She did not seem to find it strange that Lavenham should have abandoned his bride to go and dance attendance on the Court, nor that he and Camilla had their own independent apartments in the house. If no one else appeared to find this odd, then neither would she. Perhaps, Camilla thought, she was too happy to notice much. Freed at last from the tyranny of the schoolroom, she blossomed each day into new life and gaiety. She was not endowed with a particularly deep or serious nature and it was indeed remarkable how happily ignorant she had contrived to remain after all those years of forced study. Her genius was for happiness, not learning, and she contrived to find and convey to Camilla a fresh delight in every detail of their new life. Presently, Camilla feared, she might, since she had so few resources within herself, begin to find their simple daily round monotonous, but by then, no doubt, Lavenham would have returned and Portuguese society would provide a new scene of pleasure and interest.

As for Camilla, she, too, was very happy in her own, quieter way. This breathing space of Lavenham's necessary absence could be given up to the pleasure of being a married woman, someone with a place in the world at last. And it was all Lavenham's doing. There was a deep, quiet pleasure in setting his house in order against his return, which, she hoped, would not be much longer deferred. A feeling of tension hung about Lisbon these hot days of early summer: rumours ran the streets in the daytime, as packs of scavenging dogs did by night, and Camilla did not know which she found more disturbing, the whispers that ran, incomprehensibly, through the Great Square by day, or the desolate howling of the dogs at night. She would be glad when Lavenham returned, with his understanding of the language and the situation.

The Prince Regent came back at last, rowing down the Tagus in the royal barge on the eve of the Festival of Corpus Christi. Chloe was delighted and spent the morning watching the animated scene on the river from the terrace of the house, running in, from time to time, to urge Camilla to come out and join her, or to ask if there had been any news of Lavenham. Her anxiety for his return was considerably heightened by the fact that Camilla had positively refused to take her to see the procession next day unless he should be there to escort them.

When he arrived at last, tired, and travel-stained from a morning's jolting over the rough Portuguese roads, Chloe rushed to throw her arms around him and put her request. "Lee, you are here at last! Oh, Lee, you will take us tomorrow, will you not? Camilla will not go without you, she is grown positively matronly while you have been gone. Oh, Lee, we can go, can we not?"

With something half-way between a laugh and a groan, he disengaged himself from her embrace and held her at arm's length, looking over her head to Camilla, who had followed her, more calmly, into the carriageway behind the house. "Quiet, child, a moment." To Camilla's relief, the rebuke was a gentle one. "You are both well, I can see," he went on. "I must ask your pardon for leaving you so long alone," he was addressing Camilla now; "we have been expecting, daily, the order to return, but Dom John, excellent man, has a perfect genius for vacillation. I am only relieved that his beloved church has brought him at last. It is, I collect, unthinkable, that one of the great festivals should take place in his absence." And then, to Chloe: "So you wish to see the procession tomorrow? I promise you, it will prove disappointing and tawdry enough, but if you have been behaving yourself, why, we shall see."

"Oh, Lee, I have been a perfect angel, a model of all the virtues, have I not, Camilla? We have hardly stirred from the house, and I have sewed, and studied, and slept like an absolute paragon. Truly, I deserve a treat, and so does Camilla, who has been so busy and domestic that I doubt you will not recognise the house. Why, it smells almost like Haverford Hall, instead of the stables it seemed when we arrived."

Laughing, he took an arm of each and led them indoors, through the enthusiastic crowd of servants who had hurried out to welcome him. In the main salon, Chloe seized his hand and hurried him enthusiastically here and there to see the improvements Camilla had made, but Camilla, who had noticed the telltale furrow between his eyes, soon intervened, partly, she realised, to protect Chloe herself from the explosion she could see was imminent.

"Your brother is tired, my love," she said, and then, to Lavenham, "Would you not be glad to retire for a while and recover from the fatigue of the journey? We do not dine till six; it will be time enough then to hear your news and talk of tomorrow."

Chloe laughed. "I told you she was the complete matron, Lavenham. You had best do as she bids you."

It was spoken thoughtlessly enough, but Camilla coloured up to the eyes at the suggestion that she was acting the part of a managing wife and began a stammered apology.

Lavenham cut her short, addressing Chloe in repressive tones. "I shall indeed do as Camilla bids me," he said, "since she has suggested the very thing I most desire, rest. As for tomorrow, we will talk of that later. In the meantime," he had reached the door, but now turned to speak once more to Camilla, "are you very busy, or could you, perhaps, spare the time to give me some more of that massage that proved so miraculous for my head at Exeter? I have been plagued with the headache since I saw you last, and if we are to take this bad child to see the procession tomorrow, I had as lief be rid of it."

Camilla, who had been longing to volunteer her services, was equally delighted at his request, and at the kinder tone he used towards Chloe. Besides, she was glad of the chance to accompany him to his rooms and talk to him alone. She

had done her best to keep her anxiety about the state of
things in Lisbon to herself, considering Chloe too young to be
burdened with such worries, but it was an immense relief to
be able to ask Lavenham whether he thought an invasion by
France, or Spain, or even both, to be imminent. It was an
even greater relief to have him pooh-pooh her fears. "Do you
think I would have left you and Chloe alone if there had
been any chance of it? No, no, there will be much more of
the kind of political blackmail of which Bonaparte is such a
master before he moves to the attack. I do not expect any
trouble before autumn. Ah, that is better," and he gave
himself up, with a sigh of relief, to the soothing pressure of
her hands.

Camilla was waked at first light next morning by a hideous
din, which, as she came gradually to complete consciousness,
resolved itself into the jangling of all the church bells in the
city, mingled with the rolling of drums and the harsh braying
of trumpets. The Festival of Corpus Christi had begun. They
met early for their breakfast of excellent coffee and coarse,
indifferent bread and Camilla was glad to see that Lavenham's brow was clear and to have him assure her that he had
quite slept his headache away. She had given up the effort to
persuade the servants to produce an English breakfast for
herself and Chloe, but was amused to see ham and eggs
appear, as if by magic, for Lavenham. Clearly, she teased
him, men were still the lords of creation, at least in Portugal.

Chloe's thoughts, of course, were all on the procession this
morning, but, warned by Camilla, she managed to refrain
from mentioning it until her brother had finished his breakfast. She was rewarded for her patience when he rose from
the table Camilla had had set up in the sunshine of the
terrace, smiled from one to the other of them, and asked,
"And now, how do you ladies wish to celebrate my first day
at home?"

Chloe, who had been wandering restlessly to and fro between the garden and the terrace, ran to him at once. "Oh,
Lee, by going to see the procession, please ... It is quite
near, I have found out all about it, and it starts from the
Church of St. Vincent at our end of the town. We could
almost walk there, and everybody says it is something quite
out of the ordinary."

He turned to Camilla. "What say you, my dear? Shall we
gratify this child's passion for spectacles?"

Camilla, who would gladly have done anything for him
when he called her his dear, agreed at once.

"Very well, then, we had best start as soon as you ladies
can make yourselves ready. Is it not fortunate that my friend
Dom Fernando has arranged to make a balcony available to
us in the square opposite the church; I fear you would be
sadly crushed if we had to watch from the street itself."

Chloe reached up to give him a resounding kiss on the
cheek. "You monster, Lee, you had planned to go all the
time. What a tease you are to be sure. I do not know how
Camilla abides you!" And she danced away to fetch her
shadiest hat and most becoming scarf.

Alone with Camilla, Lavenham seized the opportunity to
explain to her that Dom Fernando da Casa Molinha, who
had arranged for them to have the use of the balcony, was
one of the leaders of the British party in Lisbon, and to ask
her to try and make sure that Chloe did not, as he put it, "fly
off in one of her mad starts" and offend him. Camilla
promised to do her best, though she felt slightly daunted
when he reminded her that an unmarried Portuguese girl of
Chloe's age and position would be immured almost as completely as a Turk or Moor. She hurried away to fetch her
own hat and sunshade and pass on the warning to Chloe, who
promised that butter would not melt in her mouth all day.

Their mule-drawn carriage made its way with difficulty
through the crowded streets towards the square in which the
church of St. Vincent stood, and they had to leave it some
distance off and walk through back streets to the building
from which they were to watch the procession. Dom Fernando greeted them in fluent French, and Camilla breathed a
secret sigh of relief, having discovered, with surprise, that
Chloe knew none. It would be difficult, even for her, to
shock their hosts with her few words of Portuguese.

Looking down, she forgot anxiety in amazement. All round
the crowded square, balconies were hung with damask, tapes-
try, or cloth of gold, and the rich fabrics, gleaming in the
sun, made it look more like an Eastern encampment than a
European city. Opposite them, the church's vast flight of
steps was lined with Yeomen of the Queen's Guard, brilliant
in their parti-coloured uniforms. When the great doors were
flung open at last, and the Patriarch of Lisbon appeared
under his canopy, with the church dignitaries in their scarlet
vestments and the Prince Regent and his court in all the

splendour of full dress, Camilla and Chloe alike were silenced as much by the magnificence of the scene as by the roar of guns and the clangour of all the church bells of Lisbon.

After some inevitable Portuguese confusion, the procession got under way at last across the square and wound slowly away to disappear down a winding street. Chloe caught Camilla's hand: "May we not follow it?"

"I'm afraid not." But Camilla was distracted by a question from Dom Fernando. She threw together enough French adjectives to satisfy him, and turned to see, with dismay, that Chloe had vanished. Below them, the square was emptying fast as the crowd hurried after the procession. Was that Chloe's Italian straw bonnet whisking off round the corner? Camilla's heart plummeted. What should she do? What would Lavenham say? With a half-intelligible apology, she left Dom Fernando and crossed the balcony to where her husband stood talking animatedly in Portuguese.

"My dear." She spoke in English. "Chloe—"

He looked quickly round. "Where is she?"

No use beating about the bush. "I am very much afraid she is run off to follow the procession. I was talking to Dom Fernando." She blanched at his frown. "I beg you will forgive me."

"Forgive *you*? What's that to the purpose? I should have known better than to bring her."

"But will you not go after her?"

"How can I?" He kept his tone casual, but she could sense the anger seething below. "She has played us this trick, and must take the consequences. Because she is a reckless hoyden, am I to leave you here alone? Besides, I have invited Dom Fernando and his friends to come home with us."

"But what will you tell them?"

"About Chloe? That she was overcome by the heat and is gone home already." It was settled. He turned away to speak to Dom Fernando.

The rest of the afternoon was slow agony for Camilla. Acting hostess for the first time, offering the wine and sweetmeats Lavenham had ordered, and automatically exchanging polite French nothings, she did her best to hide her gnawing anxiety for Chloe. When their guests left at last, she turned impulsively to her husband. "I'm so worried," she said. "For Chloe. But did I manage to hide it? Did I do, Lavenham?"

His smile was reward enough. "You were perfect. My grandmother would have been proud of you."

She would much rather he had been proud of her himself, but there were more important things to think about. "And now, will you not go and look for Chloe?"

His face hardened. "And where, pray, should I begin? Am I to blazon her disgrace by enquiring her out through all the public haunts of Lisbon? Impossible. I am afraid she must pay the penalty of her folly and find her way home as best she can."

When Chloe finally appeared, dusty and tired but shockingly cheerful and quite unharmed, Camilla's heart-felt relief was qualified by dread of what Lavenham would say. He looked his sister up and down from under furrowed brows, then turned to his wife: "You would oblige me by leaving us. What I must say to this termagant is not for your ears."

Chloe never told Camilla what he had said, but seemed to avoid him, spending much time wandering in the alleys of their garden and even among the tangled shrubberies of the empty house next door. When Camilla mildly queried the wisdom of this, she was up in arms at once. "Oh, pshaw, Camilla, must you play the prude so unmercifully? Were you never young yourself? And anyway, if I wish to be alone sometimes, so, surely must you? I am not quite blind, though I collect you think me so."

Camilla was silenced. It was true that she found their trio awkward enough these days. It was not only that her husband and his sister were on such bad terms. She could not help feeling that but for her own impulsive invitation of Chloe she might by now have come to what she thought of as more human terms with her formidable husband. Would he never stop behaving to her with a stranger's calm courtesy? Walking back now, alone, through the orange and lemon groves of their garden, she tasked herself, for the thousandth time, with folly. Lavenham had promised her a marriage of convenience and had kept his word. But had she ever believed him, or wanted to? Like so many other women before her, she had deluded herself that marriage would change everything, particularly her husband. He hated women, and with cause, but she would change all that. So she had thought, without quite admitting it to herself. Now, she admitted failure. And (she plucked a rotten lemon and threw it, furiously, downhill towards the river) there was worse than that. Lavenham still disliked women, herself included, and she, fool that she was, had fallen in love with him.

Admitting it made it worse. She hurried back to the house and stopped short at sight of Lavenham himself awaiting her on the verandah.

"You look flushed." His cool solicitude was the last straw. "Surely you have not been hurrying in this heat? It is high time we moved to the country. The Prince Regent, Dom John, leaves for his palace of Mafra next week, and Lord Strangford is finding us villas at Sintra. You will be glad, I am sure, of the cool and quiet of the hills. But where is Chloe? I thought her with you."

"In the garden." For the first time Camilla found herself prevaricating with him, but why make trouble by saying she was actually in the garden next door? "I have just left her. She is picking a bunch of jasmine for the house."

"Touching and domestic." His tone held irony. "I wish I might consider her a reformed character, but, if I know her, it is only skin deep. I wish she may not lead you a dance when I am away."

"Away?" She seized on the important point.

"Yes. I must leave you tonight, and do not exactly know when I shall return. Lord Strangford will make our apologies to Dom John. Your presentation will have to be postponed till we have moved to Sintra. Perhaps, by then, Chloe's conduct will have justified her inclusion in the party. I can only hope so." He did not sound optimistic.

Chloe took the news of her brother's departure, and their consequent return to a life of almost cloistered seclusion, with equanimity. It was a sad comment, Camilla thought, on how relations between brother and sister had worsened since Corpus Christi. As for her, she was glad enough to escape the heavy round of Portuguese hospitality, but missed Lavenham more than she liked. Besides, she was anxious about him. He had avoided telling her where he was going, and she had forborne to press him, but knew, somehow, that it was into danger.

So when Chloe, the afternoon he left, stretched herself like a luxurious little cat in the sunshine, and said, "Now I call this peace and quietness," she was surprised at the sharp answer she got.

Restless and unhappy, Camilla was pleased when Chloe actually suggested that they spend some of their time study-

ing French and Portuguese. They settled down to domesticity, spending long hours on the verandah, sewing and exchanging French and Portuguese verbs. Only, towards evening,
Chloe would grow restless, jump up, drop her book, and say
she was going for a stroll in the garden. Once or twice,
Camilla went too, but it was never a success, and she soon
gave up. She remembered well enough what it had been like
to be seventeen in Devonshire House, where, however lonely,
one was never alone. And when Chloe came back, at dusk,
from her solitary rambles, with flushed cheeks and happy
step, she congratulated herself on her decision. The child was
growing up, finding herself. She must be left to do it her own
way.

It certainly seemed to be working. In her own anxiety
for Lavenham, Camilla was sometimes almost irritated by
Chloe's visible, bubbling happiness. She did not walk, she
danced; even her voice was a song. Monstrous that this
child, with her gift for enjoying life, should have been cooped
up for so long, learning little or nothing from a parcel of old
women. In her sympathy with Chloe's past, she was prepared
to bear with her present heedlessness. Sometimes she found
herself wishing that Chloe was not quite so set on these
evening walks of hers. For with the approach of night, the
air, intolerably hot all day, began to cool and a fresh little
breeze sprang up off the harbour. Now would have been the
time to order out the carriage for a drive along the shore.
But Lavenham had explained, before he left them alone for
the first time, that if they wished to drive out, it must be
together, chaperoning each other. He had been equally firm
about any chance of their being benighted in the sudden
dark. And by the time Chloe came wandering back from the
garden, her golden curls in disorder, her arms full of jasmine
or myrtle blossom, the first shadows of night would have
begun to creep along the terrace and it was too late to think
of anything but candles and bed.

Camilla was brooding about this, one golden afternoon,
and wondering whether she was allowing Chloe to overin-
dulge her passion for solitude, when she was disturbed by a
servant announcing Dom Fernando and his sister. Surprised
and alarmed, for she had thought them already at Mafra
with the Court, she hurried to greet them and offer refreshments, waiting impatiently, as they completed the solemn

ritual of meeting, for the moment when she could ask the question that had flashed at once to her mind.

"You have news, perhaps, of my husband?" she said in French.

"Why, no." Dom Fernando seemed ill at ease. "That was what I had come to ask you. Can you tell me, perhaps, where I could get in touch with him? The Prince Regent is anxious to speak with him."

Camilla, explaining that Lavenham had not told her where he was going, found much to disquiet her about this speech. Dom Fernando was supposed to be a friend of the English, but she knew enough already about the Portuguese Court to be aware that his message from the Prince Regent must be a mere pretext. Why, then, was he so anxious to know where Lavenham was? A creeping feeling along her bones confirmed her earlier certainty that he had gone on a mission of danger, and one, it now seemed, unknown even to his Portuguese friends. But there was no time for anxiety; she was too busy concealing it, laughing with Dom Fernando and showing herself the kind of giddy wife to whom no man in his senses would think of giving precise information.

"He said he would be back—presently." She fluttered her eyelashes at Dom Fernando in the best imitation she could manage of Chloe. "Perhaps Lord Strangford would know where he is. I have not seen him this age."

"No," said Dom Fernando. "He is away too." The words fell coldly on Camilla's ear and she was relieved when he put down his wine glass and said something in Portuguese to his plump and docile sister. They rose together and took their leave, only, as Dom Fernando kissed Camilla's hand in parting, he paused for a moment. "Ask him to come to me as soon as he returns. I am," he paused for a moment, "I am anxious about him."

Chloe, returning, late and glowing, from the garden, found her sister-in-law so short-tempered that she retired at once to the dreamy seclusion of her room.

CHAPTER 6

The anxious days that followed were made no easier for Camilla by the constant visits she received from Dom Fernando and his family. He brought his sister again, he brought his grandmother, he brought his plump and widowed aunt and his three giggling sisters-in-law. If a day passed without his visiting her, urgent messages would summon her to his house, where, among an indescribable medley of sounds and odours, she was expected to join them in their oily and indigestible meals of fiercely flavoured rice. Dom Fernando's pretext was the enormous fancy his sister had taken to Camilla, though since, as Lavenham had warned, none of the females of the family spoke either English or French, it was difficult to see what satisfaction they could get out of her company. An aged, wrinkled priest, part father-confessor, part hanger-on, acted, when Dom Fernando was absent at court, as interpreter on these occasions, translating Camilla's French formalities into Portuguese and then, laboriously, conveying his mistresses' trite answers. It would all have been comic enough if Camilla had not been racked with anxiety for her husband, and convinced that all this solicitude on her behalf merely masked Dom Fernando's curiosity as to Lavenham's whereabout. Every day, regularly as clockwork, if with careful casualness, came the question from one or other of the family: Had she heard from milord yet? And every day, equally casual, she replied, with perfect truth, that she had not. It was galling enough thus to have to expose Lavenham's neglect, and yet she had to admit to herself that if he had expected this kind of inquisition on her, he had been well advised to tell her nothing of where he was going. It would have been hard work, if she had known where he was, not to give something away under this courteous barrage of apparently trivial questions. On the other hand, her anxiety for him was exacerbated by the thought that he did not trust her to keep his secret. He might at least have warned her what to expect.

Chloe was no help these long, anxious days. Her one idea was to escape visiting the Molinhas, with whose cloistered daughters Dom Fernando had done his best to force her into reluctant friendship. After one session with them in their private apartments, Chloe told Camilla frankly that if she was compelled to go again she would not be answerable for the consequences. "I do not know which is worse, the girls' giggling or their brother's laboured attentions." Camilla found herself reluctantly sympathising with Chloe. So far as she could see, the Molinha girls' entire occupation was to sit on the floor of their apartments searching each other's jewelled hair for lice and gossiping about possible husbands, while their brother had so obviously been instructed by their uncle to lose no opportunity of paying court to Chloe that Camilla felt faintly anxious lest, in Lavenham's absence, Chloe, whose position as a comparatively emancipated young English girl obviously left her open to misapprehension, might not be in some way compromised. So when Chloe pleaded unconvincing headache or unlikely fatigue, or just vanished into the garden when it was time to go to the Molinhas', Camilla usually took the line of least resistance and went alone. She did however insist on Chloe's accompanying her when Dom Fernando arranged a party to cross the river and go to a bullfight on the other side. Camilla had done her best to be excused, saying with truth that she thought it of all things what she would like least, but Dom Fernando overruled her, insisting that she must take the opportunity which might easily not recur before the impending general move to Mafra and Sintra. When she hoped to nonplus him by querying the propriety of her attending it in her husband's absence, he silenced her by telling her the Prince Regent's wife was a constant spectator. Of course, he admitted, if Chloe had been a Portuguese young lady, it would have been unthinkable that she should have accompanied them. "But your English young ladies have such liberty, have they not?" And, since Chloe had gone with them to see the Corpus Christi procession, Camilla could only agree with him, while feeling privately that if she must go she would be glad of Chloe's support.

The day of the bullfight dawned fine and clear, with a welcome little sea breeze to temper the heat, and Camilla and Chloe, festive in their freshest muslin and shadiest hats, found themselves immensely enjoying the crossing of the Tagus, which they made in the Molinhas' sumptuous, if shabby, private galley, rowed by twenty oarsmen. They landed in a pleasant hilly country shaded by pines and overgrown with a wild shrubbery of low aromatic bushes, and Camilla would gladly have remained there to explore the little paths that wandered beside rivulets among a tangle of wild orange and bay trees. But mule-drawn carriages awaited them and they had to climb in for a stuffy jolting over hill roads to the amphitheatre, where they were hurried straight into a box and had hardly time to agree that the place was about the size of Ranelagh but very much less splendid, when a dozen hideous Negroes dressed in a sort of Indian-Chinese style tumbled into the ring driving a placid herd of bulls. A tawdry procession introduced the matador, who proceeded to slaughter one passive bull after another until Camilla and Chloe, sickened alike by the bloody spectacle and the remorseless heat, had to beg Dom Fernando to let them retire. He, it seemed, was a devotee of the ring—or had to pass as one in deference to his royal mistress—but he deputed his eldest nephew, Dom Pedro, to accompany them, and they retired, grateful, for once, for the escort of this very young man, to the shady garden of a nearby monastery. To Camilla's relief, it was quite impossible for females to enter the monastery, so they were able to sit in the shade of a gigantic cork tree and recover something of their spirits before they were rejoined by Dom Fernando and his sister. As Dom Pedro's attentions to Chloe were very much less pressing when his uncle was not present, the interval was refreshing enough, and they were able to enjoy the homeward journey across the Tagus in the cooling evening among a throng of other boats from some of which rose the strains of song, the catchy Brazilian *modinhas* for which Chloe had developed a passion.

Reaching home late in the afternoon, Camilla was able to put more conviction than she had expected into her thanks to Dom Fernando. The bullfight itself might have horrified her, but the rest of the day had been pleasant enough. To her relief, he merely left them at their door, but then spoiled it by promising himself the pleasure of calling on them later to make sure they had not suffered from the fatigues of the day.

She would gladly have dispensed with this courtesy, but forced herself to welcome it, putting an extra touch of enthusiasm into her voice to make up for the defection of Chloe, who, after the briefest of thanks, had already vanished into the garden.

Glad to be alone, Camilla settled herself with a book on the terrace, but was soon aroused by the sound of a horse's hoofs on the carriage drive behind the house. Her first thought was of Lavenham, but he had left by carriage. Still, she jumped to her feet; this might, at last, be a messenger from him. She hurried through the main salon and reached the front door in time to see Lavenham himself being helped to dismount by one of the servants. The fact that he needed help was alarming enough, but his pale face and torn and dusty clothes told their own story.

Camilla hurried forward: "My dear, you are hurt?"

He managed an apology for a smile. "A trifle. Nothing to signify." But he let the man help him towards the house, while another servant led away the exhausted horse.

Once in the salon, Lavenham dropped with a sigh into a chair and dismissed the man with a few rapid sentences. Then, once again, he did his best to smile at Camilla. "Lord, it's good to be home. But I must ask your pardon for so melodramatic an entrance. Where is Chloe?"

If Camilla suffered a little at this evidence that his first thought was for his sister, she did not show it, merely replying, "In the garden as usual, and you, I'm sure, should be in bed."

"All in good time. First I must eat. I rather think I have not done so since yesterday. No, no," as she jumped to her feet, "never trouble yourself; I told the man to bring it presently. In the meantime, I am glad Chloe is out of the way. I need your help."

"It is yours."

"I knew I could count on you. You are not, I am sure, one of the young ladies who faint at the sight of blood."

She was on her feet at once. "You are wounded! I knew it. Of course I do not mind the sight of blood. I used, often, to assist the surgeon who attended the poor Duchess of Devonshire. Only come to your room and I will fetch ointment and bandages. But should we not send for a doctor?"

He had risen somewhat shakily to his feet and now gratefully accepted the support of her arm. "No, no. We cannot have a doctor, and indeed it is not necessary. You will see it is but a scratch, but has bled most confoundedly. I am in a sad state, I fear, and no object for a lady, but the deuce of it is I cannot afford a doctor and his gossiping."

More and more alarmed, she was relieved to get him to the privacy of his room, where a servant had already brought warm water. Bidding him sit quiet until she returned, she hurried off to her own apartments to fetch salve and bandages. Returning, she found him shrugging himself awkwardly out of his dusty blue jacket and hurried to help him, letting out a gasp of horror when she saw the clotted blood through an awkward-looking bandage around his left arm. But this was no time for talk; she set at once to work and was relieved, when she removed the bandage, to find that the bleeding was from a clean sabre cut.

"You see," he said, clenching his teeth as she gently sponged the wound. "I told you it was nothing. Ah, that feels better. What an admirable woman you are, to be sure. Not a question yet?"

She laughed with relief at his stronger tone. "I have no doubt you will tell me what you wish me to know in your own good time. For now, I would rather see you in bed than talking. You must be fatigued to death."

"I am a little weary," he admitted, "since I have been riding all night, but, tell me, you do not expect company?"

"Oh, I forgot. Dom Fernando is coming. He has positively haunted us since you have been gone, Lavenham, and is coming to see we are not unduly fatigued by the bullfight we went to this afternoon."

"A bullfight! But you shall tell me about that later. In the meantime, you must help me to my clothes. If he is coming, I must see him. No one—I tell you no one, not even Chloe, chatterbox that she is—must know that I am wounded."

Now she could not forbear a question. "But, Lavenham, why?"

"Because I have been where I should not have. Tell me, does the wound on my head show?"

"On your head?" She had finished binding up his arm now and noticed for the first time the place where his dark curls were matted together. Gently probing, she found an enormous lump which, luckily, had bled only a little so that she was able by gentle bathing with spirits of lavender to remove all traces of it. By the time she had finished, a servant appeared with a tray of food and Camilla was able to appreciate her husband's forethought in making her hide away the bloodstained bandages as she worked. Lavenham, in a clean shirt over his dusty buckskins, merely looked as if he was tired out with travelling. Camilla was the devoted wife bathing his temples with lavender water. When the man had gone and she had seen Lavenham take his first few hungry bites, and a good draught of wine, Camilla ventured another question.

"But where is Jenks?" she asked. For Lavenham's valet had accompanied him on the journey, as well as several Portuguese servants.

He put down his fork. "Dead, I am afraid. We were taken by surprise. I thought no one knew where we were. No one should have. Jenks was on the box; an easy mark. I was able to use the coach as a defence—I do not think they had looked for so stout a resistance. At all events, when I killed their leader, they soon took to their heels, and I was able to avail myself of his horse, since the carriage was useless."

"And the other servants?" She kept her voice calm, aware that any exclamation from her would be intolerable to him in his exhausted state.

"One dead, the others fled. We shall not see them again. Nor, I hope, will they come back to Lisbon to tell tales of the encounter."

"But, Lavenham." Now that he had eaten she must ask it. "Who? Why?"

"Who but the French? It would suit their book very well to have me out of the way. They know, I am afraid, more than I could wish about the real purpose of my coming to Portugal."

"The real purpose? Is it not, then, to help Lord Strangford in his negotiations?"

"Not entirely. I suppose I should have told you sooner, but it is a secret to be shared by as few as possible. No, my main purpose in coming is to get in touch with the various military agents in this country and in Spain, to get what information and make what preparations are possible against the outbreak of war with France. I am not, you must know, quite the do-nothing I must have seemed, but have had to play the court butterfly to conceal the real purpose of my coming."

"I see. And these journeys of yours—"

"To meet the various agents. This time I have been to

Spain. I only wish I knew who blew the affair to the French, but I have been beginning to wonder, for some time past, whether Dom Fernando was quite the friend of Britain he would have one think."

"He has certainly been most anxious for news of your whereabouts, and has positively haunted the house for tidings of you. To tell truth, I was quite glad Chloe and I did not know where you were, or it would have been hard, without rudeness, to have concealed it."

To her moved surprise he took her hand and kissed it. "I owe you many apologies, Camilla, for having done you less than justice, and you are generosity itself not to chide me for leaving you so in the dark. But you, with your good sense, will realise, I am sure, that it was not a secret to be entrusted lightly to a stranger."

She managed a laugh. "What a mortal inconvenience it must have been to you to find yourself saddled with a parcel of females."

"Not altogether." He considered it. "You and Chloe have provided me with a most admirable cover, and will, I hope, continue to do so. Though I am afraid you will find it harder now that you know what you are doing."

"Yes, I shall be anxious about you. As for Chloe, of course she must know nothing of this. And now, if you are convinced you must give Dom Fernando the meeting, I had best act valet, and find you your evening dress. Is there none of the servants you could trust to help you?"

"I think not. But if you will find me what I need and leave me to my struggles, I can, I think, make shift to dress myself. And indeed, I shall have to, for there, if I mistake not, is Dom Fernando now. Go to him please, and tell him I am a trifle fatigued from travelling but will join him forthwith."

"Very well, and for good measure, I will tell him I am quite exhausted with the bullfight and have the headache, and if that does not shift him soon, do not be surprised if I suffer a public attack of the vapours. After all, a bullfight is a trying experience for an English young lady."

"Admirable girl." He pressed her hand gratefully. "But have you a headache?"

"Not the least in the world. I have never felt better—since you are safe home." And then, colouring fiercely at her own unexpected vehemence, she left him hurriedly and ran down the shallow marble stair to the great salon, where she found Dom Fernando awaiting her.

After assuring himself, and her, that she was in most remarkable looks and clearly none the worse for her exhausting day, he came quickly to the point. Complimenting her on her colour, he continued archly. "But I am not coxcomb enough to think you fly these flags on my account. I understand that milord is most happily returned. I hope you have chided him for his long absence from so charming a bride."

"Oh yes." She gave her best imitation of Chloe's laugh. "I have read him a fine lecture and he is a chastened man. He is making himself presentable, for indeed he was sadly travelstained, and bids me tell you he will be with you directly. What a fortunate thing that so good a friend should be here to welcome him home."

He made her a gallant rejoinder, and she continued to keep the stream of small talk alive, while all her thoughts were with Lavenham. Would he really be able to shrug his wounded arm into his dress jacket? Not for the first time, she congratulated herself that he was not one of the town dandies who insisted on a fit so rigorous that it was impossible to put on their own clothes. But time was passing.

"I trust," Dom Fernando said, "that milord is none the worse for his journey. You are wishing me no doubt at the devil for troubling your reunion, but I must just wait long enough to welcome him home. That is, if you think him well enough to see me?"

"Well enough? But why should he not be? I hope he is not such a weakling as to be tired out by a long day's journeying, though he is, in truth, more than a little fatigued and I shall certainly do my best to ensure that he retires early."

"I am sure you will." And then, seeing her colour, he changed the subject. "But, tell me, where is the charming Mademoiselle Chloe? I trust that she is not worn out with the exertions of her day, or disgusted with me for taking her to the bullfight."

"Oh no." For some time no anxiety for Chloe had been mingled with that for Lavenham. What could be keeping her out so long? "She is out, I think, walking in the garden."

"In the garden? So late?" And indeed a servant had just brought in candles which made the terrace and garden below suddenly a place of twilight shadows. Camilla moved restlessly over to the window, while throwing back over her shoulder

to Dom Fernando: "I know you must think our English girls
sadly unprotected, but Chloe will come to no harm in our
own garden." She only wished she was sure of it. "Ah, here
she comes." And she opened the folding door that led on to
the terrace to call, "Chloe, what are you doing out in the
dew so late? Here is your brother home, and Dom Fernando
come to enquire after our health."

"Oh!" Chloe's *moue* was for the second half of the sentence. She had clearly been intending to skirt round the house
and go in by the other door, but now came reluctantly up the
terrace steps, where candlelight from indoors caught golden
lights in her tousled curls and showed up the brilliance of her
complexion and the rich red of the roses she carried. Pausing
in the doorway, she greeted Dom Fernando with what
Camilla could only think deplorable casualness and then
looked about her. "But where is Lee?"

"Here." He appeared in the doorway, dead pale but erect
and with a courteous speech of welcome for Dom Fernando
and a quick smile for Chloe, who, Camilla saw, was about to
rush towards him for one of the quick fierce embraces he
tolerated from her. But not tonight. Camilla caught the hand
that was not full of roses. "Your brother is tired, Chloe. He
has been riding all day. And you, my love, are in no state to
see company. I beg you will tidy your hair and your dress
before you rejoin us." Thus positively commanded, Chloe
made a little rebellious face for Camilla alone, smiled brilliantly at Lavenham, and withdrew, with the merest sketch of
a curtsy for Dom Fernando.

He was already pressing Lavenham with courteous questions about his long absence. His friends had missed him ...
Had he found the roads passable? ... Had his business not
taken him longer than he had expected? ... One must hope
that at least it had proved prosperous ... And so on, with
each half question circling closer to the crux of the matter—
the purpose of Lavenham's journey.

To Camilla's relief, a servant interrupted one of Lavenham's courteous, vague replies by appearing with the wine
and cakes she had ordered, and she made a little business of
being sure that the men were served with what they liked
best, then took advantage of the interruption to change the
subject, bursting into an exclamatory description of Dom
Fernando's kindness during Lavenham's absence and then
proceeding to a detailed and falsely enthusiastic description

of the bullfight. Dom Fernando listened with his usual grave politeness, then returned to the attack. If they had only known milord was to return today, they might have extended their journey to ride out and meet him. Or was he wrong in assuming that milord had come from south of the river?

Lavenham laughed and parried the question by replying that he had been in no mood to be met by a party of pleasure. "Your roads and your inns do not leave one in festive spirit."

The men's glasses were empty. Camilla rose to her feet to replenish them, hoping that this would give Dom Fernando his cue to leave, but he let her fill his glass and sipped at it absentmindedly as he returned to his questioning. Lavenham, too, was drinking quickly, and a little flush of colour had mounted in his cheeks. Camilla, who knew him to be moderate to the point of abstemiousness, watched anxiously and was relieved when Chloe danced back into the room, her crumpled muslin changed for a fresh one, her golden curls agleam with brushing. But the distraction she provided was only half successful, for she, too, wanted to know where her brother had been and what had kept him so long away. Since her questions were put in English, Dom Fernando could not, presumably, understand them, though Camilla, watching his absorbed expression, found herself wondering whether his ignorance of English was as complete as he had led her to suppose.

Lavenham was taking no chances, but rebuked his sister roundly in French for talking a language their guest could not understand, and then, breaking into English with an apologetic glance at Dom Fernando, continued, "And if you do not understand that, I will tell you in plain English that I am tired out and have no wish to discuss my travels tonight."

Chloe, always unpredictable, amazed Camilla by bursting into a golden peal of laughter. "Why, Lee, you are disguised! I have not seen you so since your coming of age. Did you know you had a toper for a husband, Camilla?"

Camilla had been watching Dom Fernando throughout this interchange and was now convinced from his expression that he understood every word they were saying. She noticed something else, too. A dark patch was forming on the sleeve of Lavenham's evening jacket. His wound was bleeding again and had already soaked through the bandage. It was only a matter of time until either Dom Fernando or Chloe noticed;

and Dom Fernando had just poured himself another glass of wine and seemed to have settled down for the night. She rose to her feet, exclaiming: "My head aches so," and moved towards the window, then, as she passed the chair where Dom Fernando was sitting, swayed on her feet and fell towards him. To her intense relief, he caught her, and laid her on a nearby sofa with exclamations of solicitude and alarm, in which the others joined. For a few minutes, she let herself lie there with closed eyes, listening to the little tumult her collapse had caused. Then, as Chloe held a vinaigrette under her nose, she let her eyes flutter open, looked vaguely around and tried to sit up, with a murmured apology: "The heat ... the blood ... Dom Fernando, what will you think of me?"

Lavenham had taken his cue. "I was afraid the bullfight might prove strong meat for English stomachs," he said. "Chloe, ring for your sister's maid. She will be best in bed."

Camilla allowed herself a sigh of pure exhaustion. "Oh yes," she said, "I fear the excitement of the day has given me the vapours. All that blood . . . Lavenham, you'll not leave me?"

He took her hand in his, which burned ice cold. "Of course not. You must forgive us, Dom Fernando. Perhaps we may continue this most interesting conversation tomorrow?"

Thus directly applied to, Dom Fernando took his leave at last, and Camilla, who had been thinking rapidly, allowed herself to be supported to her room by Lavenham and her maid. Better that Chloe should think her a weakling and a neglectful wife than that she should guess at her brother's condition. Chloe showed signs of lingering with further offers of smelling salts and spirits of lemon, but Lavenham disposed of her with a husband's firmness before turning to Camilla, whose maid was busy on the other side of the room.

"Admirably acted." He pressed her hand. "At least," anxiously, "I trust it was acted? You are not really unwell?"

"Not the least in the world. I will come to you as soon as I can rid myself of Frances. Your wound needs dressing again. Best get to your apartments before it is noticed."

He looked quickly down at the dark patch that was spreading over the cloth of his sleeve, pressed her hand once more, and then, as Frances approached with her negligee, made her a speech of husbandly solicitude and took his leave.

By the time Frances left her the house was quiet. Camilla

jumped out of bed and put on the swansdown-trimmed blue satin negligee Lady Leominster had chosen for her. What a mockery, she remembered, it had seemed at the time. Now, impatiently sliding her feet into the matching slippers, she was glad of it with its look almost of a morning gown. In the main hall, a night light burned dimly; no light showed under Chloe's door; the house seemed asleep. She tapped gently on the door of Lavenham's apartments at the end of the hall and opened it quietly. The light of his guttering candle showed that he had managed to struggle out of his bloodstained jacket before collapsing, exhausted, on the bed. Now he slept heavily, his flushed face and loud breathing bearing witness to the unusual quantity of wine he had drunk under the strain of Dom Fernando's visit. For a moment, beside his bed, Camilla hesitated. It seemed wicked to rouse him. But the blood was still seeping through the bandage on his arm, and besides, it would be dangerous to let him lie all night like this.

Very gently, she shook his good shoulder: "Lavenham, it is I, Camilla."

He stirred in his sleep, then woke all at once, gazing at her with wild and startled eyes, then, obviously remembering: "Oh, it is you—I was dreaming."

"Yes, I am come to change your bandages. I will not disturb you for long." And she began deftly unwinding the bloody bandage.

Involuntarily, he winced at her touch. "This is no work for a young lady," he said. "You will be wishing that you had seen me at Jericho before you married me." And then, wincing again as she reached the wound itself, "Pour me a glass of wine, will you? And one for yourself. It will make the work go better."

Reluctantly, for she was convinced that he had already had more than was good for him, she poured two glasses from the decanter that stood on a side table, and brought him one, leaving hers where it stood. But he insisted, with the obstinacy of fatigue and near-intoxication, that she drink with him before she finished bathing and binding up his wound, and toasted her solemnly: "My invaluable wife."

Colouring with pleasure, she raised her glass to his and drank, recognising, as she felt the strong wine bloom within her, that she needed it. It seemed to have revived him too, for as she began once more to work on his wound, he began to talk, quick and freely, as she had heard him do in Portuguese but never, before, in English.

"Do you know," he was saying. "Out there, when they attacked the carriage, I was afraid? Afraid of death. I have never feared it before. Do you think I can be beginning to wish to live?"

"I hope so. There." She had finished and laid his arm gently on the pillow. "Now I wish you will let me help you to bed. You will catch cold, lying thus."

He caught her hand with his good one. "No, do not dismiss me so. I will be your obedient patient presently, but tell me first one thing; when you so admirably pretended to swoon, you called for me. 'Lavenham do not leave me,' you said. Of course, that was feigning too?"

She sat there for a moment by his bedside, looking at his flushed face, wondering what to say. Pride, which had stood by her so well, told her to lie, to tell him it had all been pretence, but something else in her, was it the wine, or something stronger, would not be denied. "No," she said, "that was not feigning, Lavenham."

"Then drink up your wine." He drained his glass as she obeyed him. "Perhaps there is no need to be afraid any more." And with a sudden, fierce movement of his good arm he pulled her down on the bed beside him while his lips closed hungrily over hers. For a moment, some sober instinct made her resist, then, as his kisses became fiercer and more demanding, she felt her need of him rise up to meet his. On the table beside the bed the two glasses stood empty, the candle guttered out, and cool moonlight shone into the room as there, among his bloodstained sheets, she found herself, at last, his wife indeed.

CHAPTER 7

Waking, much later, to quick happiness and the first morning sound of birds, Camilla was alarmed at once by Lavenham's restless tossing and muttering at her side. He was all too evidently in a high fever, his broken murmurings part dream, part delirium. She slipped quickly out of bed, pulled the bedclothes closer around him, and shut the large casement through which cool morning air was pouring into the room. Returning to the bed, she found Lavenham's pulse rapid and disordered. His hot forehead and flushed cheeks added to her anxiety. But what should she do? Her first instinct was to summon a doctor, but it would be impossible for him to tend the invalid without discovering his wound. For a moment she thought of explaining this away as a domestic accident of some kind, but who would believe her? And besides, there was Dom Fernando to be considered. It would be well nigh impossible to invent an accident that could convincingly have happened after he had left. No, she would have to pray to God and nurse Lavenham herself. She was slightly encouraged in this determination by memory of his strictures on Portuguese medicine. Perhaps after all she would be saving his life by keeping the doctor from him.

Only the deep, unspoken happiness of her new relation with Lavenham carried her through the anxieties of the next few days. He continued half conscious or, worse still, delirious, while his fever resisted all the medicaments she had brought with her from England. The only point of consolation was that, miraculously, his wound continued to heal, and she thought the fever must be due mainly to exhaustion and, perhaps, to the blow he had received on his head. As he continued deliriously calling out for his mother and, it seemed, acting over again the duel of long ago when his father was killed, she became increasingly anxious lest his brain should have been affected. If only she could get expert advice. But Lord Strangford was still away and there was no one else to whom she felt she could turn.

Chloe's anxiety and Dom Fernando's daily visits of polite inquisition exacerbated her misery. For them, as for the servants, she had to pretend that Lavenham's illness was merely trifling, a matter of overfatigue and inevitable recovery. But as the anxious days passed, it became increasingly difficult to keep up the pretence, and on the third day, as she sat by his bed bathing his hot forehead with spirits of lavender, she had almost made up her mind to give way to Dom Fernando's pressure and let him summon a doctor. Lavenham's mind was wandering again. Surely she was a murderess to keep expert attention from him. And yet, she was sure, a Portuguese physician would bleed him at once, and he had lost enough blood already. She was sitting there, a prey to the most agonising kind of uncertainty, when he suddenly reached out and grasped her hand, "Mother," he said, "Mother, you will not leave me?"

"No, never." How truly she meant it. "Lie still, my love, lie still and rest."

"You never called me that before." To her delighted surprise, he seemed to have taken in what she said, though attributing it, no doubt, to the mother he had lost so long ago. "Stay with me," he went on, "stay with me always."

"Of course." Very gently, still holding his hand in hers, she used the other to stroke the disordered curls away from his brow. Was she imagining it, or did this feel cooler to her touch? Scarcely daring to hope, she sat there and watched as he fell at last, still holding her hand, into a deep and refreshing sleep. Time passed. The shadows lengthened in the room and Chloe came scratching at the door to whisper that Dom Fernando was below, asking for her. Camilla did not stir from where she sat, merely turning to whisper over her shoulder that Lavenham was better, but she could not leave him.

Towards night, he woke at last, a characteristic apology on his lips. "I have been ill, and a monstrous trouble to you, I fear."

"No trouble, my love." The endearment slipped out without thought, and she saw a look of faint puzzlement cloud his face. Was she going too fast for him? Hastily recovering herself, she went on, "Do not trouble yourself about anything; I have not had the doctor to you; nobody knows what has been the matter with you."

"No one knows? No doctor?" He looked more puzzled than ever. "But why not?"

A cold finger of fear touched her heart. "But do you not remember?"

"Remember? Let me see." His head moved restlessly on the pillows. "I was dreaming of my mother . . . but that's not it. Ah, now I have it. I went to Spain, did I not? And was attacked, returning . . . Poor Jenks, was he killed, or did I dream it?"

"You told me so." She watched his restless movements anxiously.

"And then—what? I remember nothing more. I must have come home somehow, for here I am. And you have not had the doctor to me— Of course, it was all to be secret. I remember planning it with Strangford. He thinks Dom Fernando less than a friend. Has Fernando been here?"

"Yes, soon after you arrived, but do not trouble yourself, he knows nothing, although, I think, he suspects much."

He managed a flicker of a smile. "So you have nursed me single-handed and kept the world at bay. I see I am more indebted to you than ever. It was a lucky day for me when my grandmother made us marry. But you must be worn out. Tell me, how long have I been ill?"

"Only three days." Her thoughts were in a turmoil. His tone, as much as his words, told her that he remembered nothing of the night that had changed her world. What could she do?

He was looking at her anxiously. "Have I been so great a trouble? I wish I could remember . . ." Again his head moved restlessly among the pillows. His colour was rising.

She reached out to feel his pulse: "Do not trouble yourself about anything. You must rest. You will remember soon enough." Deeply and desperately she hoped it was true, as she sat and watched him drift off again to sleep. If he did not? What could she do? The answer was obvious: nothing. That moonlight night must be forgotten. She must return to the old formality, the old pretence. She had never known such chill despair before, but sat there, quietly, by his bed, watching him as he slept, while, silently following each other, the tears ran down her cheeks.

There was at least some consolation in his rapid and continued recovery, but with it came no blessed return of memory. In answer to his questions, she had told him of his exhausted return and of how, between them, they had kept Dom Fernando's curiosity at bay, but this did not, as she had hoped, rouse any answering gleam of remembrance. "So you got me to bed and I turned lunatic on your hands," he concluded. "What a plague I must have been to you. It is no wonder you look exhausted. We must lose no time in moving to Sintra, where I hope the cooler air will refresh you."

She laughed. What an effort it was to get back the old lightness of touch. "You are scarce flattering. Am I indeed looking so haggard?"

He reached out to press her hand. "You look like someone who has just saved her husband's life," he said.

She slept better that night. Surely, it was only a matter of time, and all would be well. Dreaming she was in his arms again, she woke to fresh hope and renewed resolutions of patience. Lady Leominster had said she must be patient as Job and had come nearer the mark than she knew, for by now Camilla had learned only too well how an unguardedly tender word or look could startle her husband back into his lonely shell. At all costs, she must keep up the light and teasing relationship she had managed to evolve between them, and leave the rest to time.

Luckily for her, as soon as Lavenham was well enough to go out, he plunged into the arrangements for their move to Sintra, and indeed the idea of a mountain change after the dusty July heat of the city was most welcome to Camilla. But to her surprise, Chloe proved almost mutinous. They were well enough where they were, she said. What was the use of going off to ruralise in the mountains and exposing themselves at the same time to all the tedium of attendance on the Court. For the villa Lavenham had taken would be all too convenient both for attendance at the Prince Regent's court at Mafra and for visits to his estranged wife, who was living on her estate of Ramalhao in Sintra itself. It was in vain that Camilla pointed out how necessary such attendance was for the success of Lavenham's mission. Chloe refused to be comforted and sulked ostentatiously until Camilla could have shaken her. Not for the first time, she found herself grateful for Lavenham's detachment, which kept him from noticing his sister's bad behaviour.

He came home early one evening to announce, rather sooner than Camilla had expected, that all was ready: they could make the move to Sintra next morning. Camilla's own preparations were well in hand, but she suspected that Chloe had done little or nothing about getting ready, and hurried out into the garden to break the news to her. Not finding her in the shady walks of their own garden, she crossed the little stream that separated their estate from the deserted gardens of the Marvila palace next door and wandered through the overgrown thickets of myrtle and jasmine calling softly for Chloe. But the evening wind, fiercer than usual tonight, was tearing early fruit from the plum trees and her voice was lost in its wailing among the branches.

So it happened that she turned the corner of one of the orange groves and came, unawares, on Chloe, sitting on a rustic bench, her arm entwined with that of a man Camilla had never seen before.

"Chloe!" At the sound of her voice, the absorbed couple sprang to their feet, and apart. Chloe coloured crimson; the man, who was thin, brown, wiry and considerably older than she, made a low bow and stood his ground, still holding Chloe's hand in his, somewhat, Camilla suspected, against her will. For a moment, the silence stretched out. Chloe was tongue-tied; Camilla could think of nothing to say that would not seem unduly melodramatic; the stranger looked, she thought angrily, faintly amused. It was he who broke the silence at last.

"Well, *mon ange*," he said to Chloe, "will you not make me known to your sister—and mine?" He spoke in English, but with a marked French accent.

Camilla would not believe her ears. "What do you mean?"

He made her another bow, elegant, courtly—infuriating. "I would have known you anywhere," he said. "Your likeness to our lamented mother is startling. But it seems I have the advantage of you, and since this dear child will not do it, allow me to present myself: M. Boutet, the butcher's son, or, being translated, your long lost brother. Is this not a touching reunion?"

"I do not understand. Chloe, what does this mean? When did you meet this gentleman?"

Chloe spoke at last. "At Corpus Christi," she said. "He brought me home, when Lavenham would not even trouble himself to look for me. I was like to sink when he told me he was your brother, Camilla. Is it not the most romantic circumstance? Of course, it is tedious that he is one of the enemy Lee fusses about, else I would have made him known to you long ago. Indeed I am glad you have discovered us now; you can give us your counsel as to how best to make Lee see reason. How can I be expected to come to Sintra when my heart," she made a wide dramatic gesture, "my heart is here."

Camilla had never been so angry. She looked at her brother and wished that his strong and discouraging likeness to their father did not convince her of the truth of his claim. "I do not know what to say to you."

"Why, what but, 'Welcome, long lost Brother'? It is, as Chloe says, a somewhat inconvenient circumstance that we should find ourselves, for the moment, in opposite camps. But time will put that to rights—and soon enough, I can tell you. It is but a matter of months until England is a province of the French Empire, and then, little Sister, you will be glad enough to have a friend in Bonaparte's army. In the meantime, I agree with you that we had best say nothing to your husband, who seems, from all I hear, to be a marvellously stiff-necked English prig and would doubtless make an international incident of me forthwith, which, I know, is what you would not at all wish for any of our sakes."

Though it was infuriating thus to have him take her course of action for granted, she had to admit the sense in what he said. To present Lavenham with a brother-in-law in the enemy's camp would be enormously to complicate his position, and at the same time, inevitably, the discovery of Chloe's clandestine romance would put him fatally out of patience with her. Thus provoked, he might do anything— would almost certainly send Chloe back to England, and Camilla, who flattered herself that by now she had at least some influence over her volatile sister-in-law, dreaded the consequences of any such drastic action. This affair with her brother was bad enough, but who could tell what mischief Chloe might get up to alone in England? As these thoughts flashed through her mind, she also remembered, with relief, the reason for her coming to look for Chloe. After all, they were leaving for Sintra tomorrow: this would put an end to the lovers' meetings that had been carrying on, she realised with a shock of dismay, since Corpus Christi.

She had been looking at her brother gravely as these thoughts hurried through her mind, and finding little in his appearance to reassure her. No use to appeal to his better nature, everything about him proclaimed him a gambler like their father, but, she feared, a gambler not so much with money as with life. He was becoming, she noticed with satisfaction, somewhat restive under her prolonged scrutiny, while Chloe, incredibly, had drifted away to pick and nibble at a ripe apricot. Nothing could have brought home so forcibly to Camilla her sister-in-law's basic childishness. She simply had no idea of the gravity of the situation in which she had plunged her.

It was time to speak: "Come, Chloe," said Camilla, "your brother is looking for you."

This recalled Chloe's wandering attention at once. "Lee? You will not tell him, Camilla? Promise! I dare not face him, else."

"It is a pity," Camilla said, "that you had not thought of that sooner. But do not cry, child," as the easy tears began to roll down Chloe's cheeks. "I shall not tell Lavenham—yet. M. Boutet is right. Silence, for the moment, will be best. But I must have both your promises that you will not meet again." No need to tell them this would be impossible anyway because of the impending move to Sintra.

After a quick exchange of glances, both of them promised so readily that Camilla was convinced they had not the slightest intention of keeping their word. It was lucky that circumstances were likely to make them more scrupulous than they intended. She hurried their farewells, ignoring a protest from her brother that she was heartless in calling him M. Boutet like a stranger. "Am I not to be Charles after all these years?"

"I will call you Charles when you behave to me like a brother," she said austerely. "So far, I see no reason to consider you anything but a stranger. I only wish you were one. Come, Chloe," she said again. "Your brother will come looking for us if you do not hurry."

This threat was effective on both Chloe and Charles, whom Camilla began to suspect of being as much of a cowardly braggart as his father. For all his slighting words, he clearly had no wish to encounter Chloe's formidable brother. One swift look passed between him and Chloe, promising, Camilla was sure, a meeting on the morrow, whatever obstacles might be placed in the way. She merely smiled and took

Chloe's hand. "Goodbye, M. Boutet," she said. "Give my regards to your friend M. Mireille when you next see him."

The shot went home. He coloured angrily and withdrew down a shady walk of lemon and orange trees. Alone with Chloe, Camilla did not hurry her away at once. Her threats of Lavenham's impatience had served their turn, but she did not, in fact, think he would come looking for them. When she had left him, he had been busy sorting papers ready for tomorrow's move. So occupied, he would not notice the passage of time. And before they went in, she must find out how deeply Chloe had committed herself. Anxiously, she began her questioning and to her relief Chloe, who obviously felt that she was being let off lightly, answered readily enough. Yes, they had met almost daily since Corpus Christi, but in answer to Camilla's delicate but persistent catechism, she maintained that her beloved Charles had behaved to her with the most perfect propriety, had hardly, in fact, done more than kiss her hand. The naïve irritation that she showed in revealing this went far to convince Camilla that she was speaking the truth, and she decided, with a deep inward sigh of relief, that, whatever unprincipled game her brother had been playing, it had not involved actually disgracing Chloe, or at least not yet. It was with an anxious heart and an almost absentminded air that she administered the scold Chloe expected, trying to convey, as she did so, that this was a business too serious for mere scolding. In vain she tried to show Chloe how her behaviour might endanger her brother's position as a diplomat. Chloe merely sighed, shrugged, and asked what importance the behaviour of a mere girl like herself could have. At last, Camilla lost her temper. "Well," she said, "fortunately, it is not of the greatest importance that you insist in playing the fool. We leave for Sintra tomorrow. I hope you will have time there to come to your senses."

Now the tears came in good earnest, convincing Camilla once more that Chloe had not for a moment meant to keep her promise not to see Charles again. For once, she could not find a scrap of sympathy for Chloe's presentation of beauty in distress, but merely shrugged and turned to lead the way back to the house. "You had best dry your tears, if you do not want Lavenham asking questions."

Tossing on her sleepless bed that night, Camilla wondered over and over again whether she had been right in what she had done. Should she not have taken this deplorable piece of news at once to Lavenham, whose chief concern, after all, it was? She could not make up her mind. If things had been right between them, she would not have hesitated for a moment, but as it was, she could be sure of nothing—except that he was still overtired from his illness and that she could not bear to put another strain upon him. No, she decided at last, this burden must be borne alone, at least for the time being.

To her relief, Chloe seemed to have decided she had best conceal her reluctance to go to Sintra, fearing, no doubt, that any recalcitrance on her part might end in Camilla's telling Lavenham the whole story. As a result, the drive to Sintra was less of an ordeal than Camilla had feared and she was even able to enjoy the wild and romantic views of valley and mountain, parched and dry from the summer drought, the occasional aloes, splendid in yellow bloom, and the strange aromatic perfumes that were wafted into the carriage by a fitful breeze. Lavenham, too, bore the rough journey better than she had feared, though he was pale and tired by the time they crossed the desolate heath at the foot of the Sintra mountains and reached the house that was to be theirs.

But here, to her dismay, an urgent messenger was awaiting Lavenham to summon him, at once, to a conference with Strangford and the Prince Regent, who were visiting the mad old Queen at Queluz. At her insistence, Lavenham delayed long enough to drink a glass of wine and eat a handful of dried fruits, but rest longer he would not, starting at once for the ride back to Queluz. Left alone, she and Chloe plunged once more into the business of house cleaning, for here, as at Lisbon, they found the apartments intended for them scarce fit for habitation by a well-bred English pig.

Lavenham did not return until late at night, and then his face was grave as he told them the news. France and Spain together had presented an ultimatum to the Prince Regent, demanding once again that Portuguese ports be closed to British shipping and that British residents be arrested and their property confiscated. This had plunged the Prince Regent into an agony of indecision and all the English ministers' representations of the folly of acceding to so unreasonable a request had merely prevailed upon him to delay his answer. The Spanish and French representatives in Portugal were threatening to ask for their passports if Dom John did not agree to their demands, and this, Lavenham explained, would mean war. Undecided himself, he paced about the room, pale with exhaustion and anxiety, as he debated part with himself, part with Camilla, what was best for her and Chloe to do. Ideally, they should leave for England at once, but how? The regular sailings of the packet had been discontinued and he knew of no other ship on which he would trust them unescorted. Camilla seized on this at once. If he did not propose to accompany them, how would he return if war did break out? When he explained that a battleship would certainly be sent to pick up the British ministers, she urged that it would be best for her and Chloe to wait with him, pretending a greater reluctance than she actually felt at the idea of travelling unescorted. For she could not bear the idea of leaving him to the casual mercy of Portuguese servants in his still uncertain state of health. Besides, she did not want to leave him. But this must not be said. Instead, she talked of the hazards of a journey alone and was enthusiastically seconded by Chloe, who had, of course, her own reasons for not wishing to leave Portugal.

In the end, he gave in, reluctantly, and insisting that if a suitable ship should, by any miracle, arrive at Lisbon before the port was closed to the British, as he feared it soon would be, they must agree to sail with her. To this, Camilla yielded readily enough. It would be time for argument when the ship appeared. Besides, Lavenham looked more and more exhausted and had told her that he must be at Queluz again early the next morning. This was no time for unnecessary talk.

From then on, she and Chloe lived a strange life, marooned, as it were, in their country villa. Although the Prince Regent had still not answered the French and Spanish ultimatum, Lavenham was increasingly afraid that he would, in the end, yield to the demands made upon him. In these circumstances, he thought it best that Camilla and Chloe should not appear at Court, but remain as quietly as possible in the country. As for him, he spent every day adding his arguments to Strangford's in the vain attempt to persuade Dom John that an attack by Bonaparte was inevitable and that his best and indeed only course was to move his entire court to his American province of Brazil and wait out the coming storm in safety there. When Camilla protested at this defeatist advice, Lavenham explained that the Portuguese army was negligible, while both it and the country in general were riddled with secret supporters of France who still believed in Bonaparte as a liberator. Only bitter experience, he thought, would convince them of their mistake and this they were all too likely to have. Strangford, too, who rode back once or twice with Lavenham to dine and sleep at the villa, was gloomy about the prospects and made no secret of his doubts as to the wisdom of Camilla's and Chloe's remaining. But as the hot August days followed each other, and the surrounding hills grew more and more parched and brown, no English ship was reported at Lisbon, and Camilla and Chloe remained where they were, force perforce, much to Camilla's relief. For she was increasingly anxious about Lavenham, who continued pale and withdrawn beyond what the situation seemed to her to merit. He was brief with her, almost abrupt with Chloe, their earlier teasing relationship a thing of regretful memory only. It was almost a relief when the Prince Regent moved his court back to Mafra and the distance was too great for Lavenham to return home every night. Alone together, Camilla and Chloe resumed a seemingly peaceful life of reading and work. The French lessons, whose purpose had been only too obvious to Camilla since she had discovered Chloe's affair with her brother, had been tacitly discontinued, but both were making rapid strides with their Portuguese. As for Charles, or, as Camilla insisted even on thinking of him, M. Boutet, they never mentioned him. Camilla felt she had nothing to add to the scolding she had administered on the day of discovery, and was indeed only too grateful that Chloe seemed to be bearing the enforced separation so placidly. She wondered, occasionally, whether the lovers still contrived to correspond, but thought it best not to provoke an explosion by enquiring too closely. After all, they would undoubtedly be leaving for England soon enough and this would put an end to everything. For Lavenham, on the rare occasions when he contrived to visit them, was more and more gloomy. Arriving, one night, drenched with the first September rain, he announced that the French and Spanish envoys had, as they had threatened, packed up and left Lisbon. And instead of taking this as the signal for positive action, the Regent continued to hesitate and temporise, now asking the English for assurances of his safety and convoy to the Brazils, now hovering near to granting the French requests, refusing to admit that the time for this—if there ever had been one—was past.

It was later that rainy night, after Chloe had gone off, as usual, early to bed, that Lavenham, who had been pacing restlessly about the chilly room, came suddenly to stand beside Camilla as she sewed. She put down her work and looked up at him in suddenly anxious enquiry.

"I have been meaning to ask you," he paused for a minute, took another rapid turn about the room, and returned to stand over her again. "The day before we left Lisbon," he said. "You remember it?"

"Of course." She was cold with more than the chill of the fireless room. What could be coming?

"You were out in the garden—not ours, the one next door. I came to look for you." He spoke in short, disjointed sentences. "It was growing late. The dew was falling. I thought it time you and Chloe were indoors." Again he stopped, listening to the desolate patter of rain on the marble terrace. Then, in a rush, "Who was the man you were talking to?"

"The man?" At all costs, she must have time to think.

"Yes. Do not, I beg, think that I was in any sense spying on you. I heard your voices: that was all. I thought I saw someone with you. I did not wish to seem to intrude. I should have asked you sooner." He passed a hand over his forehead. "You do not, I think, quite understand, you and Chloe, what a nest of spies we live among." He was looking at her now, almost, it seemed appealingly. What a blessed relief it would be to tell him. But how could she, now, so long after the event, expose poor Chloe, who thought herself safe, to the explosion of his wrath? It was all over: let it be forgotten. And yet, how she hated to lie, and to him, of all people. She looked up from her sewing, where it lay, neglected in her lap. "What man?" she said. "I remember no one." She regretted the lie as soon as it was spoken, but, to her relief, he seemed to accept it.

"Strange," he said. "Can my memory have been playing me tricks again? I was positive . . . You are sure you were not talking to one of the gardeners?"

"So late at night? You know they would not think of working after evening. But ask Chloe, if you are still in doubt."

"What?" He took her up on it at once. "As if I would not trust your word. No, no . . . I must have imagined it. I shall be glad when we are back in England. My mind has not recovered its tone since my accident ... it is the pressure of events, I suppose. I am wretched company for you and Chloe, I'm afraid. I only wish I could send you home."

She rose and put away her sewing. "You are worn out," she said. "That is all the trouble. Let me give you some laudanum to make you sleep."

"No, no, thank you just the same. My mind is troubled enough. I will not tamper with it further. But neither will I keep you up talking here. It is too cold to be sitting so late without a fire. I only wish we could move back to Lisbon, where the house is more fit for cold weather, but the Prince Regent seems fixed at Mafra and so long as he stays, I must. Nor do I think it safe for you and Chloe to return without me."

"No, anything rather than that." His sudden questions had reawakened all her anxiety on Chloe's behalf. She hoped, of course, that M. Boutet would have left with the rest of the French mission, but nothing was certain. Much best not risk exposing Chloe once more to his dangerous proximity.

Lavenham was looking at her strangely. "You really prefer it here, with all the discomfort of draughts and cold?"

"Of course. So long as you are here." So much, surely, she could say.

He smiled at her more kindly than he had done for some time. "Very well, that is settled, then. So long as I remain, you and Chloe shall do so too. We will all freeze together."

Alone in her own apartments, Camilla allowed herself the relief of a passion of tears. If only she had had the courage to tell Lavenham the truth ... Now, looking back on it, she was sure she had been wrong to shield Chloe at the expense of a direct lie. It was frightful to have convinced Lavenham that his memory was playing him false, while his kindness, his confidence in her and refusal to apply to Chloe for confirmation of what she had said were more than her guilty conscience could bear. If he should ever learn that she had lied to him, he would never trust her again.

She woke next morning feeling ill and wretched, her first thoughts of the unlucky interview of the night before. But it was too late now for regret, she had committed herself to the lie and must stick to it. Resolutely putting the thought of it out of her head, she dressed and went down to the breakfast room, where she found Lavenham already eating a hurried meal preparatory to leaving for Mafra. She sat down across the table from him, but the sight of food sickened her. She crumbled at a roll, pretended to drink her coffee, and made an early excuse to leave the room. To her relief, Lavenham appeared to notice nothing. He was busy giving last-minute orders to the steward, for this was to be an absence of some duration. He had had news that Antonio de Araujo, the Minister for Foreign Affairs, had been urgently summoned to Mafra, and as he strongly suspected Araujo of belonging secretly to the French party, neither he nor Strangford would think it safe to leave the palace so long as he remained there. But he urged Camilla to have everything ready for a sudden move to Lisbon in case this should become necessary. She promised to do so, said the formal goodbye that was all she allowed herself, watched him anxiously as he rode away along the hillside, and then retired to her room to be sick.

CHAPTER 8

TTTTTTTTTTTTTTTTTTTTTTTTTTTTTTTTTTTTTTTTTTTTTTT

September passed, the sun came out to shine on hills that were green from recent rain. The heather on the plain below them was in splendid blossom, and Camilla and Chloe, in their afternoon rambles, were delighted to find enormous pink and white lilies blooming among the wild moss under the cork trees of a nearby valley. But all the sunshine could not warm Camilla, who continued chilly and wretched, shaken by alarming fits of nausea and faintness. It was Chloe, one golden afternoon, when Camilla had been compelled to sit for a time on a mossy bank to recover from a giddy spell, who suggested an alarming explanation of her state.

"Can it be that you are breeding, Camilla?" she asked, with her devastating schoolroom frankness. "How delighted Grandmamma would be."

Camilla, with a sinking heart, pooh-poohed the idea. She was merely suffering, she said, from nerves and the intolerably greasy Portuguese food. She convinced Chloe easily enough, but convincing herself was another matter. More and more, as September darkened towards October, she began to fear that Chloe was right. If so, what should she do, how break it to Lavenham that she was to bear his child? How bitterly, now, she regretted that she had not told him the whole story of their night together when he first recovered his senses. And yet, in the face of his total oblivion, his almost unbearable return to the old formal relationship, how could she have? Would he, even, have believed her? Wary as she knew him to be of female guile, might he not have thought she was taking advantage of his admitted forgetfulness? No—it would have been impossible to tell him—and yet, now, how she wished that she had. If it had seemed impossible, before, to tell him that he had broken through a

100

lifetime's suspicions and slept with her, how much more so, now, when she must tell him, as well, that in that one ecstatic, forgotten night, he had got her with child.

How could she hope that he would believe her? Distrustful, always, of women, he must inevitably think this a ruse on her part to conceal her own unfaithfulness. As she grew, morning by morning, increasingly, despairingly certain of her condition, her one, pitiful consolation was that there was no one else, after all, whom Lavenham could possibly suspect of being the father.

But even this forlorn consolation was snatched from her, one mild October morning, by an unexpected visit from Dom Fernando. Chloe, to whom Camilla had allowed increasing liberty since the departure of the French mission, was out gathering arbutus berries on the nearby hillside, and Camilla, welcoming Dom Fernando with apologies for her husband's absence, found herself, alone with him, unaccountably ill at ease.

As always, they spoke French, and it was in that language that he assured her that he had known Lavenham was still at Mafra, had, in fact, left him there that morning to return to his own house in Lisbon. He had not been able, he told her, to pass so close to her villa without calling to find out how she did. And then, to her appalled surprise, he seized her hand and burst into a speech of passionate love. He could no longer bear, he told her, to stand by and see how Lavenham neglected her, how carelessly he exposed her to danger. Why, at any moment, the French might be over the border, and here she remained, on their very line of march to Lisbon. It was enough to make a man mad, he said, to see so much beauty and goodness so treated. How pale she was, how thin, her appearance distracted him! He had not meant to speak, had meant to love on in silence, but, seeing her thus, how could he help himself? He must tell her how completely he was her slave, how entirely hers to command.

She had contrived, at some point in this long and vehement speech, to withdraw her hand from his, but there was no stopping him. When he was silent at last, looking at her with a mixture of hope and despair, she found herself strangely moved. He asked nothing, seemed to hope nothing. For the first time in her life she found herself the object of disinterested affection—but with what disastrous possibilities. Here, ready made, if he should not believe her story, was a suspect for Lavenham. Every moment that she continued talking with Dom Fernando was fraught with danger, and yet, she could not bring herself to be less than gentle in dismissing him. She did her best to convince him of the injustice of his criticism of Lavenham, assuring him of her devotion to her husband and explaining that it was at her own insistence that she remained at Sintra. He listened to her patiently enough, but refused to be convinced, and continued to beg her to call upon him if she should find herself in any difficulty. "For, say what you will, I will not believe that husband of yours as devoted to his wife as he is to his politics."

This came uncomfortably near the bone, and it was a profound relief to Camilla when she heard Chloe singing "Lady Fair" in the garden. When she appeared with her basket of arbutus berries, Dom Fernando stayed only long enough for the necessary polite speeches, then took his leave, begging Camilla, once again, to let him know if he could be of the slightest service to her.

"Do you know," said devastating Chloe after he was gone, "I really believe the old goat is sweet on you, Camilla. And if he did not stink so of garlic and salt fish, he would be a proper enough conquest." She was quite surprised and hurt when Camilla rounded on her, telling her to mind her manners and try to speak like a lady, if she could not think like one. And Camilla herself was so taken aback by her own vehemence that she ended by bursting into tears, apologising to her sister-in-law and retiring to bed.

Morning brought no comfort. Ill and wretched as usual, she wandered from room to room under the pretence of making arrangements for the sudden move Lavenham had warned them might be imminent, but in reality driven by the restlessness of despair. Until yesterday, she had continued to hope that it might yet be possible to tell her story to Lavenham and be believed. Dom Fernando's outburst had changed all that. When she remembered how he had haunted the house while Lavenham was away, she could not bring herself to hope that Lavenham would not suspect him. In fact, now that her eyes had been opened, she felt that she had been mad not to have thought of him as a possible suspect sooner. Perhaps it was as well she had not tried to tell Lavenham . . . and yet, how she wished she had. Her thoughts went round and round like this, till, finding them and the house alike intolerable, she made her way out on to the terrace and down into the sloping walks of the garden. The day was fine, with a new crispness in the air that helped to revive her spirits, and she drifted up and down the alleys, trying not to think, and noticing instead the mosaic patterns of the fallen leaves, red, black, and yellow, that strewed the walks. They were another reminder that winter was coming, and she found herself passionately hoping that before it began in good earnest the crisis that had been looming over them for so long would break. Anything would be better than this desperate inaction. If only the French would attack, they might at last go home. At the thought, a pang of fierce home-sickness overwhelmed her and with it the glimmering of an idea. It was cowardly, perhaps, but might she not persuade Lavenham that she was not well enough to stay? At home, she might be able to convince his grandmother of the truth of her story. Old Lady Leominster would be a powerful ally, and surely her desire for an heir would help to persuade her. And yet ... it would mean leaving Lavenham, for however eagerly she had defended him against Dom Fernando's criticisms, she was sure he would put his work first and stay to see it through. And quite right, too, she told herself angrily, particularly as her illness must seem to him nothing but an affliction of the nerves.

Returning at last, reluctantly, to the house, with nothing decided, she found Chloe looking for her. Her first words chimed oddly with Camilla's thoughts. "I have been looking everywhere for you," she said reproachfully. "Do you think you are well enough to be wandering off alone? The girl tells me you have eaten no breakfast. I wish you will sit down and take something now. And will you not let me send a messenger for Lavenham? You do not sleep, you do not eat ... Camilla, do you not think we should go home?"

"But how?" Camilla had sat obediently down, enlivened by a faint amusement at this odd reversal of their roles, and had begun to pick idly at a bowl of fruit.

"Someone told me there was an American boat at Lisbon. We could take passage on her. I know you do not wish to leave Lavenham, but truly, Camilla, he is much better; it is about your health that we must be thinking now. Do, pray, send for him at once. The *Jane* has already unloaded her cargo, I believe. There is no time to be lost. Oh, Camilla, think of London, the blessed English food and clean sheets at night. Or we could go to Brighton; I know you would recover your spirits there: it is the enervating Portuguese air, I am sure, that has made you ill. Please, let us go home, Camilla; I am tired of it here: I do not wish ever to smell garlic again, and as for their sunshine, they are welcome to it: I would give anything for a comfortable London fog."

Camilla could not help laughing. "Ungrateful girl, I am sure you will sing another song when we do get home and encounter one. But, tell me, how do you know about this American boat—the *Jane*?"

Chloe was elaborately casual. "Oh, somebody told me— one of the men, whose family is in Lisbon. Was it Pedro? Or Jaime? I vow I do not recall, but it is certain enough, I tell you, and no time to be lost. Only let me send for Lavenham and he will arrange everything."

Camilla knew Chloe well enough by now to be sure that she was lying. Who, then, had told her about the *Jane*? Could it be that she was still seeing—or at least corresponding with —M. Boutet? Had he not gone with the French mission after all? With a chill memory that his friend M. Mireille was a self-acknowledged spy in England, she wondered what sinister role her brother filled in Portugal. "Chloe." She had just begun the essential question when they were interrupted by an excited servant who announced that milord was riding up the hill.

Inwardly noting Chloe's look of relief, Camilla ran with her to welcome Lavenham, who had just dismounted from his exhausted horse. He, too, looked infinitely weary and Camilla hurried him indoors to comfort and a glass of wine, before she would do more than exchange the most routine greetings. Sitting, he sighed with relief. "Ah, I was ready for this. I have been to Lisbon and back since yesterday," he explained. "And on a fool's errand, too, I fear. There is an American ship in the harbour." Camilla and Chloe exchanged glances as he took another long draft of wine. "The *Jane*. I hoped to get you passage on her, but my information came too late. She was loaded to the gunwale when I arrived; her captain said he could not take aboard so much as another child. They are paying twelve hundred pounds for one family's passage to England. I wish I had heard of her sooner. I am afraid I have done wrong, gravely wrong, in letting you stay so long."

He looked so tired and depressed that Camilla forgot her

own anxieties and hurried to comfort him, reminding him that it was she who had insisted on staying. "And, besides," she went on, "surely there will be other ships? It is true that Chloe and I have been saying, only this morning, that we should be glad to get home. Should we, perhaps, move to Lisbon and await the next one?"

He made an impatient gesture. "But that is the whole point," he said. "Dom John has signed the edict. Tomorrow all Portuguese ports will be closed to British shipping, and who knows how long it will be before another American boat touches here? No, I have done wrong," he said again, "and regret it too late. For I fear that now he has yielded this point, the Regent will soon give way to the other French demands. It is only a matter of time until he orders the arrest of British subjects that remain and the confiscation of their property."

"But surely," protested Camilla, with sinking heart, "that will not apply to us? You have diplomatic immunity. He cannot touch us."

"I wish I could believe it. I fear I have let Araujo lull me into a false sense of security. I am increasingly convinced that it is he, not Dom Fernando, who is playing the French game. I only wish I had realised it, and listened to Dom Fernando's warnings sooner. He has been urging me, this month or more, to send you both home without delay. And now it is too late. I shall never forgive myself—" He stopped in the middle of this gloomy sentence and changed his tone. "But there is one crumb of comfort. Strangford has received information that a British squadron, under Sir Sidney Smith, is on its way to Lisbon. We must hope that they arrive before conditions here become impossible, or before the French invade, which, I am sure they intend to, whatever last-moment concessions Dom John may make. In the meantime, I think you had best move back to Lisbon: this house is too lonely, and too close to what must inevitably be the French line of attack, for it to be a suitable home for you now. Can you be ready to leave this afternoon, for if so I shall be able to give myself the pleasure of escorting you."

Camilla assured him that they had everything in readiness and could easily make their final preparations in time for an afternoon journey, but could not help asking, "And you? Will you be able to remain with us in Lisbon?"

"Not beyond tonight, but at least the Prince Regent plans

to move his court tomorrow to Queluz, to join his mother. So at least I shall be only an hour's journey from you."

Comforted by this news, Camilla set about her preparations with a will, and felt better, so occupied, than she had done for some time, so that when, over a light luncheon preparatory to departure, Chloe raised the question of her health with Lavenham she was easily able to scout their anxieties. It had been, she assured them, nothing but an affliction of the nerves: the move back to Lisbon would doubtless be a cure in itself. And indeed the drive back, in mellow afternoon sunshine, was a pleasant one. The heath below their house was still brilliant with a profusion of wild flowers and when they reached the Valley of Alcantara, which had been so parched and dry when they last traversed it, they found it resplendent with an almost springtime green. The orange and lemon trees under the pillars of the gigantic aqueduct that crossed the valley were vividly green again and brilliant with ripening fruit. When, at Chloe's insistence, they stopped the carriage for a few moments so that she could pick some of the flowers that enamelled the close and fragrant turf, they could hear larks singing, far above them. Camilla, who had found the carriage's jolting over the rough roads far from pleasant, was delighted at the excuse Chloe had given her to sit for a while in the benevolent sunshine with Lavenham beside her. He seized this opportunity, when Chloe had wandered away a little in search of some particularly luxurious myrtle blossoms, to question Camilla more closely about her indisposition, and did it so kindly that she was on the point of risking all and telling him the truth when Chloe came running back with her armful of blossom, and the opportunity was gone.

Still, it was a happy day, with Lavenham kinder than he had been for some time, teasing Chloe and taking care of Camilla so that she began to feel that, if this had been achieved by her lie to him on his last visit, it was almost worth it. She was relieved, too, to find that he no longer seemed to suspect Dom Fernando of spying on him and began to hope that before he left she might have the chance, and the courage, to tell him her secret. But the chance never came. They found the servants they had left to look after the Lisbon house in a state of panic, the house itself in rack and ruin with a family of toads six inches across in the cellar. Lavenham was busy all evening putting some heart into the

servants, who had been convinced they would never see
master or mistress again, while Camilla and Chloe had their
work cut out for them in making the house habitable once
more.

And first thing next morning Lavenham rode off to visit
Dom Fernando, explaining to Camilla that, since he had no
reliable English manservant to leave as their protector, he
intended to entrust their safety to Dom Fernando. "He will
be, I am sure, a reliable protector, for really, Camilla, I
believe him to be more than a little in love with you," he
finished teasingly. And Camilla, laughing and blushing, longed
to seize the chance to tell him of Dom Fernando's amazing
declaration. But Chloe was there, and Lavenham's horse
awaiting him: once more she let the opportunity slip.

Lavenham returned to assure them that Dom Fernando
promised to watch over them like a brother, and that he
himself would come at once if any new crisis arose, and then
took his leave urging Chloe to look after Camilla, and Camilla to take care of herself. "I hope to see your health quite
re-established when I next visit you."

Camilla, who was now thoroughly convinced that it would
be nine months before her health was re-established, found
cold comfort in this speech, with its suggestion that her
husband was only on visiting terms with her. Left alone once
more, she resumed the old round of "if onlys." If only she
had told Lavenham in the first place ... If only she had
seized that chance in the Valley of Alcantara ... If only ...
If only ...

A visit from Dom Fernando was almost a relief, because a
distraction, and she was grateful for his assurances that she
and Chloe should come to no harm that it lay in his power to
prevent. To her relief, too, he made no reference to the scene
he had made her two days before, behaving once more
merely like her husband's friend. As such, she found him easy
and entertaining company and was surprised when he rose to
take his leave and commented on Chloe's prolonged absence.
Apologising for her, and bidding Dom Fernando a grateful
farewell, Camilla found herself a prey to renewed apprehen-
sion. Surely it was impossible that M. Boutet was still in the
country? Or, if he was, secretly, he would never risk visiting
Chloe here? And yet—Chloe had been out in the garden for
over an hour. She wandered out on to the terrace and stood
there irresolutely unable to decide whether to go and look for

Chloe. After all, she told herself, Chloe had never made any
secret of the boredom Dom Fernando's visits caused her. She
might well have seen him arrive and contrived to avoid him.
So hesitating, Camilla accused herself of cowardice. Her real
reason, she knew well enough, was that she could not face
the possibility of another scene with her brother, for whom,
on the strength of one brief meeting, she felt an aversion so
strong as to amount almost to terror. Even thinking of him
brought on one of her faint spells; she was compelled to
hurry indoors and lie down on an uncomfortable chaise
longue in the salon. And it was thus that Chloe found her
when she came running up the steps from the garden, her
cheeks flushed, her arms full of late gleanings from the
rose-bushes.

She was all contrition at sight of Camilla. She had left her
too long alone; she would fetch smelling salts and the cordial
Camilla found reviving. Dropping her roses on a small table,
she hurried upstairs, to return almost at once with the medicaments and a light mohair shawl which she folded lovingly
round Camilla. "There," she said, "now you will be better,
will you not, Camilla? But I wish you would let me fetch a
doctor to you: I am sure Lavenham would wish it if he knew
how often you were having these giddy spells."

"What?" Camilla's spirits were reviving. "And be dosed, as
like as not, with crushed snails and viper's broth? No, thank
you, Chloe, I will wait to call a doctor till we are safe home,
which I hope will be soon now."

The light went out of Chloe's face. "Very soon?"

"I hope so. But are you not glad? Chloe," the question
came out almost despite her, "have you been seeing him
again?"

"Him?" All too obviously Chloe was playing for time.

"The Frenchman ... M. Boutet ..." and with a final
effort, "my brother. Is he not gone with the others? Chloe,
tell true! I must know." And she sat up on her couch with a
look of such feverish anxiety that Chloe, alarmed in her turn,
hurried to take her hand and offer the smelling salts once
more. But Camilla waved them away. "No, no; I am well
enough; if only you will tell me the truth. I must know,
Chloe," she said again, "or else I will send a messenger to
Lavenham telling him the whole."

Thus threatened, Chloe dissolved into one of her fits of
easy tears. "Why are you so hard to me, Camilla? One would

think you had never been in love in your life." And then, drawing herself up proudly, "Yes, I am this minute come from Charles. He has stayed in Lisbon, at great risk to himself, merely in the hope of seeing me again. Camilla, I beg you will try to understand. We have so little time. Who knows when we shall meet again? I know Lee would not understand, but that you—Charles's own sister—that you should be so hard, so unsympathetic: it is beyond bearing! Sometimes I think I shall go mad. And I thought you would be so pleased: I shall never understand you: to treat your own brother as if he was an enemy."

"But he is one, Chloe. I fear I have done wrong in not telling Lavenham of this affair long since. But I tell you now that unless I have your solemn word that you will not see M. Boutet again, I shall send to Lavenham tonight." And yet, she told herself, this too was cowardice. What was the use of extorting promises from Chloe, who would break them as lightly as the leaves she was stripping, as they talked, from one of her roses?

"Oh." She had pricked herself and put her finger into her mouth to suck away the blood, then smiled reassuringly at Camilla. "No need to promise," she said. "Charles leaves tonight: I do not know when I shall see him again."

"For good?" Camilla could not conceal her relief.

"Oh no, but for more than a week." Chloe made it sound an age. "You do not think we shall be gone before then, Camilla? If I did not see him once more, to say goodbye, I think my heart would break." And Camilla, wryly amused, found herself, of all things, consoling her incorrigible sister-in-law for the absence of her untrustworthy love. And so the scene between them ended with nothing settled, though Camilla, thinking it over afterwards, told herself that next time Lavenham came he must be told, at whatever cost either to herself or to Chloe.

But when Lavenham did ride up to the house a few days later, he looked so distracted that Chloe and Camilla, after a quick exchange of glances, devoted themselves entirely to his comfort, without daring even to ask the questions that trembled on their lips. At last, setting down the glass of wine he had hardly tasted, he spoke. "You do not ask my news?"

"I fear it is bad," Camilla said.

"Yes, the worst. It is but a matter of days before Dom John signs the decree confiscating British property. And the squadron we were promised, under Sir Sidney Smith, has not arrived. But there is worse than that."

"Worse?"

"Yes. At least for me . . . for us, I should say. Chloe, I beg you will leave us."

Chloe protested, but her brother was firm. "No, this is no concern of yours, thank God. I must speak to my wife alone."

With an anxious glance at Camilla, Chloe rose and left them. Closing the door behind her, Lavenham took another distracted turn about the room before he came back to stand over Camilla. "Do you remember my asking you, some time since, at Sintra, about a man I thought I saw you talking with in the garden here?"

"Yes?" Camilla's voice shook on the word.

"And you denied having done so?"

"Yes," she said again.

"God, I should have known." He stood beside a tall vase of myrtle, systematically stripping the white blossoms from their stalks. " 'Trust the devil before you trust a woman,' my father told me as he died. Why did I not listen? Now I am disgraced—a laughing-stock. I hope my grandmother will be pleased with what she has done to me. 'No, no,' you said, you had talked with no one. My poor mind, you hinted, must have been deceiving me again . . . And so it was—when I took your word. I must have been mad. The Court has its spies, you must know, on all of us foreigners. I collect you did not think of that. And most particularly have there been agents about you, being the Frenchwoman, God forgive me, that you are. This morning, when I was urging Araujo to persuade Dom John to throw in his lot with ours and sail at once for the Brazils, he turned on me. 'Is that the advice your wife wishes me to give?' I did not understand what he meant. 'My wife?' I said. 'Yes,' he said, 'that French wife of yours. Or did you not know she has been constantly in touch with a notorious French spy? I have no doubt it would suit the French admirably to have us run away, bag and baggage, leaving our country for who will to snap up, but we'll not do it, I tell you, and so you can tell that wife of yours you have kept so close—and no wonder, a spy and the accomplice of spies.' " Lavenham broke off and took another furious turn about the room, while she watched him, speechless. At last he returned to loom over her more threateningly than ever.

"And I—poor fool," he went on, "I spoke up for you, refusing to believe what Araujo said—only to be faced with proofs, the reports of his men who have watched you."

"Araujo's men?" she asked, grasping at a straw. "But did you not say he was for the French?"

"What's that to the purpose? No, no, do not shilly-shally with me like that. You have ruined me, and there's an end of it. I trust you are satisfied with your work."

Camilla had been thinking the rapid thoughts of despair. If they had indeed been spied on, surely the informer must know perfectly well that it was Chloe, not she, who had been receiving the Frenchman's visits. His reports must have been deliberately falsified in order to give Araujo the strongest possible hold over Lavenham. Or could it be that Charles Boutet himself was the source of the information and had deliberately misinformed Araujo for some sinister purpose of his own? Groping among these possibilities, each one more desperate than the last, she sat tongue-tied under Lavenham's furious stare. What could she say, what do? Useless to tell him that Boutet's visits had been to Chloe: they remained just as damaging, and anyway she felt herself responsible in that she had let them continue. But there was one question she must ask. "And Strangford," she said, "does he know?" Before the words were out of her mouth, she realised how he would take them.

"Ah," it was something between a sigh and a groan. "So you admit it. As calmly as that. Is it nothing to you that you have destroyed everything I had hoped for in life? Do you know—it will make you laugh, I have no doubt—do you know that I had begun to think we might find happiness together, you and I. I had begun to believe a woman could be trusted—might even be safely loved. Yes, have your laugh, for you have earned it. I had begun to love you, poor fool that I was. And all the time, you were laughing at me with that French accomplice of yours. Tell me, accomplished wife, is he your lover, too? But I've not answered your question. No, Strangford does not know, nor will he, Araujo tells me, if I will but contradict everything I have ever said; change my advice to the Regent. Urge him to stay in Portugal, and my secret is safe. If I betray my country I may continue respected there; if not, I must be ruined. And this you have done to me. You, the girl I picked up in the gutter and gave my name—and almost my heart, too. But I have learned my lesson. Only tell me, mistress spy, what shall we do now? Do you propose to continue gracing my board—never my bed—or do you intend to join your Frenchman when he welcomes Bonaparte's armies into Portugal—all too soon? I had best know, had I not, that I may guide my conduct accordingly." His eyes glittered dangerously as he bent still more closely over her, but she was too angry now for fright.

"I thank you, my lord," she said, "for your confidence in me. So I am to be tried, judged, and condemned, am I, on the word of Araujo, whom you have always proclaimed a French agent! You do not come to ask me if there is any truth in his accusations. Oh no, merely to tell me that I am false, and pour out your accumulated spleen against womankind on my innocent head. Yes, I said 'innocent' and it is true, though I can see you will never believe it. I have been foolish, I admit, and would ask your pardon, if you were in any state to listen to me. As for Araujo, go to him, tell him he has been misled by his agents, if that is the story they have told him, and see how he takes that. As for me: I have no French accomplice and never have had. Your board I have shared—and your bed too, though you have paid me the compliment of forgetting the occasion—and carry the consequences with me now. It is a little late in the day to talk of banishing me from your bed when I am carrying your child. Oh, I grant, you were drunk—not yourself at the time—you would doubtless never have touched anything so loathsome as a woman else. Well, I too have learned my lesson. I have had my delusions too; my hopes of a happy marriage, but, believe me, my lord, they are at an end. Let us but get back to England and I promise you my child and I will never trouble you more."

"Your child? What madness is this?"

"Yes, my child—and yours, though I can see you will never believe it. Well, so much the better for it, poor baby. Better no father than one as incapable of human feeling as you . . . a man who will believe anyone rather than his own wife."

He was silent for a moment, white-faced and shaking, then, as she succumbed to a passion of tears, he broke out again: "A likely story, madam, and told in a most happy hour. So I am to acknowledge some French spy's bastard as my heir . . . You say I believe Araujo before you: well, why should I not, when I have, to confirm his story, the evidence of my own eyes. Did I not—though, in my folly, I let you persuade me I was mistaken—did I not, myself, see you with your French paramour in the garden?"

He was interrupted by a voice from the doorway, where Chloe stood, white-faced and trembling. "Oh, Lavenham," she said, "it was I."

He looked at her, for a moment, in appalled silence, then, at a cry from her, turned back to catch Camilla as she fell.

CHAPTER 9

For Camilla there followed an interval of blessed unconsciousness. The doctors came, sighed, and shook their heads. It was brain fever, said one, and recommended shaving off her hair. It was merely the culmination of a nervous affliction, said another, and urged frequent bleeding. It was homesickness, said a third: Lavenham had best send her back to England without delay. In the same breath he warned that it would mean certain death to move her. None of them discovered her condition, and Lavenham, racked with an intolerable uncertainty, at once cursed and congratulated himself for his silence on this point. If she was false—as he mostly believed—what better than that she should die, undisgraced, here in Portugal? But—suppose her story was true? Pacing the house, sleepless, night after night, he tortured himself with the doubt, and the vain attempt to remember. It was true enough, that when he had waked, the morning after he came home wounded, he had remembered nothing of what had happened the day before. Camilla had had to tell him. And how could she have told him this? And yet—how easy for her to use his brief forgetfulness to mask her own guilty secret. True, Chloe had confessed the whole of her affair with Charles Boutet, though suppressing, from a delicacy of her own, the fact that he was Camilla's brother. But there were other men ... Suspicious of women since childhood, Lavenham found it impossible to believe one now.

And yet, as Camilla lay there, day after day, so white, so silent, so nearly dead, it was impossible not to be moved by that strange feeling—could it be love?—that had crept upon him, almost unawares, since the first day when he had seen her in his carriage, drooping, exquisitely asleep—his wife. Sometimes, as he paced his room, those still, intolerable nights, he found himself praying for proof of her innocence, for another chance, for life ... But still she lay there silent, the doctors came, their advice conflicted on every point, and Lavenham and Chloe, united in an uneasy truce over the sick-bed, agreed tacitly to ignore it. As for the maid, Frances, she had fallen into such a state of panic since the first decree against the British that she was worse than useless and the main burden of the nursing fell inevitably on Chloe and Rosa, the plump, kind-hearted Portuguese girl who acted as her maid.

Despite his racking anxiety and tormenting doubt over Camilla, Lavenham still had to spend much of his time with the Prince Regent at Queluz. Things were moving rapidly to a crisis. It was only a matter of days, perhaps of hours, he told Chloe, before the Prince Regent signed the decree confiscating British property. And still the promised British squadron had not arrived—not that its coming would do them much good, as Chloe gloomily pointed out, since the one point on which all the doctors were agreed was that Camilla could not be moved without grave risk to both life and reason. Fortunately, when the decree was signed, it excluded the property of diplomats, and Dom Fernando, whose solicitude for Camilla's health had been unfailing, and had added considerable fuel to Lavenham's suspicions, arranged for a police agent to be stationed at their house to ensure that they were not molested. But it was uncomfortable enough, just the same, to hear of the forced sale of such British possessions as had not been already disposed of, and Chloe was not surprised when Frances' nerve gave way entirely and she accepted an offer of a passage home with an Englishwoman who had contrived to bribe her way on board an American ship.

Chloe was glad enough to see her go. She had been more of a liability than an asset for some time, and, besides, it was a relief to have no English ears to hear the bitter scenes between her and her brother. For the discovery that it was Chloe who had been associating, all the time, with a known French spy had combined with Lavenham's suspicions of Camilla to reawaken all the old bitterness against his mother, and through her, against women in general. Only the fact that most of their meetings took place over Camilla's sick-bed saved Chloe from the full tide of his wrath. Inevitably, he blamed her more than himself for Camilla's illness and found her devoted nursing the smallest of amends. Conscience-stricken herself, she bore his reproaches for some time with the patience of guilt, but gradually her spirit reasserted herself and she turned on him roundly. Whose fault, after all, was it that she and Camilla were still here? "I do not blame you on my own account," she went on, "since I begged to come and must take the consequences, but as Camilla's husband I should have thought you would have taken more thought for her safety. The truth of the matter is you want a wife for your convenience but do not propose to yourself to take any responsibility for her. And besides," she was well and truly roused now, "if you ask me, the main cause of Camilla's illness has been your continued neglect of her. She has borne it like the angel she is, and therefore, I have no doubt, you have not even perceived that she felt it, but I have. It has never, I collect, since you are incapable of such a feeling yourself, occurred to you that she loved you and suffered from your treatment of her. If you could not *feel* towards her as a husband, you might at least have compelled yourself to *behave* like one. I only wish I knew what madness made you propose to her in the first place—or her accept you, for the matter of that."

Thus roundly attacked, Lavenham was silenced for once, and he left soon afterwards for Queluz with much to think about. It was a relief, both to him and to Chloe, when circumstances kept him there for several days. When he next came to Lisbon, it was to announce the imminent arrival of the British squadron and to bring bad news arising from it. Lord Strangford had felt compelled to ask for his passports and intended to go aboard Sir Sidney's flagship as soon as he arrived to begin his blockade of Lisbon harbour. To make the gesture complete, it was essential that Lavenham should accompany the Minister Plenipotentiary. He came to ask Chloe whether she thought it safe to take Camilla. Once more the doctors came, and once more they shook their heads. There had been no change in Camilla's condition, she still lay in the stupor into which she had fallen, accepting Chloe's ministrations passively, like a child, or, more frightening, an imbecile, but otherwise entirely withdrawn into some shadow world of her own. The doctors looked grave, each one blaming her failure to recover on Lavenham's refusal to take his original advice. As for moving her—and on board ship at that—they were unanimous in agreeing that it was out of the

question. Death or madness were the alternative consequences. Then, gravely accepting their fees, they shook their
heads a last time and took their leave.

Alone with Chloe, Lavenham turned to her in despair. She
had had the main charge of Camilla; what did she think?
Reluctantly, she found herself compelled to agree with the
doctors. "But do not trouble yourself, Lee. I shall stay with
her. We will do well enough. Dom Fernando will protect us,
and you will be within easy call, will you not? If the worst
comes to the worst, and, for any reason, Sir Sidney proposes
to leave Lisbon, we will have to risk moving her, but until
then, I think she and I had best remain here."

However reluctantly, Lavenham found himself compelled
to admit the sense of what she said. Since the terrace of their
house commanded a clear view of the harbour, he arranged a
code of signals by which Chloe would be able to communi-
cate with him on Sir Sidney's flagship, and promised to seize
every opportunity of visiting her. At last, reluctantly, he took
his leave, all his earlier fury forgotten in the unwilling respect
he found himself feeling for her. But when he tried to say
something of this, she just laughed at him: "Never mind,
Lee, you will have plenty of chances to be in a passion with
me again before we are old and grey and gouty."

He returned to Queluz, to join Strangford in making arrangements for their move aboard ship, with an uncomfortable feeling that he was not, somehow, showing up very
well in contrast to his flibbertigibbet younger sister. It was a
new experience for him, and one, like his torturing doubts of
Camilla, and Chloe's own disconcerting attack on him as a
husband, that kept him awake for many an uncomfortable
night's tossing on the uncertain water of Lisbon harbour.

His only comfort, those wretched days, was that he had at
last told the whole story of Chloe's indiscretion to Lord
Strangford. The confession, though painful enough, had at
least been an easier one than if it had concerned his wife
instead of his sister. Luckily for his peace of mind, Chloe had
not thought it wise to tell him that her French lover was
Camilla's brother, and Camilla had been in no state to do so.
He had been soundly rebuked by Strangford for not keeping
his household in better order, had felt, with dislike, that he
deserved the rebuke, but had at least had the consolation that
Araujo's blackmailing overtures had not been repeated. His
career was safe, but as the gloomy November days passed, it

seemed more and more likely that it had been saved at the expense of his wife's reason. Night after night, the signal Chloe flashed from the shore indicated no change in the invalid's condition, and night after night Lavenham paced the decks for hours, in turns blaming and excusing himself. If only he could *remember*. If Camilla was indeed carrying his child, how different the world would be to him ... And yet, how could he believe it? Never trust a woman, his father had said. What cause had he to do so now? And yet ... and yet ... Camilla had *seemed* so different, so calm, so good ... so lovable. Still, despite himself, he loved her, and his love, stronger than any reason, argued the truth of her story. If it was indeed his child ... and he had destroyed mother and child together ... So he went on, suffering, doubting and arguing with himself, hour after hour, in a squirrel's cage of wretchedness, until Strangford, increasingly anxious about him, was almost relieved when an urgent messenger summoned them to the Prince Regent at Queluz.

The news was as bad as possible. A French army, under Junot, who had once been French Minister in Lisbon, had entered Portugal. And now, at last, the Prince Regent had been forced to open his eyes. By some freak of luck an old copy of the Paris *Moniteur* had reached him, and in it he had read Bonaparte's announcement that his house of Braganza had ceased to reign in Europe. Even he realised that the time for compromise was past. He summoned his Council of State and announced his immediate departure for Brazil; a Provisional Government, of which Dom Fernando was a member, was named to rule Portugal in his absence.

The news brought chaos to the city, and despair to Lavenham. It was to be his honourable task to accompany the Portuguese royal family on their arduous voyage to the New World. Out of the question that Camilla should accompany him, but equally imperative that, at whatever risk, she be placed on board one of the British ships that were to return to England. With Strangford's permission, he made a detour on his way back from Queluz to visit Chloe and tell her the news. She received it with unconcealed anxiety. There had been no change in Camilla's condition; the risk of moving her was as great as ever. She led her brother upstairs to Camilla's bedroom, where she lay, white and still, her only movement a restless convulsive clutching and unclutching of her fingers.

"What is she holding?" Lavenham asked.

"Her wedding ring. She has been doing it for some days. It is the only change."

They stood together, silently, for a few minutes, then Lavenham spoke with a brisk cheerfulness he was far from feeling. "Perhaps it is a good sign. Should we have the doctors again? No?" As Chloe shook her head vigorously. "I am inclined to agree with you. Very well, then. We must simply arrange to move her, as gently as possible, and at the very last moment. It will take some days for the Court to embark ... many of their ships are still fitting for the voyage; the provisions of others need replenishing. We can count, I think, on four or five days' grace ... and, besides"— he looked gloomily out the window and across the harbour— "if the wind does not change, it will be impossible to sail anyway."

"You mean Junot may catch us here?"

"It is possible. By all reports, he is only a few days' march from the city and no attempt has been made at stopping him. General Freire and his troops are still on the coast. So far as I know they have not even heard of Junot's advance. They have certainly made no move to check it. Not," he added with his usual fairness, "that they would have the slightest hope of doing so. Junot's troops, I understand, are something of the rawest, but the Portuguese army can hardly be said to exist at all. The fact remains that Araujo has made no move to alert it. I am more and more convinced that it has been he, all the time, who has played the traitor. I owe Dom Fernando a hearty apology for my suspicions of him ... and hearty thanks, too, for his care of you and Camilla."

Chloe smiled wickedly at him. "I am not sure that it is not Camilla who should be thanked for that. If he is not head over heels in love with her, I miss my guess very sadly. But what are we going to do, Lee?"

"Why, leave her here until the last possible moment. This movement of her hands is new, and I don't like it. Who can tell what other change it may presage? Come out on the terrace every night at first dusk. If the fleet is ready to sail, and the wind favourable—if, in short, I feel that the time has come when, at whatever risk to her, you and Camilla must come aboard, I will burn a green and a red light, together, on the stern of the *Hibernia*. That is your signal to get the men to carry Camilla, as gently as possible, down to the cove below the house. I will meet you there, with one of the

Hibernia's boats. We must just pray God that the movement does not hurt her."

"Yes," Chloe said, "I do not see what else we can do."

Camilla's dreams had been troubled and restless. Now, waking suddenly, she was relieved to see Chloe bending anxiously over her. Chloe had been in the dreams, surely? And Lavenham, too? She was sure of it, yet could remember no detail. She was tired, too tired for remembering, or even for thought. But she must think. She must consider Chloe, who looked thin and pale, and who was, unaccountably, crying. To confirm this, a large tear splashed on to Camilla's right hand, which was clasped, she noticed, over her left, the fingers rubbing feebly over—oh, her wedding ring of course. Lavenham ... Chloe ... bad dreams. It was no use, she could not remember.

Chloe's voice distracted her "Camilla! Can you hear me?"

What an effort it was to speak. "Of course. Why not?" The question left her exhausted and she lay with closed eyes, trying to take in Chloe's answer. She had been very ill: that was why she was so tired. Of course, that was all ... She was beginning to remember now; a little, slowly. And at once there was another question. "Lavenham?" she asked.

"Coming for us tonight," Chloe said, and then, in a rush that sounded more like her usual self: "Oh, Camilla, I am *glad* that you are better. But no more questions now. Rest ... try to sleep. It will be tiring enough tonight."

It was good advice. Camilla was glad to close her eyes. Only, as she did so, another memory came to her and she opened them again. "And the baby," she asked, "what does Lavenham say now?"

Chloe's look of puzzlement was answer enough. "The baby? Camilla, what do you mean? . . . Are you? . . ." and then, in a rush, "Oh, those doctors! ... Oh, Camilla!" Again her tears began to fall and then, unaccountably, she was laughing. "Oh, Camilla, I am so *pleased*—and Lavenham kept it to himself! ... Just wait till I see him."

"No, no ..." It was all too much. She was relieved when her protest was interrupted by the girl, Rosa, who brought Chloe a note. Chloe read it, coloured, and rose to leave the room, telling Rosa to watch by Camilla and urging Camilla, once more, to rest. Drifting off to sleep, Camilla found herself a prey to a vague anxiety. Chloe had had a note ...

Why not? ... What was there frightening about that? ... It was no use; she gave up trying to think and drifted off again into a place of troubled dreams.

When she next woke, Chloe was back by her bed watching her anxiously. The room was full of evening shadows and Camilla could hear, outside, the steady rush of rain. She shivered. "It is cold," she said, and then, "how long have I been ill?"

"Not long; though it seems an age. A little more than two weeks. Camilla, are you really strong enough to talk?"

"Of course. But, tell me, where is Lavenham? You said he was coming for tonight. Why? Where are we going?"

"Home, I hope. As for Lavenham, he is aboard the *Hibernia* with Strangford and Sir Sidney Smith, and mad, I can tell you, with anxiety for you. The doctors said you could not be moved, you see."

"So you stayed here with me? Thank you, Chloe. But I still do not understand ... " Once more, her hands began their restless movement, and Chloe, noticing it, hurried to give her a brief explanation of the events that had taken place during her illness, of Junot's approach and the Prince Regent's belated recognition of danger. "You should just have seen the harbour two days ago, when the Court were going on board: I spent all day at the window here, watching: you never saw anything like it. The whole Court, the archives, the treasury—everything, out there in the pouring rain. The mad old Queen, they tell me, crying, '*Ai Jesus,*' harder than ever, the Prince Regent with tears running down his cheeks, the proudest ladies of the Court wading into the water to beg for passage ... And many of them without a scrap of baggage to their name. It will be an unhappy enough voyage even for those who have managed to beg or bribe their way on board."

"But when do they sail?" asked Camilla.

"Why, that's the rub. They have been ready for two days now, but the wind is against them. They cannot stir. And all the time, Junot is getting nearer. That is why Lavenham is coming for us tonight. He thinks it possible Junot may be here tomorrow and dares not risk a further delay. We are to meet him down at the little harbour. What a happy man he will be when he sees you recovered. Tell me, are you strong enough to dress? The men will carry you down, but you would be better dressed."

Camilla laughed. "I should rather think I would. Well, let us make the effort."

She found it an exhausting enough business, but with Chloe's loving assistance managed, at last, to put on a warm travelling dress of dark green sarsenet and its matching pelisse. After the effort, she was glad enough to lie back on her bed while Chloe hurried away to make her own preparations. Lavenham had told her that they must bring as little as possible, but her jewels and Camilla's must be packed into the smallest compass, together with a minimum wardrobe for the voyage back to England. "We shall be nothing but a pair of waifs and strays when we get home," she told Camilla, "but luckily Grandmamma will be so delighted with your news I am sure nothing will be too good for you."

"My news?"

"Why, the baby. Or were you funning? Oh, Camilla, surely not?"

It seemed an odd enough kind of a joke to Camilla, although she was tempted, for a moment, to pretend that it had been a misunderstanding. But what was the use? The truth would have to come out sooner or later. If only she knew whether she had succeeded in convincing Lavenham in that last dreadful scene, of which she had only fragmentary memories. But the fact that he had not spoken of her condition, even to Chloe, was anything but hopeful. Her hands resumed their nervous movement as she begged Chloe to say nothing about the baby to anyone. "Do not, I beg of you, tease Lavenham about it ... there will be time enough on the voyage home."

Chloe looked appalled. "Oh, Camilla, how could I be such a muttonhead! Did I not explain? Lavenham does not come with us. He has been appointed to escort the Prince Regent to the Brazils. It is a great honour, of course ... " Chloe was dwindling to an unhappy silence when she was interrupted by an agitated servant who announced that there were men below who insisted on speaking with the ladies.

"Men? What men?" Chloe was beginning, when she saw another figure enter the darkening room behind the servant. "You?" she said.

"Myself. And entirely at both your service." Charles Boutet removed his hat with a flourish, dismissed the man in fluent Portuguese, and advanced towards the window where Camilla sat transfixed. "My dear Sister, I am delighted to see you better. When our beloved Chloe told me the good news I was transported with joy—for many reasons."

"What do you mean?" It was no comfort, in her cold terror, to see that Chloe shared it.

"Just what I say. That I am glad to see you better. Whatever risks milord your husband might have been prepared to take with you, I should have been most reluctant to move you against the advice of the doctors. But now, everything is altered, and just in time. I am come to offer you asylum, my dearest Sister, and to you, my ever beloved Chloe, my heart and hand."

"What can you mean?" For all her illness, it was Camilla who spoke.

"Why, that I am come to take you home. You did not, surely, think that I would stand by and let you return to England with that tyrannical husband of yours? No, no, I am a better brother than that, and a better lover, too, as my dearest Chloe will admit, I am sure, before many days are past. For the moment, there is no time to be lost in talk. You, I am sure, have no more desire than I have for an encounter with your braggadocio husband, in which he must inevitably be defeated. So come, you are packed and ready, I see. We have not far to go: I am much too considerate a brother and," once again there was a proprietorial smile for Chloe, "lover for that. We will just take you to a safer shelter far enough sway so that milord the husband cannot find you, and there, for tonight, you may rest. Tomorrow, Junot will be here, and all Lisbon yours. You will find it somewhat different from playing the beggarly British suppliants, I can tell you."

Chloe spoke at last. "Traitor," she said. "I should have known. And all your talk of love was time-serving and treachery. Camilla, will you ever forgive me? It was I—I am the traitor. I told him all our plans. I wanted—God help me—I wanted to say goodbye to him. Because, you see, I loved him. Or," she was standing beside Camilla now, one hand protectively—or for protection—in Camilla's, "I thought I did."

Charles Boutet smiled mockingly. "A pity to change your mind now, when everything is in train to make me the happiest of men. But come, we are wasting time. Tell me, ladies, do you propose to accompany me willingly? It will be very much your wiser plan. I should be sorry to have to mar our relationship with any show of force, but, believe me, I shall not hesitate to do so, if you make it necessary. Dom Fernando's officer has been dealt with; your servants have taken our hint and fled; there is no other house within earshot; my carriage is outside. And I am sure you, my love," he turned to Chloe, "will agree with me that any scene of violence will be the worst possible thing for our dear sister's precarious health."

Chloe and Camilla exchanged despairing glances. It was all too evidently true. The house was silent, and Chloe, white with rage, could see that Camilla was near fainting. Charles Boutet settled it. "Of course," he went on, "if your pride compels you to make some show of resistance, I shall feel myself constrained, however regretfully, to separate you from our sister, who would, I am sure, sadly miss your nursing."

Once more the girls exchanged glances. Then Camilla spoke, "Very well," she said. "We will go with you, but do not imagine that we will ever forget or forgive this outrage."

"No?" He raised mocking eyebrows. "Speak for yourself, my dearest Sister. Perhaps you may be so foolish as to continue resenting my freeing you from an unloving husband, but I am sure my beloved Chloe will forgive me soon enough when once we are man and wife."

"Never," Chloe began, but he had turned to summon his men. Speechless with indignation, she nevertheless found herself helping in the business of carrying Camilla down through the deserted house to the closed carriage that waited outside. To the last moment, both girls had expected a miracle, had refused to believe that this could really be happening to them, but no miracle took place. With a careful solicitude that was, somehow, the last straw, Charles Boutet's followers laid Camilla down on the back seat of the carriage, where Chloe supported her as best she might. Charles Boutet stepped in beside them, gave an order to his men, pulled down the shades, and settled himself on the front seat with a little sigh of satisfaction. "*Bon.*" He lapsed comfortably into French. "Now no one will disturb us. Besides, the world has other things to think of, today. Come, my dearest Sister, do not fret," for tears were slowly following each other down Camilla's cheeks. "I have left a note for that bullying husband of yours telling him not to derange himself on your account since you have followed your heart, to France."

It was too much. Camilla, who had been fighting for

consciousness with every breath she took, slid once more into a faint. When she came to herself again, she was lying on a hard bed, with Chloe once more anxiously beside her. "Was it a nightmare?" she asked.

"No," Chloe said. "It is all true, and all my fault. But if it has not killed you, Camilla, perhaps there is some hope for us yet."

"Hope?" Camilla asked sardonically. Then, looking around the darkening room, "But at least we are alone."

"Yes. That is why I dare speak of hope. When we reached this house—and God knows where it is, for I certainly do not—there was a messenger waiting for Charles, an urgent summons to join Junot on the march. I am glad you taught me some French, Camilla, for Charles thinks I do not understand it. He has left us here, with only two of his men on guard. We are locked in, of course, and they think us safe till morning. I heard them say so. They are downstairs, in the servants' quarters, with a cask of wine. We are at the very top of the house; they think we cannot possibly escape."

"Well," Camilla said reasonably, "how can we?"

"By climbing down the vine that grows up this side of the house. You should just see it, Camilla, it has branches as big as your arm. It will be a ladder for us—a ladder to freedom. Camilla, say you can do it."

But Camilla, all too evidently, could not. When she tried to rise to her feet, it was only to fall back, half fainting, on the hard bed. "It's no use," she said. "I cannot do it. Chloe, you must go alone. If you cannot get to Lavenham, go to Dom Fernando. He will help us, I am sure."

"But, Camilla, how can I leave you?"

"You must. It's our only chance. And besides, consider. Charles can only hold me to ransom, but he means to marry you."

It was a clincher. Chloe kissed Camilla, asked her once more for her forgiveness, pinned her skirts up carefully around her knees, and disappeared, with one last near-smile, out of the window. Camilla, listening desperately, heard a continued rustling, then silence. No sound of a fall; no sound of pursuit. Perhaps there really was hope. Amazingly, she slept.

She woke to morning light and the sounds of altercation downstairs. And also to an almost forgotten feeling. She was actually hungry. I must be better, she thought, and then

suspended even thinking in her effort to make out what was
going on below. A few more anxious moments and she heard
voices on the stairs. Chloe burst into the room, followed by
Dom Fernando. "Thank God," she said, "you are still here.
We are safe, Camilla."

"But Lavenham?"

Chloe's face fell. "You must be brave, Camilla. He was
gone when I reached the house. And—the wind has changed;
the fleet is putting out of the harbour. Listen!" A volley of
gunfire sent her running to the window. "It is the British and
Portuguese fleets saluting each other," she said, "and, oh,
Camilla, I fear Lavenham must be aboard. He must have
believed that lying note Charles left. Though how he could
leave us so passes my imagining."

"I collect he could not help himself." As always, Camilla
rallied to her husband's defence. "He has his duty, after
all."

"Duty! And leave us to the mercy of the French! Were it
not for Dom Fernando we would be in their hands tonight."

"And may be yet," interposed Dom Fernando himself, "if
we lose more time talking here. I am told that Junot's
advance guard is already on the hills above the town."

"Oh." Camilla sank back despairingly on the bed. "Then
how can we be safe? Lavenham gone ... Junot coming ...
what hope have we?"

Chloe took her hand. "Do not despair, Camilla. It is bad, I
know, but not so bad as it might be. Dom Fernando has an
admirable plan for us: we are to pose as his two mad nieces,
who used to live on his estate south of the Tagus. It is but to
row across the river—and vanish. Charles will think we
succeeded in rejoining Lavenham and have sailed with the
fleet. Besides, the French will be occupied enough for some
time in taking over Lisbon. By the time they get south to
Almada, we will be perfect in our disguise; I promise you,
they will never find us."

"And then what?" Camilla asked.

"Why, then," Dom Fernando said, "as always, we must
trust in God."

CHAPTER 10

While Camilla and Chloe were being hurriedly rowed across the Tagus by Dom Fernando's servants, Lavenham was pacing up and down the deck of the *Marlborough* in an agony of indecision. The combined British and Portuguese fleets were clear of the harbour now, all except one frigate that had had difficulty in crossing the bar, and as Lavenham stood, looking longingly back towards Lisbon, he saw a puff of smoke from the cannon in the fort of St. Julian. The French advance guard must have taken the fort already and had lost no time in turning its guns on the last straggler from the fleet. But their shot fell short, and the frigate crossed the bar at last and joined the rest of the squadron.

Realisation that the French were already on the outskirts of Lisbon gave the final twist to Lavenham's anguish. He had not been quite a reasonable man since he had found Charles Boutet's note pinned to the door of his house the night before. His sense of duty had made him return to the *Hibernia* after his fruitless search of the house and garden and even of the deserted Marvila palace next door. Of the servants there was no sign, and everything he found in Camilla's and Chloe's rooms seemed to indicate that they had indeed left of their own free will. Searching almost frantically among their possessions he had found that each had taken her jewels and, he thought, a few personal necessities. Camilla's enamelled hairbrushes, a wedding present from Lady Leominster, which she had particularly treasured, were missing, and various other things that he remembered. And yet—how could Charles Boutet's message be true? How could Camilla have left him voluntarily, when she was not even conscious? It was at this point that he had heard movement in Chloe's room and, throwing open the door, discovered the

127

maid, Rosa, who had come back to collect her possessions. What she told him merely confirmed his despair, although he found himself oddly comforted by the news that Camilla had recovered her senses. But what was that to the purpose when the first use she had made of them was to leave him? For Rosa insisted that she had hidden in the bushes and watched Camilla and Chloe go. They had not been forced, she said. Milady was carried, it was true, but Dona Chloe had walked beside her freely enough and had seen to it that she was comfortably settled in the carriage. Throughout, the Frenchmen had behaved with the greatest possible courtesy, brutes though, of course, they were. At this point, something in Lavenham's face had frightened her, and she had taken flight, not even pausing long enough to remove a few coveted trifles of Chloe's that had been the real reason for her return.

And Lavenham had gone, almost mechanically, back to the *Hibernia*, to be greeted with the news that the wind had changed and they were to sail at dawn. Hardly knowing what he was doing, he had accompanied Lord Strangford and Sir Sidney Smith when they went to pay their respects to the Prince Regent on the *Principe Real* and only returned to full consciousness when he heard the Prince request once more that he be detailed to accompany the Court to the Brazils. He had had no chance to tell Strangford of the disaster that had befallen him, and his training forbade him to breach Court etiquette with an instant protest. There would be time enough later, he told himself, to explain his predicament to Strangford and ask for an exchange from the *Marlborough*, which was to accompany the Court to the Brazils, to one of the ships that were to continue the blockade of Lisbon. It had been a blow when Lord Strangford had accompanied Sir Sidney Smith back to the *Hibernia* without giving him a chance for a private word, but he had reassured himself that the fleets would be sailing together for some time yet. Now, with the wind rising, and Lisbon dwindling in the distance, he cursed himself for a vacillating fool. He should have spoken up roundly at once, royal presence or no royal presence. But it was still not too late. Determined to lose no more time, he hurried to the captain of the ship to ask for a boat to take him over to the *Hibernia*. The captain's answer was short and brutally to the point. They were in for a storm—a hurricane perhaps. The very idea of launching a boat was madness. He had no time for landsmen's idiocy. When they had survived

the storm would be time enough to talk of boats. He turned
from Lavenham to shout an order against the roar of the
wind, then turned back, for he was a kind man at heart, to
answer Lavenham's last question. "When will it blow out?
God knows. Best ask Him."

The storm raged for four days. The fleet was scattered and
the *Marlborough* alone in a hell of wind and green water.
For Lavenham, the private hell was worse. The captain,
pitying his evident distraction, had told him that their only
hope was to run before the wind. With luck, they would
reunite with the rest of the Brazil-bound fleet when the storm
was over. But for better or worse, they were committed to
the long journey to the New World. How much of the fleet
ever reached it was, he said, another question. The Portuguese ships had been unready and ill-equipped; they were
grievously overloaded; only the hand of God could bring
them safe to shore. "And trust you in Him, too," said the
captain, who had heard something of Lavenham's story.

But Lavenham was beyond trust, beyond hope. Alternate-
ly, he blamed, with desperate rage, himself, Chloe, Camilla.
He could not sleep; he could not eat; he was not even
granted the distraction of sea-sickness, but prowled about the
boat, a Jonah, the sailors whispered to each other, if ever
there was one. And yet, though he sometimes half hoped it
would, the ship did not sink. On the fourth evening the wind
began to fall, and on the fifth morning they woke, those of
them who had contrived to sleep at last, to a brilliant sunrise,
and sight of the *Principe Real* on the horizon. Gradually, in
the course of the next calm days, the little fleet reassembled
and exchanged bad news. Surprisingly, no ship had sunk, but
the sufferings of the refugees, crammed into the ill-equipped
Portuguese fleet, had been frightful and there had been many
deaths, including that of the aged Duke of Cadaval. Lavenham, harvesting what news he could, learned that his old
enemy, Araujo, was on board the *Medusa* and, with relief,
that Dom Fernando had remained behind in Lisbon. If
Camilla and Chloe should need a friend, he told himself, they
would find one in him. And then, in one of his fits of bitter
rage, he told himself to quit his folly: Camilla and Chloe
were very likely in Paris now, fêted by the Emperor. But he
could not imagine Camilla curtsying to Bonaparte, could not
help remembering her voice the first night they met: "I am
as English as you, sir, perhaps more so, because I know how

lucky I am." Had he not been mad to believe Boutet's note? And yet, what else had there been to think? Camilla and Chloe had gone willingly enough, the girl, Rosa, had said. He was back, once more, on the round of doubt and self-blame, half realising that his very rage at Camilla and Chloe as renegades was an attempt to ease his own conscience. Had he failed them, or they him? Would he ever know? The voyage, in calmer waters now, was an eternity of wretchedness, his only comfort the knowledge that his application for recall was already written and sealed, waiting only the chance of despatch.

This came at last at the end of January, when they sighted land and the tattered little fleet sailed into Bahia where the once proud Portuguese Court tottered to shore, thin, emaciated, and dirty. Dom John's estranged wife, the Spanish Princess Carlota Joaquina, who had travelled with her children on the *Affonso D'Albuquerque*, came ashore, like them, in a white muslin cap to hide her head, shaven in the endless unavailing battle against lice and infestation on board. The exhausted Court decided to rest for a while at Bahia before sailing on to a formal welcome at Rio de Janeiro, and Captain Moore seized the opportunity to send a ship home with the news of their safe arrival. By this ship, too, went Lavenham's impassioned plea for recall, and then there was nothing for it but to settle down to count the days and, as the kind captain had suggested, to pray.

Meanwhile, in Portugal, Camilla and Chloe had had their share of terror and of prayer. They had hardly landed on the south bank of the Tagus when the storm broke, and their first few days in the little house Dom Fernando had given them were made horrible by the lashing of wind and rain against the shutters and by their fears for Lavenham at sea. In Lisbon, they were told, the storm had been so fierce that even in the sheltered harbour boats were thrown up on the steps of Corpo Santo. Was it possible that Lavenham could have survived? And, if he had, what must he be thinking of them? Could he really have believed Charles Boutet's note? But if not, how could he possibly have sailed without them? These speculations were as painful as they were useless, and they soon abandoned them by tacit consent. Chloe could see that the mere mention of Lavenham's name was calculated to renew the hectic flush in Camilla's cheek and start once more that restless, anxious movement of her hands. And Camilla, for her part, felt too truly sorry for Chloe to wish to remind her of the part she had played in their disaster. Besides, maternal instinct was at work in her now, warning her that agitation was bad for the child she carried. The only way not to be agitated was not to think, and she was amazed how successfully she managed.

Of course, they had enough of a practical kind to do and think of. Dom Fernando had not dared accompany them himself to their new home, but had sent his steward with them and had given them a letter to his cousin, the Prioress of the convent in whose grounds their house was situated. Its two previous tenants, his mentally defective illegitimate nieces, had lived there, inconspicuously, most of their lives and had recently died there just as quietly, of typhoid. The Prioress, who received Camilla and Chloe with the greatest kindness, told them she thought they would be perfectly safe. Dom Fernando's nieces had hardly stirred from their house except to visit the convent, whence they had obtained all their supplies. The nearest village was some miles away and its inhabitants had thought the two women witches and had given their cottage a wide berth when they visited the convent. Their superstitious terrors could be relied on to keep them away from it now. Like them, Camilla and Chloe would receive all their supplies from the convent and should be safe enough so long as they did not stray beyond its grounds. Only—here the Prioress looked doubtfully at Chloe— perhaps they had best assume the habit of lay sisters. It was unusual for a Portuguese young lady to be conspicuously blond and at all costs they must avoid drawing attention to themselves. In gowns and hoods, they might walk safely where they pleased. Chloe pulled a face but had to admit the sense of the Prioress's argument and in fact she and Camilla found the voluminous robes surprisingly comfortable and a great blessing in their cold little house. As the slow months passed Camilla was increasingly grateful for their robes' lavish, concealing folds. She had told the Prioress of her condition and had been amused, despite herself, at the worldly calm with which the reverend lady took it. "Admirable," was all she had said. "If questions should be asked, I shall put it about that you are a young lady of family saving her good name by a timely retirement—it happens often enough, I can tell you." She urged Camilla robustly not to worry about anything: when her time came, the sister who cared for sick nuns would come to her. "And she is not without experience, I promise you."

Amazingly enough, Camilla found that she was not worrying. As the days passed, and she and Chloe settled into their almost primitive daily round, her strength and spirits improved. "Take no thought to the morrow" might have been her motto, so successfully did she live from day to day, while her colour crept back, her quivering fingers relaxed, and her child stirred to life within her.

"Chloe, he kicked me!" she exclaimed, one mild morning in earliest spring when she and Chloe were out together working in their little garden.

Chloe straightened up and laughed. "He?" she asked.

"Of course. How shall I face Lady Leominster, if it is not an heir."

"Well," Chloe said reflectively, "it is true that, in our family, the first child always *is* a boy. First Maurice, then Edward, then Maurice, then Edward and so on, back to William the Conqueror and forward—who knows, till kingdom come, I suppose. Oh, Camilla, I wish I might see Lavenham's face when he hears the news." For they had heard, at last, that none of the fleet had been lost, and felt themselves safe in assuming that Lavenham was alive and, probably, in the Brazils. If they both, in their different ways, found this knowledge of his distance rather restful, they did not discuss the matter.

There was something that Camilla had been waiting a chance to ask. "Chloe," she said now, after a moment's consideration of her sister's brown and cheerful face.

"Yes?" Chloe dropped her primitive spade and ran earthy hands through her tangled hair. How would they ever be young ladies again?

"Chloe, tell me, do you still think of Charles?"

"Think of him!" Chloe exclaimed. "I should rather think I do. I have guillotined him, and boiled him in oil, and—oh, a thousand torments, but it is all no use: it still exasperates me, just to think of him. Camilla, how could I have been such a fool? To imagine I loved him! It makes me mad, merely to think of it."

"You do not mind any more?"

"Mind? You mean, do I still love him? Camilla, I don't think I ever did. Is it not shameful? To have made all this trouble for you, just out of a whim, out of liking flattery, wanting to be important ... when I think of it, I am so ashamed ... "

"Then do not think of it," Camilla said. "What's the use? And, besides, it is foolish to talk of making trouble for *me*—the misfortune is just as much yours as mine, and you have made up for it a thousand times in all you have done for me since . . . After all, he is my brother. I am only grateful to learn you are not suffering too much."

"Suffering? Do you know, Camilla, I do not think I have ever been so happy before, in my life. Does that surprise you very much?"

"Why no," said Camilla, "for I believe I have not either." And they returned contentedly to their digging.

News came to them rarely, by way of the Prioress, for Dom Fernando, much concerned with the problems of the French occupation of his country, did not dare visit them in person, nor write often. They knew, however, that the French were behaving more like the masters they were than the liberators they pretended to be. "We are unable to entertain you as friends, nor to resist you as enemies," Dom Fernando had told them, but, as time went by, their behaviour proclaimed them all too clearly as enemies. It was a long, hungry winter for the Portuguese, who found themselves penalised by severe laws and heavy, enforced contributions to the war chest of France. Writing of this, Dom Fernando told Camilla that, for them, and for all true friends of Portugal, it was good news. "The spirit of revolt is growing," he said. "It will not be long now." He had other good news for her, too. Her brother had been recalled to France on the very day Junot had taken over Lisbon, and had not returned. "So long as he is away, I think you safe enough."

Reading this, Camilla found herself blushing. How extraordinarily good Dom Fernando had been to her; it was reassuring just to think of it. The very fact of his keeping away from her now was proof of his thought for her. He had never referred again to that scene at Sintra. No doubt his cousin the Prioress had told him of her condition and his only thought was to make things as easy as possible for her. How different from Lavenham's behaviour. And then, angrily, she repudiated the thought. After all, Lavenham had never asked her to love him. She had taken him on his own terms and must abide by them. Or, must she? Alone in the garden, she thought that their child must change all that. If she ever lived with its father again, it must be on her terms, not his. But then, the chances of their ever doing so were slight enough. But Dom Fernando wrote encouragement: it was only a matter of time before he would contrive to smuggle them out of the country and home to England. He was still in touch with the English fleet that continued to blockade Lisbon, and hoped that, sooner or later, the French's vigilance would relax and he could find a way to get them home. Later was soon enough for Camilla. She was very big now, very placid, and more than ready to wait out her time in this quiet corner of Portugal, where no one expected anything of her except Chloe, who merely wanted her to drink goat's milk and rest in the afternoons.

They were excellent friends now, each of them glad of the sister she had never had. Chloe had grown up a great deal since the shock of discovering what a fool she had made of herself over Charles Boutet, or rather, as Camilla insisted, how he had contrived to fool her. Camilla blamed herself as much as Chloe for their plight. She should have suspected that Chloe and Charles were still meeting and done something about it, but, absorbed in her own relations with Lavenham, she had been almost wilfully blind. Chloe would not allow this, insisting that the fault had been entirely hers, and they soon abandoned the fruitless subject. Nor did they talk about Lavenham, since each, in her heart of hearts, could not help but feel that he had failed them, and either would have died rather than admit it. So they lived contentedly enough from day to day, baking their bread and working in their garden, and turning, as Chloe often exclaimed, into a quite capital pair of housewives. No one had ever taught her anything more useful then beadwork and embroidery, and as Camilla's domestic education at Devonshire House had been almost as frivolous, they found themselves shamefacedly compelled to go to the fat and jovial convent cook for lessons in cookery, which involved their learning a good deal of Portuguese, since she spoke nothing else.

Dom Fernando, paying them one of his rare visits early in April, congratulated them heartily on the progress they had made in the language. It would be invaluable when the time came for them to make their escape. For he had almost abandoned hope of being able to get them out to the blockad-

ing fleet, and thought they would have to make their way
northward across country to make contact with one of the
British ships that called, from time to time, to drop spies,
or—as they were more politely called—military agents, in the
little harbours around Oporto. Their chances of getting successfully across so much occupied territory would be much
increased if they could speak enough Portuguese to pass as
visitors from the Brazils, who might be expected to speak
with an outlandish accent.

The news Dom Fernando brought them was mixed bad
and good, with the bad preponderating. No word had been
received from the Brazils, but no news, he said, was good
news. In Europe, Bonaparte seemed all powerful. Russia and
Austria had given up the struggle, and England faced him
alone. But in Spain and Portugal, he told them, the scene was
changing. Spain, too, had been occupied, treacherously, by
Bonaparte's armies and there, as in Portugal, the people at
large were awaking slowly to a realisation of disaster. Passive
at first, the people of both countries were rousing to fierce
resistance under the goad of French tyranny. "They have
learned at last," Dom Fernando said, "that France is not the
saviour they hoped. Now, when it is too late, they begin to
sigh for their lost rulers. I think we shall have a hot summer
of it in Iberia; I only wish I could see you safe home before
the fighting really begins. How long do you think ... ?" He
stammered to a halt.

Camilla laughed. "Not long now," she said. "Sister Maria
says it is a matter of days."

"Good." He rose to take his leave. "I confess I shall
breathe more freely when you are safe away from here. I
find that your identity is an open secret in the village by
now: they are all your devoted friends and I hope you have
nothing to fear ... but," he shook his head and repeated, "I
shall feel safer when you are gone."

Camilla laughed. "And so shall we! It seems little less than
a miracle that we have been unmolested so far."

He smiled at her very kindly. "Perhaps it is one. Who
knows?" And took his leave.

Two days later, Camilla roused Chloe in the small hours of
the morning. "Chloe, I think it is time to go for Sister
Maria."

Chloe was out of bed in a flash. "Are you sure? Will you

be all right while I am gone? Oh, Camilla, I wish we were at home."

"So do I, but never mind; it has happened before, and will again. I have no doubt I shall do well enough ... only, hurry, Chloe."

Chloe ran all the way to convent, but Sister Maria, who was as lazy as she was good-tempered, refused to be hurried. "Time enough, time enough," she said, in her broad, country Portuguese. "These first mothers always think the end of the world is at hand, but, I promise you, we will have time for breakfast—yes, and lunch too, before we see his young lordship." Wheezing with the exertion, she packed up her sinister-looking tools, and Chloe, equally alarmed by her grimy equipment and the delay, could finally bear it no longer and ran on, alone, to their cottage. As she crossed the garden, a sudden almost unrecognisable scream from Camilla gave wings to her feet. She entered the tiny bedroom, gasping for breath, just in time to receive her squalling nephew. Sister Maria, arriving placidly ten minutes later, found herself with nothing but the tidying up to do and could hardly forbear scolding Camilla for her unlady-like speed. But Camilla, white and exhausted, was too happy to care. "Edward," she whispered, and fell asleep.

It was Sister Maria who first noticed the thin webbing between the baby's smallest toes and pointed it out, with eldritch shrieks, to Chloe. Chloe, an aunt and entirely grown-up now, merely dismissed her from the house with unearned thanks and a string of beads the sister had admired and now accepted with enthusiasm: "For the blessed Virgin, of course." Then she returned to the little room where Camilla and the child slept peacefully. If she could help it, Camilla should not be troubled with news of her child's deformity before she was strong enough to bear it.

To her delighted surprise, Camilla's return to strength was very much more rapid than she had expected. It almost seemed that there was something to be said for bearing a child in an atmosphere of domesticity and gardening and without society's benefits of laudanum plaisters, devoted relatives, and straw in the streets. At any rate, by the fourth day, Camilla insisted that she was tired of lying in bed and wanted to bathe her son herself: "You are not to have all the care of him, Chloe. Aunts have their rights, I know, and you have most certainly earned yours, but his mother must come first."

Chloe protested, but in vain, and watched in anguished expectation while Camilla removed little Edward's clothes with loving unskilful hands and held him gently in the large cooking pot they used for a bath. In a moment, Camilla looked up at her. "I see," she said. "That is why he was always dressed. Did you think I should mind it, Chloe? I shall only love him all the more. Do you know, I was beginning to be afraid there was something really *wrong* with him, but this—who cares about this?"

"Not I, for one," said Chloe robustly, but could not help adding. "I only wondered—Lavenham and Lady Leominster . . . "

"Who cares what they think, or the world for that matter? And, besides, why should anybody know? It is not yet the fashion that I know of for gentlemen to dance barefoot, is it, my precious?" And she bent to concentrate on the intricate and unfamiliar task of washing her son, who was beginning to wriggle in her hands like the fish he resembled.

He was a wonderfully well-conducted baby, but then, as Camilla said, so he should be, with the entire attention of a devoted mother and aunt. When Sister Maria called to see how he and Camilla were going on, she was amazed to find them both out under a huge cork tree in the garden and raised her hands in horror, prognosticating all kinds of disasters from such an early risking of fresh air. As for the baths, when she learned of them she was convinced the baby would not survive its second week. "And perhaps as well," she said to Chloe, who was shepherding her out of the garden, "poor little monster. What good can come of it? Let me but baptise him and he will be better off with the angels."

Grateful that Camilla had not heard, Chloe paid a visit to the convent that night and begged the Prioress, who had always been their understanding friend, to prevent Sister Maria from visiting them again.

The old nun nodded her comprehension. "Yes," she said, "perhaps it would be best. Sister Maria is well enough for the peasant women, and even for our own girls when they go astray, but perhaps I will take her place from now on. She has told me, of course, about the poor little boy. We can only pray that it will prove, by God's grace, a blessing to him in disguise."

Chloe could hardly see how it could do so, but was too relieved at the success of her mission to care. From then on, the Prioress visited them daily, cheering them with her robust common sense and her hearty and convinced praise of the baby, who grew and throve in daily contradiction of Sister Maria's prophecies.

He was a month old, and a picture of placid health, when Dom Fernando paid them an unexpected visit. He arrived late in the evening, when the shadow of the cork tree had lengthened across the sunny garden and they were beginning to think about bed. One look at him told Camilla that something was wrong, and she helped him to hurry through the formal greetings and congratulations as fast as possible. He came quickly to the point: "I am more relieved than I can say to find you so well, for I fear I bring bad news."

Camilla turned white. "Not Lavenham?"

"No, no. How could I be so stupid? I have good news of him. We have heard at last that the Court are arrived safe at Bahia, though after a sufficiently grievous voyage, poor things. Your husband is alive and, so far as I know, well. No, my news is not of him but of Charles Boutet, who is returned to Lisbon and who, I fear, must have learned that you did not escape with the fleet as he first thought. I discovered only this afternoon that he has been tampering with my servants, asking them all kinds of questions about my movements. That is why I am come so late; I did not dare let anyone know where I was going. But now he has started making enquiries it is only a matter of time—and not very much at that—until he discovers your whereabouts and then, I gravely fear, I would be powerless to protect you."

Camilla had taken Chloe's hand. "But what shall we do? Where can we hide?"

He answered her with another question. "Are you truly better? Strong enough to face a journey, and, I fear, an exhausting one?"

"To go home?" Camilla asked. "I could face anything for that. And indeed I am entirely recovered. Chloe will tell you that I have been working in the garden all afternoon, and none the worse for it."

"I cannot tell you how relieved I am to hear it. No hope, now, of getting you out to the blockading fleet. Since Boutet arrived, the French vigilance in the harbour has been redoubled. It was with the greatest difficulty that I made the crossing to visit you tonight. To attempt to get out to the British ships would be to court disaster. But I have another plan which I begin, now I see you so well, to think may be possible. There is a British agent, a Mr. Smith, who is returning from a visit to Spain. He is to be picked up by a British frigate north of Lisbon, where the French watch is less close, and I have suggested to him that you might accompany him."

"You have seen him, then? Where is he? Can we really go with him? What did he say?"

He smiled a shade reprovingly. "One question at a time, I beg. Or rather, the fewer questions, the better. The less you know, in fact, the safer for you. But, yes, he has agreed to take you with him, always provided that you are strong enough to stand the journey. He has vital information to take home to England and asks me to warn you that he must travel fast and can stop for nothing. Luckily his rendezvous is not for another three days or he could not wait for you. But as it is he will be delighted to escort you and, indeed, thinks that your company will much improve his chances. The French are, we believe, on the lookout for him, but are not likely to suspect a family travelling together. Only," he paused to look anxiously at Camilla, "are you strong enough? And what of the baby?"

"To get home," Camilla said again, "we can face anything."

CHAPTER 11

‏‎ⵍⵍ

Neither Camilla nor Chloe slept that night. Excitement would have prevented it, even if there had not been so much to do. Before he left them, Dom Fernando had explained that Mr. Smith could not risk the detour to join them; instead, they must make their way along the south side of the Tagus and would find him waiting for them at the crossroads just before the first bridge across the river. He would, of course, recognise their little party easily enough and would identify himself by asking them, in Portuguese, "What news, today, in Setúbal?" To make assurance doubly sure, Camilla must then answer, "None worth the hearing."

After they had met Mr. Smith, Dom Fernando warned them that they would have two days' hard riding over rough country, if they were to keep their rendezvous with the frigate. His cousin the Prioress would provide them with mules, peasant costume, and a man to escort them to the meeting place with Mr. Smith: after that, they would be in his hands. He left at last with many good wishes for what seemed a mad enough venture, and promises of a happier meeting when Bonaparte was defeated and peace restored. At the last minute, he came back with a final injunction: "I had almost forgot. Mr. Smith urges that you make yourselves look as much like peasant women as possible. The clothes my cousin will provide will help, but can you, perhaps, bring yourselves to dirty your faces and untidy your hair?" And on this semi-comic note he left them.

The Prioress came bustling over soon afterwards and added her advice to his. Better than advice, she brought a jar of black and viscous fluid with which she urged Chloe to dye her hair: "Those golden locks of yours are as good as an advertisement that you are a foreigner." Chloe made a face,

but agreed, and by morning her hair had been turned a
muddy black and her face liberally streaked with the glu-
tinous dye. She insisted, somewhere between laughter and
tears, that Camilla, too, daub herself with this strong-smelling
substitute for dirt, and by the time they had put on the
bedraggled clothes the Prioress had brought them, and tied
dirty black shawls over their heads, they made, in their own
opinion, as convincing a pair of filthy peasant women as
anyone could wish to see. The Prioress, however, was not so
sure, and insisted, at the last moment, that the baby, too,
must be wrapped in one of the grimy shawls she had
brought. Camilla nearly rebelled at this, but her good sense
made her yield soon enough, and she even rubbed a very
little of the black dye on Edward's pink and somnolent
cheek, where it stood out like a clown's paint.

By now, it was morning, and the man was waiting outside
with the mules, of which, they realised at the last moment,
the Prioress was making them a present. Protests were vain.
There was no possible way to arrange for the animals'
return, and they left with a warm feeling of gratitude and the
kind old nun's blessing in their ears. They rode for the most
part in silence, since Dom Fernando had urged them to speak
as little as possible, and never in English: "Imagine that the
very aloes have French ears."

They had to admit the justice of his advice, although the
enforced silence added very considerably to the misery and
fatigue of the day's journey. In order to be sure of their
rendezvous, they must ride steadily through the noontide
heat, pausing only for brief rests, to feed the baby and to
encourage themselves with the lavish refreshments the Prioress had provided. Their guide was silent to the point of
taciturnity, the sun blazed down, their only consolation was
that little Edward, carried first by his mother and then by his
aunt, slept like an angel, soothed, no doubt, by the rocking
gait of the mule.

Towards evening, however, he woke and began to whimper
in his mother's arms; the fatigue of the journey had made
him hungry earlier than usual. But their guide rejected
Camilla's suggestion that they stop to feed him with a sur-
liness that was all too evidently the mask for anxiety. They
were late already, he said. There was an hour's hard riding
still to the crossroads and Dom Smith would be already
awaiting them there—if he waited, added the man gloomily,

troubled by visions of having to escort his awkward companions back to the convent.

The last hour's ride was a silent misery. Both Camilla and Chloe were proficient riders, and had had plenty of practice on mule-back over the rough Portuguese roads, but neither of them had realised what an awkward addition little Edward would be to the party. Even asleep, he was a problem to carry; now that he was awake, crying and wriggling, it was all that they could do to hold him and still keep their beasts on the road. "Truly, my angel," Chloe exclaimed as she handed him back to his mother, "if I did not adore you, I should be in a fair way to thinking you a little pest."

She had spoken in English, and Camilla was beginning a reply in the same language when a warning exclamation from their guide silenced her. Absorbed in the handover of the baby, they had neither of them noticed that they had come to the outskirts of a village. It was an encouraging sight, for the crossroads at which they were to meet Mr. Smith was only a mile or so further. But just as Camilla and Chloe were exchanging glances of mutual congratulation, their guide's hand on the knotted rope that served as bridle halted Camilla's mule. Without a word he turned its head towards a filthy alleyway leading past a group of hovels and away from the Tagus. A fierce glance silenced the question that rose to Camilla's lips, and she and Chloe followed him without a word down the stinking lane and into the untidy orange grove to which it led. There, at last, he let them come up with him. "You did not see them?" he asked.

"Who?"

"The French soldiers." He spat expressively. "The village was full of them. I hope it does not mean they have caught Dom Smith. But it certainly means we must avoid the village. How long it will take to go round it, God knows. I only hope Dom Smith will wait—if he is not already in French hands."

The next hour or so was pure nightmare. Camilla and Chloe had thought the riding over country roads bad enough, but now they were following mere goat tracks. Brambles slashed their faces; even the sure-footed mules slipped and slid on the rocky ground; carrying the baby was so difficult that when their guide, with an impatient exclamation, snatched him from Camilla, she was simply grateful. When they finally returned, down a precipitous slope, to the little road on the far side of the village, they were already two hours late for their rendezvous. Their guide's face was a picture of gloom; Camilla and Chloe were both near tears and the baby, in Chloe's arms now, wailed on the despondent note of exhaustion.

A sudden turning of the road showed them the crossroads—and a small group of French soldiers camped at it. They had been seen already; there was nothing for it but to go on, with sinking hearts and as bold an appearance as possible. The soldiers, they now saw, were grouped around a tattered figure and his dejected mule. Camilla and Chloe exchanged quick glances. Impossible that this vagabond, who was holding forth to a French officer in rapid Portuguese, could be Mr. Smith, the British agent. But he had seen them, and broke, all of a sudden, into a loud wail of thanksgiving to all his patron saints, whom he named in exhaustive catalogue, while the French officer listened impassively. "Mary, Mother of God, and all the saints be praised," he concluded, when he was sure that Camilla and Chloe were within earshot, "here, at long last, are my beloved wife, my sister, my child." He ran towards them, mule and Frenchmen alike following him closely, embraced Camilla in a cloud of garlic and salt cod, and then, to her utter amazement, gave her a resounding slap across the face. "And that," he said, "is for keeping me waiting. As for you, neighbour Tomas, I'll not ask you to escort my wife again! Two hours I have waited for you, here in the sun," and he turned on their guide in such a threatening manner that the man kicked his mule into a gallop and disappeared around the corner in a cloud of dust.

The French soldiers found all this highly entertaining, and laughed still harder when their prisoner, for such he obviously was, fetched Chloe a box on the ears, and then snatched the baby from her and covered it with dirty kisses, calling it his lamb, his only son, his treasure, his hope in heaven. Handing little Edward back to Camilla, he turned to the French officer and broke into what seemed an endless tirade against the whole of womankind, describing their shortcomings in such a wealth of unprintable detail that Camilla and Chloe were grateful for the dirt that hid their blushes, and for their limited Portuguese, which spared them full comprehension of what he was saying.

At last, the officer grew impatient. "Enough," he said. "I am sure your wife and sister are everything you say, and more so," he spared them a quick, contemptuous glance, "but we have work to do. Away with you, and do not let me find you loitering about the highways again." He gave him a push that sent him staggering into the filthy ditch, shouted an order to his men, and wheeled his horse back in the direction of the village.

The man lay in three inches of stinking water and watched them go, muttering a mixture of prayers and curses, while Camilla and Chloe sat speechless on their mules. Of their guide, there was no sign; he had taken his cue and vanished. At last, when all the Frenchmen were out of earshot, the man crawled out of the ditch, shook himself, and approached Camilla and Chloe with a smile that gave a sparkle to grey eyes and revealed startling white teeth in his filthy face. "Well," he said, "what news, today, in Setúbal?"

"None worth the hearing." Camilla, who had noticed with fury that he had contrived to filthy the baby's face all over, controlled her voice as best she might. "Is it really you?" she went on, still in Portuguese.

"Yes, and never more glad to see anyone. If you had not kept your tryst, I should have been a dead man. I apologise to you both," he made an awkward peasant's bob, "for the blows I gave you, but you must admit that they saved you questions I was afraid you might not be able to answer. There is nothing more husbandly than a few matrimonial slaps. And now, we must lose no more time." And without more ado, he mounted his bedraggled mule and led them at a brisk pace away from the village. They exchanged despondent glances and followed. He might, despite appearances, be an Englishman, but he seemed no more considerate a guide than their Portuguese one. Too exhausted to make the effort of speech in Portuguese, they followed him as best they might, drooping in the saddle. But their mules, too, were tired. They found themselves dropping further and further behind their guide. At last he disappeared into a little wood and they exchanged a glance of mute despair. Could he have decided, already, that they were too much of a liability, and abandoned them? They did the best they could to kick their unresponsive mules into a trot and reached the wood with sinking hearts, only to find Mr. Smith lying full length at the side of the road, waiting for them.

"Good," he said, "we are out of sight at last. But we will still speak Portuguese, I think. Now, tell me, have you the strength to ride another two miles—to safety? I have good friends in the next village, where you may rest in peace."

After a glance at Chloe, Camilla assured him that they would manage. "Then let me take the baby," he said. "I can see that he is an awkward burden," and then, seeing Camilla hesitate, "I know you think me a brute for blacking his face, but it was touch and go with us, then, and when did you see a clean Portuguese baby? I am sure, when he grows up, he will thank me."

There was such obvious good sense in this that Camilla handed him the child gratefully enough and settled down to concentrate all her energies on the exhausting problem of keeping her weary mule on the road. Chloe, too, was swaying with fatigue, and she and Camilla rode silently, side by side, some way behind Mr. Smith, who went steadily on ahead, hardly sparing them a glance. Added to their fatigue, there was something infuriating about this neglect, and by the time he finally dismounted outside a lonely hovel by the road and stood awaiting their approach they were both seething with silent fury.

When they drew level with him, he merely said, "Good, we are arrived at last," and handed the baby to Camilla, who had lost no time in sliding to the ground. Chloe, who had fallen a little behind, now drew up, swaying with fatigue, and sat, for a moment, too tired even to make the effort of dismounting. When Mr. Smith made no effort to help her, rage overcame her. "Pray," she said in English, "do not trouble yourself to help me dismount."

For a moment he looked as if he would strike her again, then answered in Portuguese. "I most certainly shall not. When did you see a Portuguese peasant help his women? It is far enough out of character that I should have been carrying the baby. I could not risk even that where there were people about. Most fortunately, here, we are among friends, but I warn you, if you speak English again, I shall leave you behind. The news I carry is too important to be jeopardised by a girl's foolish tongue." And he turned on his heel and began to lead his mule round to the back of the hut.

Following him in chastened if irritable silence, they were greeted by the hut's ragged owner, who kissed Mr. Smith enthusiastically on both cheeks, greeting him in a flood of Portuguese so rapid and so strangely accented that neither Camilla nor Chloe could understand him. They followed the two men mutely into the hovel and then stopped to gaze in horror at its single, filthy, earth-floored room. But their host was bustling hospitably about, drawing stools up to a rickety table and fetching dirty bread and sinister dark sausage from a cupboard in a corner.

Mr. Smith eyed the two of them coolly. "I hope," he still spoke Portuguese, "that Dom Fernando passed on my warning about the roughness of our trip."

Camilla was too busy trying to soothe the now frantic Edward to reply, so it was Chloe who answered. "Naturally we are prepared for some discomfort, but the baby needs to be fed. Surely my sister should have some privacy."

"Privacy? In a peasant's hut? Are you mad? You should be grateful that my friend here has sent away his wife and children, for fear that contact with you should endanger their lives. Be thankful for the shelter he risks his life to give us, and spare me your complaints. As for the baby; why should he not be fed? I promise you, we have other things to think about." And he drew up a stool beside their shabby host, who had just produced a bottle of local wine and filled two glasses. In a moment, the two men were deep in conversation and Camilla, who had, of course, heard everything, gave one defiant look round, opened her dress and put little Edward to suck. A contented silence replaced his previous wailings and was broken only by the murmur of the two men's voices as they disposed of their wine, which they accompanied with great slices of greyish bread spread liberally with sausage. Mr. Smith turned once to invite Chloe to join them, but she indicated haughtily that she would wait for Camilla and busied herself with unpacking the bundle of provisions the Prioress had given them, of which a lavish quantity still remained for their supper. When the baby finally fell into a contented sleep, she handed Camilla her share and they fell to with a will. Mr. Smith after a quick and, Camilla thought, hostile glance in their direction turned back to his incomprehensible talk with their host, who was busy opening a second bottle.

The talk went on and on. Camilla and Chloe swayed on their stools and still the two talked and drank, drank and talked. At last, Chloe could bear it no more, but jumped to her feet. "We wish to sleep, my sister and I."

Their host looked at her in puzzlement, and Mr. Smith merely answered, "Well, why not?"

The two girls exchanged glances, then, without a word, began to make their travelling shawls into the best approximation of beds they could manage in a dark corner of the little room. Seeing what they were about, their host leapt to his feet and produced two filthy blankets, which he pressed upon them. Chloe was about to refuse hers, when a warning glance from Camilla stopped her, and later, when the chill of midnight crept into the hut, she was glad that manners had forced its acceptance, and pulled it around her, dirt and all.

They were roused, far too early, by Mr. Smith. Even little Edward was still asleep, and Chloe, stiff and sore from exercise and the hard bed, awoke with a rebellious murmur. Mr. Smith was looking down at her with calm grey eyes. "Very well," he said. "I will leave you behind to have out your sleep, if you prefer."

She was up in a flash and began to make her morning toilet as best she might when a word from him stopped her, "No, no," he said, "Leave it. You are much better as you are. I tell you, I trembled at every step we took yesterday. This morning, you are almost convincing if you will only remember to speak in Portuguese."

Chloe turned from him with an angry *moue*, but nevertheless abandoned her efforts to tidy herself and set to work, instead, to prepare breakfast for herself and Camilla out of the remnants of the Prioress's supplies. Mr. Smith had already sat down with their host to more of the inevitable bread and sausage and as soon as Camilla had finished feeding the baby, the two girls made their own breakfast in peace. When they had done, Chloe began to pack the last fragments back into the bundle, but Mr. Smith intervened: "No, no," he said, "you have insulted our host enough. If he had not been my very good friend, I do not like to think what would have happened when you refused his bread last night, but this morning, you shall make amends." At that moment, their host, who had been out of the hut on some errand, returned, and Mr. Smith at once offered him the remains of the girls' food "as some small token of their gratitude." The man accepted with a sudden grace that pricked Chloe's conscience far more than Mr. Smith's rebuke had done and they set out on their day's journey with many protestations of affection on their host's part and gratitude on theirs—and some more of the stinking bread and sausage for their wayside luncheon.

Once more they rode through the long, hot day in silence, the two girls always some little distance behind Mr. Smith, who showed no sign of caring whether they followed him or not. When Chloe, who was very far from being in charity with him today, murmured about this to Camilla, the latter looked up from little Edward to say reasonably, "But, Chloe, look at the people we meet. The men always ride ahead. Mr. Smith is right and I beg you will do your best not to annoy him further. I only hope we are not being too great a burden for him as it is." And she kicked her mule to make it keep up with Mr. Smith's beast, which, despite its shabby appearance, seemed to be able to go steadily on forever.

When they stopped for lunch, Camilla asked Mr. Smith anxiously whether they were going fast enough, and, to her relief, his answer was reassuring. If they kept up the pace he had been setting, they would reach his friend's hut at a reasonable hour in the evening. And tomorrow they would have an easy day's ride. Their rendezvous with the frigate was not till after dark; they would have ample time to reach it. "You may catch up on your beauty sleep in the morning, if you wish," he told Chloe, but she was too irritated with him to answer.

Their afternoon's ride was uneventful and as Mr. Smith had promised they reached his friend's house early in the evening. The two girls saw with pleasure that this house, which stood alone in its orange grove, was very much larger than the hovel in which they had spent the previous night. They dismounted and received the obsequious greetings of their new host with visions of some possible modicum of comfort dancing in their heads. He shouted to one of his sons, who were playing in the dust outside the house, to take their mules to the stable, and led them indoors with an extravagant speech of welcome which Chloe, at least, found almost comprehensible. She and Camilla were delighted to find that the house consisted of three rooms, one of which was to be put at the disposal of their little party. Of course, it would have been better still if Mr. Smith could have slept elsewhere, but this was too much to be hoped. Besides— alone, for a moment, in the room that was to be theirs, Chloe whispered to Camilla, in English, "Camilla, I do not like this place."

"Not like it?" Camilla was feeding the baby. "Why not, Chloe?"

"There is something wrong here. I can feel it. Did you not hear how the man received us—as if we were honoured guests. It is absurd: we are fugitives; he endangers his life harbouring us. Remember that man last night, how frightened he was. He had even sent his family away, lest they be implicated ... What makes everything so different here? Listen to them."

She was silent for a moment, listening to the chatter of female voices in the next room, then went on, "I tell you, I do not like it. There was something wrong in his tone as he greeted us. Do you know, I am glad Mr. Smith is to share our room. I shall feel safer so."

She was interrupted by Mr. Smith himself, who entered at this moment with a look of controlled rage. "I believe I asked you not to speak in English," he said, in furiously whispered Portuguese.

"I am sorry; I forgot." Chloe refused to be cowed. "But, Mr. Smith," she too was whispering, "I was telling my sister. Do you not feel something wrong here?"

"Wrong? What do you mean?"

"About our host. I do not like him. Do you think it is safe to stay here?"

He made an impatient gesture. "What nonsense is this? I thought you would be glad to spend a night of comparative comfort and instead you start refining at God knows what imaginary terrors. I see nothing wrong with the man. It is true, he is a stranger to me, not a close friend like last night's host. Doubtless that accounts for any difference you may have noticed in his behaviour. But, come, leave these megrims and join the family at their supper. And, remember, you are to eat whatever is given you, and show your gratitude. If you do not value your life, I do mine, and both lie in our host's hands."

"Yes," said Chloe mutinously, "that is exactly what troubles me." But he had already turned to leave the room.

The evening dragged on interminably. There was the usual fierce sausage to be washed down with coarse red wine, and, tonight, doubtless as a hospitable gesture, there was salt cod, too, cooked with a lavish flavouring of garlic. But appetite was on the two girls' side and they ate their way staunchly through everything they were offered, making what conversation they could with their hosts as they did so. But it was an enormous relief when a cry from Edward in the next room, and a confirmatory nod from Mr. Smith, gave them the signal to say good night.

"Do you still say you feel nothing?" whispered Chloe, in Portuguese this time, when they were safe in their own room.

Camilla temporised. "Well, naturally, it was not the easiest evening in the world, but I am sure that is all, Chloe. You are tired, and refining too much, as Mr. Smith said. Try and sleep now, and forget it."

"Yes," said Chloe, "and wake up dead in the morning, most like." But she curled herself up in the pile of blankets that had been provided for them and seemed, by her quiet breathing, to be asleep.

Much later, however, when Camilla heard the party next door breaking up and Mr. Smith tiptoed in, Chloe stirred and sat up to whisper to him. "Lock the door, for the sake of my megrims, will you?"

He gave an impatient exclamation, but went back to the door, which turned out to have no lock. He shrugged his shoulders, made his brief preparations, and settled down among his blankets in the furthest corner of the room from Chloe. Much later, just as she was drifting off to sleep at last, Camilla heard Chloe get up and go over to the door; she remained there for a minute and then, just as Camilla was about to rouse herself and ask what she was doing, returned to her makeshift bed. It was nothing ... megrims ... Camilla slept.

She woke with a start to darkness and terror. Chloe was shaking her shoulder. "Camilla, someone just tried the door. I wedged the latch with a bit of wood; otherwise they would have been here. Do you still think nothing is wrong? Get Edward, while I wake Mr. Smith."

Half asleep, Camilla's first thought had been to pick up little Edward, who stirred as he slept, then settled once more against her breast. Meanwhile, Chloe had crossed the room, silent in the darkness, to rouse Mr. Smith. He was on his feet in a moment and listened to her whispered explanation. "Tried the door, did they? You wedged it, you say? You may have been wise. At all events, we will take no chances. It is probably nothing, but better safe than sorry. Get together your things, and come." He moved to the one window of the little room, which was closed by a wooden shutter, and began to remove its bolts. "I loosened these earlier," he explained in a whisper as the girls followed him. "When you spoke of danger. Better, always, safe than sorry. There," he had the window open, "out you go: quietly."

Obediently, Chloe slipped out into the darkness and turned to receive the baby from Camilla, who followed her. Last came Mr. Smith with their bundles. "This way," he whispered. "For the moment, we will not risk staying for the mules." And he led them along a little path, fitfully moonlit, that ran down through the orange groves towards the main road. Suddenly he stopped. "Hush!" Mercifully, the baby still slept, and they followed him down in absolute silence as he slipped off the road and into the shadow of an enormous cork tree. Safe behind it, he stopped, and touched a finger to each of their cheeks in warning. As their quick breathing steadied, they heard what he had, the sound of marching men approaching from the main road.

They stood there, as still as statues in the warm darkness, as a detachment of French soldiers marched past. They, too, were silent, moving almost stealthily through the fitful moonlight. And as the last of them went by, the moon came out more clearly, to reveal their host marching amicably beside the officer. Mr. Smith's hand on each girl's arm constrained them to stillness for what seemed an incredibly long time after the men had passed. Then, "Hurry," he whispered, and led the way back on to the track. When they reached the main road he turned back the way they had come. "Safer so," he whispered. "And I remember a side road soon."

The side road, when they found it, climbed precipitously among the foothills of the Sintra mountains, and presently, when, at long last Mr. Smith allowed them to stop for breath, they looked down and saw how wise he had been in bringing them this way. For below them lay the village from which the soldiers had come, and they could see lights moving everywhere about its streets. The hunt was up for them.

"Time to move on," said Mr. Smith, and then, matter-of-factly, to Chloe, "We all owe you our lives, Lady Chloe. And I, an apology."

She inclined her head, all at once the society beauty. "I thank you."

After that, no one had the breath for speech. If the rough roads had been hard work on mule-back, on foot, and in the dark, they were torture. But at least the little road continued to rise and to lead at once away from the village where they had so nearly been captured and towards the bay where they must keep their tryst with the British frigate. Light was beginning to show in the east, and first birds to twitter here and there around them, when Chloe voiced the question that had been in all their minds. "Have we any chance of getting there on foot?"

Mr. Smith signalled a halt and looked thoughtfully from her to Camilla before he spoke. "Yes," he said at last, "we have a chance. If you can walk all day."

Chloe and Camilla exchanged glances and this time Chloe spoke for both. "If we must," she said, "we can."

"Good. Then let me take the baby." He settled the sleeping Edward gently in the crook of his arm. "The longer he sleeps, the better. We can afford neither to draw attention to ourselves by his crying, nor to stop often for him to feed."

"If the worst comes to the worst," said Camilla, "I shall just have to feed him as we go." It was a far cry from the time when she had been embarrassed to feed him in public.

Mr. Smith rewarded her with an approving glance. "If you continue in that spirit," he said, "I have no fear of our failing to keep our rendezvous."

The sun grew higher, dust rose round them, making breathing difficult and speech too much trouble, and still they walked on, one foot placed relentlessly in front of the other, Mr. Smith, with the baby, a few yards in front, Camilla and Chloe stumbling speechless behind. Only, once, when they had climbed breathlessly for what seemed an eternity, Mr. Smith stopped at a turn of the road commanding a wide view of the sea. "There," he pointed ahead, "there is our goal."

Camilla and Chloe looked at the distant promontory and their hearts sank. Could they possibly get there by night? But they had got their second wind by now and plodded on valiantly for another hour or so as the sun rose towards noon and the heat grew more intense. At last, little Edward began to cry in Mr. Smith's arms. He looked up at the sun, then paused. They were passing a thicket of myrtle and wild orange through which ran a little laughing stream. "We will stop here for a while," he said, "and rest."

Safely out of sight of the road, Chloe and Camilla sank down with sighs of relief and Camilla began at once to feed little Edward while Chloe unpacked the bundle in which she had wrapped the scanty remains of their yesterday's luncheon. She was sharing the dry bread and now stinking sausage out into three meticulously equal, pitifully small portions when Mr. Smith stopped her. "No, no," he said, "share it between you. I have gone without food often enough; it is no hardship."

All too soon, he gave the signal to resume the march. The two girls found that their muscles had stiffened as they sat, and stumbled along slowly enough at first, Mr. Smith slackening his pace to theirs. But as Camilla got back into her stride she found that Chloe still lagged behind, walking as if each step was agony. Mr. Smith had gradually increased his pace. Now, as Chloe fell further and further behind, Camilla called to him softly.

He stopped and turned back. "What is the matter?" He spoke with the brusqueness of anxiety.

"I don't know." They waited in silence as Chloe came up.

As she approached, Mr. Smith spoke bracingly. "We must go faster than this. If your sister can keep up, surely you can?"

Chloe coloured, bit her lip, and was silent. Camilla took her hand. "It is just the stiffness from sitting," she said encouragingly. "It will pass off soon. Mine has already. Come, Chloe."

Still silent, Chloe stepped out faster and they resumed their dogged march. But soon she was falling behind again. At last she sat down by the roadside. "You go on, Camilla," she said. "Leave me here. I can go no further."

"Leave you? What madness is this?" Looking down, almost impatiently at Chloe, Camilla suddenly noticed blood oozing over her left shoe. "Chloe? What's the matter?"

"My shoe." Wearily Chloe lifted her foot and showed that the rope sole of her shoe had worn clean through. For some miles she had been walking almost barefoot on the rocky road. Her foot was bleeding from a dozen wounds and lacerations. "You see," she said. "It is no use. I cannot go on."

Mr. Smith, who had been some distance ahead, came back to join them. "What new absurdity is this? We cannot afford these delays." He saw Chloe's foot: "Good God." He said no more, but hurried to a nearby stream, brought water, and bathed the foot before bandaging it gently with strips of his shirt. "No, no," he ignored her protest, "I shall do well enough without. But—you cannot go on thus."

"No," Chloe said. "You must leave me. Take my sister, and

the baby. Remember, you said yourself that the news you carry is too important to be jeopardised by a mere girl."

He stood for a moment, looking down at her silently, then, "Wait here," he said, "rest, and, if you know how, pray. If I do not return, you must try to get back to Lisbon. Dom Fernando will look after you, if you can reach him."

"But what are you going to do?" Camilla asked.

"Beg, buy, or steal a mule—or two, or, best of all, three. If I am not back before the shadow of that tree falls across you, you will know that I have failed, and you must find your way back to Lisbon as best you may."

"But," Camilla protested, "you could go on alone without taking the risk. Leave us here. As you say, Dom Fernando will protect us."

"'If you reach him. No," he anticipated her further protest, "it is no use. I cannot reconcile it with my conscience to abandon you here. The message I carry is important, it is true, but there are other things more important still. Besides, we must hope that we will all carry it together." And then, "Goodbye. Rest well. You will need all your strength when I return."

He was gone. For a few moments, as they settled themselves in the little glade by the stream, neither girl spoke. At last, "Do you think he will return?" Camilla asked.

"Of course," said Chloe. "He said he would."

"I am glad you are so sure. We know so little about him. I did wonder whether this was not a gentler mode of leaving us."

"What? After what he said? Camilla, how can you?"

Surprised at her vehemence, Camilla said mildly, "Well, why not? We are nothing to him, the message he carries doubtless means everything, his career, his future ... Tell me, Chloe, who do you think he is? Do you realise we have never heard him speak in English, nor seen what he is really like: that filthy face—those ragged clothes—how can one possibly tell what is underneath. Do you think he is a gentleman?"

"I have no idea," said Chloe. "I only know he is a man, and will return. And now, he told us to rest. It is a pity we cannot eat first, but for myself I am tired enough to sleep through worse hunger than this. I do not believe I slept at all last night."

"And lucky for us you did not," said Camilla as she obediently composed herself and little Edward for sleep. "I suppose Mr. Smith feels he owes it to you to return. After all, as he said, you did save his life last night."

"Oh—a fiddlestick for Mr. Smith!" Chloe's burst of temper surprised Camilla. "Stop talking, Camilla, and go to sleep."

Drifting off into a doze of nervous exhaustion, Camilla thought with amusement that her position and Chloe's seemed to have reversed themselves of late. Now, it was Chloe who gave the orders, she who meekly obeyed. Well, it was restful . . . she slept.

She woke at last, to see Chloe bending anxiously over her. "Camilla? What time do you think it is?"

Camilla stretched, shivered, and tucked the shawl more closely round little Edward who still, blessedly, slept. "I have no idea. Oh! The sun has gone in."

"Yes. I think there must be a storm coming."

Camilla looked up at the tall tree whose shadow was to have been their clock. "For once," she said, "Mr. Smith has not thought of everything. Now what do we do? I have a feeling it is late, Chloe. Surely, if he was coming, he would have returned long since. And it is certainly going to storm. Should we not try and find shelter? These trees will be useless if it really rains—and dangerous if it thunders." She picked up little Edward as if ready to start at once.

"Are you mad, Camilla?" asked Chloe. "What is a wetting, compared to our chances of safety? Find shelter for yourself and Edward, if you must, but I shall stay here and wait for Mr. Smith."

"Oh, very well." Camilla sat down again faintly relieved at having her mind so definitely made up for her. "We will wait here a while longer."

"We will wait till Mr. Smith comes," said Chloe.

"But, Chloe, have you considered . . . it is not only that he may have decided to go on alone . . . he may have been discovered . . . he may be dead by this."

"I do not believe it," said Chloe.

The minutes dragged, the clouds darkened, the air grew colder, and the two girls sat close together for warmth. They were silent now. There seemed nothing to say. A few large drops of rain fell in the clearing and the wind began to grumble among the trees.

"Chloe," Camilla said, "it is getting dark."

"It is the storm," Chloe answered, and she jumped up and

arranged her shawl over the branches of a tree so that it formed a kind of makeshift tent over their heads.

"But, Chloe, you cannot intend to stay through this." For now the rain was falling fast, and the thunder rumbling nearer.

"I most certainly do." Chloe's look of white determination carried even more conviction than her words.

Camilla shrugged. "Very well, then. But I tell you it is madness. Mr. Smith is doubtless at the rendezvous now."

"I do not believe it." Once again they fell silent. Huddled together, they yet felt strange little currents of hostility playing between them as the rain began to penetrate their shelter. A large drop fell on Edward's nose and he woke with a cry as forked lightning slashed to the ground dangerously near them.

Camilla was on her feet. "Now I am going, Chloe."

Chloe was up too. "Listen," she said.

They stood, for a moment, silent in the teeming rain, and then Camilla, too, heard the terrified braying of a mule nearby. Her hand found Chloe's. "It cannot be," she said.

"It is," said Chloe.

A few moments later, Mr. Smith entered the clearing, riding a drenched mule and leading two others. "Thank God," was his greeting. "I hoped the storm would prevent you from knowing how late I was. Now, we must lose no time. You have slept, I hope."

"Yes." Like him, Chloe was oddly matter-of-fact.

"Good. Then up you go." He helped them to mount and led the way, without further words, out of the little clearing.

The rain teemed down, the thunder roared, the lightning flashed, and Mr. Smith rode on ahead as unconcernedly as if he had been in the Mall. Only, once, he turned to shout back, as always, in Portuguese, and with the flashing white grin they had come to know so well: "This is luck for us. No one but lunatics will be abroad tonight. We will risk taking the shortest way."

So once more it was nightmare on mule-back. The girls were drenched to the skin and so, despite Camilla's best efforts, was little Edward and howling resentfully as a result. But his cries were lost in the roaring of the wind and the fitful crash of thunder. There was no question of stopping; they rode on doggedly through the storm while its darkness was swallowed in that of night. At last, when they could hardly see Mr. Smith riding ahead of them, he paused to let them catch up.

"It is the next valley," he said. "One more hill, and we are there. Keep close behind me, and let the mules find their own way."

In single file, drenched and numbed beyond thought, they made the last climb and the even more precipitous descent into the valley of their rendezvous. There they found Mr. Smith, who had drawn slightly ahead during the descent, busy looking for dry bits of undergrowth. "It will be a pity," he remarked calmly as they drew up, "if I cannot light the signal fire." But even as he spoke he had it going, its flames crackling up in defiance of the slackening rain. "Watch," he said to the girls. "Watch the sea as if your lives depended on it."

"I collect they do," said Chloe, and then, "Look, there!"

And indeed far out to sea an answering flash had shown for an instant, then vanished. Once more it showed, and then again, before Mr. Smith extinguished his own fire. "No use calling more attention to ourselves than we must," he said. "Now it is but to wait."

"How long will it take?" Camilla asked.

"For them to get here? Some time, I fear, in this storm."

And indeed it was a long, cold, desperate wait before they heard the sound of muffled oars and a boat pulled into the tiny harbour. Mr. Smith had warned the two girls to lie low until he had explained their presence to its occupants and now he went down alone to meet it. There was a brief colloquy and then he returned to fetch them. "All's well," he said, with his usual calm. And then, "Come."

CHAPTER 12

Cold, drenched, and exhausted, the two girls were hauled aboard His Majesty's frigate *Indomitable* more dead than alive, past caring about their bedraggled appearance. Conducted at once to a cabin that showed signs of having been hurriedly vacated, they collapsed on to its narrow beds pausing only to strip off their soaked outer garments and settle the baby in an open sea chest. For the time being, exhaustion was more powerful than hunger. All three of them slept heavily for the rest of the night, while outside the storm raged with increased vehemence. They woke to find the little cabin a swaying inferno and the next three days were a mere struggle to keep themselves and little Edward alive and unhurt. From above, they heard, from time to time, the sound of orders and hurrying feet as the ship battled her unsteady way through the gale. Their only communication with the outside world was through the tongue-tied sailor who appeared, at irregular intervals, with meals they did not want. Questioned, he bobbed shyly, said they were weathering the storm—he did not know where they were, or when they would reach England—and left them once more to their struggle for survival.

On the fourth day, the storm subsided, little Edward turned pink again, and Chloe began to fret about her clothes. "To think that we shall have to land in England like this." She shook out the skirts of her black peasant's dress, which had been shabby when she put it on and was now merely deplorable.

"Yes," Camilla agreed, "like two bumboat women—or worse. Still, better to land in rags than not at all, and I fear it is rags or nothing. It seems hardly likely that there will be anything on board that we can borrow."

Chloe laughed with something of her old light-heartedness. "I certainly do not intend going ashore in the full rig of a first lieutenant. Mr. Smith is luckier than we are. He is doubtless on deck this very moment, enjoying the sunshine in the guise of a rear admiral."

"Or a ship's cook," said practical Camilla. "Remember, Chloe, that we know nothing in the world about him."

"Except that he saved our lives," said Chloe.

They were interrupted by a tap at the door and their sailor attendant appeared with a beaming face, and breakfast, to announce that it was a fine morning, a calm sea, and they were three days out from Falmouth. "And," he concluded, "cap'n's compliments, and will you ladies dine with him and the dook tonight?"

"Him and what?" asked Camilla.

"The dook, ma'am ... His Grace, cap'n says we're to call 'un. Can't think why, though a prettier sailor I never wish to see ... been on his legs right through the storm, he has, and never so much as turned green—and eat! I wish you could a' seen 'im. Would a' et an 'orse, he said, when he come aboard, and blimy but I believe him, only we didn't have one 'andy." He made his customary awkward bob and left them.

Alone, the two girls exchanged glances. "A duke?" said Chloe.

"Mr. Smith?" said Camilla.

"It cannot be," said Chloe.

"Then who else?" asked Camilla.

"But what shall we wear?" wailed Chloe.

She spent the rest of the day trying to persuade Camilla that they should make an excuse to refuse the captain's invitation: they were tired, they could not leave the baby, anything ... But Camilla was firm. A captain's invitation, on his own ship, she said, was the equivalent of a royal command. There could be no question of refusing. As for their clothes—he must have known how they were circumstanced when he invited them. "It is but to carry the thing off with an air—and at least we have our jewels."

But Chloe remained rebellious and it was with the greatest difficulty that Camilla prevailed upon her to do what she could for her appearance. This was, admittedly, not a great deal, for the dye provided by the Prioress had proved all too efficacious a one. Repeated washings had merely reduced Chloe's golden hair from greasy black to dirty brown. Camilla sympathised but pointed out that at least Chloe's face was now clean, as were her own and the baby's. "And, besides, Mr. Smith—I mean the Duke—I wonder, by the by, what he is Duke *of*—has seen us looking much worse than this. And who cares about the captain?"

"I do," said Chloe crossly. "As for Mr. Smith, he has already made it clear that we were nothing but an incumbrance to him: I do not care if he is a royal duke—as indeed he might well be, from his manners, or lack of them."

"But hardly from his appearance," said Camilla. "Has it occurred to you that without his disguise he might be positively good-looking?"

"No," said Chloe, and began furiously to curl her sticky hair.

Even Camilla felt a slight sinking of the heart when they were ceremoniously ushered into the captain's cabin. If anything, she thought, her diamonds and Chloe's pearls merely added a final touch of absurdity to their appearance. But she held her head high and greeted the captain with all the ease of a great lady, while noting, with sinking heart, that he was in full dress uniform, and Mr. Smith, behind him, in impeccable evening attire, and looking, as she had forecast, deplorably handsome without his mask of dirt. His bows to her and Chloe, as the captain presented him as the Duke of Weston, carried the faintest hint of laughter, and Camilla, recollecting the awkward peasant's bobs he had made them in Portugal could not help laughing herself in sympathetic pleasure at the transformation. But she could feel Chloe bristling beside her, and hurried to mask an ominous silence on her sister's part by what she herself felt to be a slightly over-eloquent flow of gratitude. Mr. Smith—or rather the Duke—would have none of it.

"If I have helped to save your lives," he said, "you—or rather your charming sister—have most certainly reciprocated by saving mine." And he told the captain the story of their adventures on that desperate last night of their journey. Camilla, taking wine, first with the captain and then with the Duke, and listening to the Duke's praises of their fortitude on their long march, was soon in charity with both men, forgiving them what had seemed, at first, their quite odious elegance of appearance. But she looked in vain for a similar softening in Chloe, who continued to act what was almost a parody of a great lady. When the Duke drank her health and called her his preserver, she merely tossed her head and remarked that he had surely changed his tune: "I seem to remember that I was a foolish girl back in Portugal."

Camilla was appalled, but the Duke merely laughed and turned back to entertain the captain with a description of their first meeting and his manhandling by the French: "I can tell you," he concluded, "if these two ladies had not arrived when they did—and looking as they did—there would have been one dukedom the less in England."

Chloe raised elegant eyebrows. "Truly," she said. "Have you then no heir ready to step into your ducal shoes?"

"Why no," he turned back to her at once, "oddly enough, I have not; we Smiths have dwindled most deplorably off into the female line."

If Camilla had not been so fond of Chloe, she would have thought she snorted. "Deplorable indeed," she said, turned her shoulder to him, and began ostentatiously to ply the captain with questions about the state of things in England.

It was not a comfortable evening, and Camilla, for one, was heartily glad when it was over and she felt that it was politely possible to plead anxiety for little Edward (who was being minded by the tongue-tied sailor) and take their leave. Back in their cabin, she turned on Chloe to administer a well-earned reproof—but found herself forestalled. Chloe had subsided on her bed in a passion of tears.

They did not see either the captain or the Duke again before they reached Falmouth. Camilla, who was beginning to fret at the narrow confinement of their cabin, urged Chloe more than once to join her in a turn about the decks, but Chloe was adamant. Nothing, she said, would induce her to expose herself once more to the Duke's censorious eye. "Did you not see, Camilla, how he took in every detail of my—I mean our appearance? No doubt it will make an admirable tale for his friends at White's, just as our meeting provided food for the captain's mirth all evening. No, thank you, I shall stay below-decks and deprive him of more grist for his humorous mill." And so, since Camilla did not feel that she could properly venture up by herself, they all three stayed in their cramped cabin, Edward increasingly fretful for lack of fresh air, Camilla suffering for his discomfort, and Chloe in what seemed a permanent fit of the sullens.

It was, therefore, with the most profound relief that Camilla welcomed their arrival at Falmouth, although she

also found herself suffering, more even than she had expected, from the inevitable memories that green harbour roused
of the last time they had been there—with Lavenham. Her
eyes filled with tears as she looked across the harbour at the
little hotel on the hill where she had stayed, with Lavenham,
so newly her husband, the day before they had sailed for
Portugal. What mad hopes she had fostered then: Lavenham
would learn to love her; in the end they would be man and
wife indeed. Well—she shook herself and picked up little
Edward—they were, and he did not believe it—perhaps never
would. And she had before her the painful task of convincing
old Lady Leominster, perhaps in the teeth of her husband's
denial, that her child was indeed the heir Lady Leominster
wanted. It was not a happy prospect, and when Chloe, who
had been miserably silent all morning, opened her mouth to
complain at the prospect of going ashore looking like a couple
of women of the town—or worse—Camilla turned on her so
roundly that Chloe, shaken at last out of her private wretchedness, suddenly put her arms round her and kissed her. "Oh,
Camilla, I am a brute; it is worse for you than it is for me,
and I have been behaving like a bear. Forgive me."

In a flood of mutual, soothing tears, they forgave each
other, and then dried them because little Edward had caught
the infection and was screaming heartily in Camilla's arms.
Chloe took up the little bundle that contained their jewels
and they went up on deck to find the captain awaiting them.
The Duke, he told them, had gone ashore at first light and
was now on his way to London with his despatches. But he
had left his carriage behind for the use of Lady Leominster
and Lady Chloe. He begged that they would allow his servants to take them wherever they pleased.

"But how has he gone to London?" asked Chloe.

"On horseback," said the captain, "he said it would be
quicker so."

"Then he lied," said Chloe, with a return of her previous
bad temper.

But she had to admit that the lie was a very handy one for
them. They had no English money, and the prospect of
pawning their pearls, one by one, in order to pay for their
journey across England had not been pleasant. Now, they
were to travel in luxury, for the Duke's elderly and formidably respectable coachman made it clear that he was to be
responsible for all expenses on the way: "It is as much as my

place is worth, my lady," he explained, when Camilla began a protest. She yielded gratefully enough—it would be time to think of repaying the Duke when they were safe home—and even went so far as to suggest to Chloe that they might borrow enough from Mr. Banks, the coachman, to equip themselves in somewhat more suitable clothes for the journey. Oddly enough, it was Chloe, who had previously complained so bitterly about their tatterdemalion appearance, who now exclaimed, just as vehemently, against the very idea of borrowing any more from the Duke than strictest necessity demanded. "Do you, if you feel you must, Camilla, but I am too intolerably obligated to him already."

Camilla gave up the idea readily enough. She was too bone weary to care for the idea of shopping; little Edward was fretful from the long journey; the sooner they got home the better. And she soon discovered that Mr. Banks had had the fullest possible orders from his master. Not only did he manage not to show the least sign that there was anything odd about their appearance, he also always contrived an excuse to go ahead and announce their arrival at the wayside inns where they stopped. When they arrived, they found themselves greeted as heroines, and their odd appearance was forgotten in the glamour Mr. Banks contrived to cast around them. England, it seemed, was war-mad all of a sudden, and Spain's unexpected resistance to Bonaparte's tyranny the subject of universal enthusiasm.

"You must confess," Camilla remarked as they remounted the coach after a positively festive meal of the best of everything a little country inn had to offer, "that the Duke is well served."

"Of course he is," Chloe replied, "tyrants always are."

Camilla sighed, shrugged, and dropped the subject. If Chloe must persist in this unreasonable aversion to the Duke, she, for her part, had worries enough of her own to occupy her. They had decided to go straight to Haverford Hall. It would be time enough, after they had somewhat recovered their strength and, incidentally, refurbished their wardrobes, to face old Lady Leominster, to whom, inevitably, they would have to apply for funds. "Unless," remarked Chloe, momentarily forgetting her own preoccupations in concern for Camilla's, "we find Lavenham home before us. I cannot believe that he will stay long in the Brazils, ignorant, as he must be, whether we are alive or dead."

Now it was Camilla's turn to be unreasonable. "I do not see why not," she said. "After all, you know as well as I do that he has always put his duty before our welfare. And quite right, too," she added belatedly, and without entire conviction.

"Camilla, I do not think that quite fair of you," Chloe protested. "If you had but seen his anxiety when you were ill, you would think otherwise."

"It did not stop him going on board ship with Lord Strangford and leaving you to nurse me," said Camilla. "If he had stayed with us, we would never have got into this scrape."

"But no more should we, if I had not been such a fool as to trust your brother," pointed out Chloe.

It was a silencer for Camilla. The part played by Charles Boutet was not one she much liked to remember; monstrous to have reminded Chloe. She put out a hand: "Forgive me?"

"Of course. Camilla, do you realise we are almost there?" The milestones were beginning to carry familiar names, and to revive, for Camilla, painful memories of that hopeful journey on which she had set out, a lifetime ago, with her new husband at her side. Where was he now, and what did he think of her? Could he possibly believe that she had gone willingly with Charles? She was actually grateful to little Edward when he burst into the tears of total exhaustion and effectively distracted her from thoughts that were equally painful and useless.

When they drew up at last on the wide carriage sweep in front of Haverford Hall, the first shadows of night had fallen, and they were surprised to see that the entire front of the house was illuminated. Camilla clutched Chloe's hand: "*Someone* is there."

For a moment, her courage failed her. Suppose it was Lavenham, how would they meet? She had not spoken to him since that desperate day when he had hurled such furious accusations at her that she had fainted. And now, she was returning with his child in her arms, a child he had called a French spy's bastard. But Mr. Banks had beaten a resounding tattoo on the big front door and it now swung open, revealing the brilliantly lighted hall. Even in this moment of tension, Camilla found time to notice, as she carefully alighted from the carriage with Edward whimpering in her arms, that old Lady Leominster had been as good as her word:

the house shone with new paint, and the servants, who were hurriedly assembling in the hall, were resplendent in new liveries. What an odd contrast, she thought as she slowly mounted the steps, she and Chloe must present in their bedraggled black.

She forgot everything as an inner door opened and old Lady Leominster appeared. More bent, more wizened, and more brilliantly garbed than ever, she hurried forward, arms outstretched. "My dears." She gathered first Camilla, then Chloe into a highly perfumed embrace, paused for a quick, satisfied glance at little Edward, who had fallen silent in the dazzle of the lights, then urged them forward into the little drawing room from which she had come. "I know it all," she said, "I had a message from the Duke of Weston this morning and hurried here to have all ready for you. You are heroines, I collect, both of you, and the Duke your servant for life." Here a sharp glance, bristling with question, flashed from Camilla to Chloe and back, before she resumed: "And my grandson, I understand, a perfect paragon among babies. Tell me," to Camilla, "has he the Lavenham foot?"

"The what?" A long, involuntary tremor ran through her and she was glad to have Lady Leominster take Edward in fragile but surprisingly competent hands. Speechless, she looked on as the old lady deftly unwound his shawls, lifted the long dress to reveal his poor little webbed feet, and let out a long sigh of satisfaction. "Ahh," she said, "most satisfactory." And then, to Camilla, "But did no one tell you? Of course, Chloe was a child—she would not know—but Lavenham? Every boy in the family—since anyone can remember. It would have been—awkward, if you had come back with an heir born God knows how in Portugal and he had not had it . . . As it is, come here, my dear, and let me kiss you." But Camilla had burst into helpless tears.

Later, she told Lady Leominster the whole story, or as much as she could bear to, and received, in return, her promise of every possible assistance when Lavenham returned. "He will not be reasonable," said his grandmother, "he never was. But we must contrive to make him so." She had told Camilla already that Lavenham had asked for, and received, permission to return to England. She looked for his arrival daily. "But I am inclined to hope, my child, that it may be somewhat delayed. I would rather you had a little colour in your cheeks, and flesh on your bones, before we have to deal with him. And now, tell me," once again the large eyes flashed questions, "what is this about the Duke of Weston?"

"The Duke?" Camilla asked, puzzled. "Why, nothing, except that he has been most kind to us."

"Kind!" The old lady snorted. "I should just about think he has! Can you really be as ignorant—or as innocent—as you seem? Do you not know that the Duke who has been so 'kind' to you and Chloe has about as sharp a reputation as any young rakehell in town? Why, I have it on the best authority that when he took it into his head to go on this dangerous mission to Portugal his family let out a sigh of relief and secretly prayed that he would never come back. And you wish me to believe that he nurse—tended you and Chloe across the country—yes, and the baby too—out of pure philanthropy? And sent you home in his own coach—thought I grant you that is more in character, since he has always been known for his wild rides across country and was doubtless glad to get rid of coach and servants as a parcel of nuisances. But to take the trouble to send and tell me of your arrival—no, no, it must be for one of your sakes, and I only hope it is Chloe. Though come to that," the bright eyes snapped, "it might not be such a bad thing after all if Lavenham were to come home and find you pursued by the most notorious duke in town. But mind you do not let him catch you. I'll not have any of your Devonshire House goings on in my family."

Half angry, half amused, Camilla did her best to convince the old lady that she was far wide of the mark in her suspicions. The Duke had never showed the slightest partiality for either of them, she said, and had indeed tended all too obviously to treat them as the encumbrances they must have been to him. "Though," her natural fairness forced her to add, "he could not, in truth, have been kinder. He even carried little Edward much of the way."

"What!" exclaimed Lady Leominster. "Best not noise that around, if you wish him to remain your friend. But I begin to think I see—treated you as encumbrances, did he? No wonder Chloe is so out of charity with him. Well, I think we had best go to London at once."

Camilla, who pined for nothing more than a long rest in the peaceful, unfamiliar greenness of the English countryside, protested in vain. Lady Leominster had made her decision and nothing would shake her. There were, she pointed out, a few weeks left of the London season: it was of the most vital importance that Camilla should make her appearance in society at once. "I wish Lavenham to find you thoroughly established when he returns."

Camilla, who could not help seeing the good sense of this, merely asked, "And Chloe?"

"Chloe comes too," said the old lady. "She has been kept in the schoolroom long enough. And, besides, who knows what may come of it?"

Chloe, of course, was delighted with the idea of London and even Camilla became gradually reconciled to it after she had won a short sharp battle with Lady Leominster about Edward. His devoted great-grandmother had found a wet nurse for him and arranged for him to stay at Haverford Hall and was quite amazed when Camilla, fierce for once in her gentle life, sent the wet nurse packing and announced, once and for all, that where she went Edward went too. "If he inconveniences you, ma'am, it is but to open our own town house instead of staying with you."

That silenced Lady Leominster, who made no secret of the fact that she wanted both girls under her immediate eye during their first tricky weeks in society.

As it turned out, she need not have worried about their reception. London was Spain-mad. Bonnets, dances, military jackets ... everything had a Spanish name, and the two heroines from Portugal found themselves taken to society's heart. No breakfast was complete, no ball a total success unless they were present. The fact that Camilla either insisted on taking Edward with her, or left early in order to feed him, merely added to the glamour that surrounded her. Not only was she a heroine: she was the best kind of modern mother. It was all very exciting, and, after a while, rather boring, since Lady Leominster insisted on their accepting every suitable invitation, and as Chloe said, yawning, one hot July morning, one breakfast was really very like another, and each conversation the same as the last. "And if anyone else asks me if I do not adore the dear Duke of Weston, I vow I shall throw something."

"Yes," came Camilla, "I do not altogether blame him for beating a retreat from London and going to join Sir Arthur Wellesley in Ireland, though I own I could wish to have seen him and thanked him before he went."

Chloe tossed her head. "If he had wanted to be thanked," she said, "he could have stayed in London till we got here."

"Perhaps he will come back when Sir Arthur sails for Portugal," said Camilla, for Wellesley had been given command of the expeditionary force that was to sail from Cork, any day now, to the relief of the Portuguese, and ultimately the Spaniards.

"Much more likely he will go too," said Chloe crossly, and as it turned out she was right. When the news came that the British expeditionary force had sailed at last, they learned that Weston had gone too as an additional aide-de-camp. "I should think he would be of the greatest assistance to Sir Arthur," said Camilla. "Think how well he knows the country and the people."

"Yes," said Chloe, "I expect he has gone back to some black-haired girl in Lisbon."

"Very likely," said Camilla.

"Or several," said Chloe.

"Why not?" said Camilla, whose heart was increasingly heavy these days. It was all very well to be the toast of the town, but where was Lavenham? He had applied for leave to return and received it weeks ago. And still time dragged on and there was no word from him. The season had drooped to an end by now and Lady Leominster had agreed at last to the longed-for move back to Haverford Hall, since neither Camilla nor Chloe had showed the slightest enthusiasm for her suggestion that they should follow the *beau monde* to Brighton.

Their determination was amply justified when they reached Haverford Hall and found a letter from Lavenham awaiting his grandmother there. She read it quickly, with pursed lips and furrowed brow, then handed it, silently, to Camilla.

Chloe watched impatiently as Camilla in her turn struggled to decipher the fine, small handwriting of the letter, which had been many times redirected and, it seemed, at some time thoroughly soaked in water. "Well," she asked at last, "what does he say, Camilla? Where is he?"

Camilla handed her the letter with a hand that shook. "In Portugal," she said, "looking for us."

CHAPTER 13

Lavenham had reached Portugal only a week after his wife
and sister left. Landed secretly, at night, some distance north
of Lisbon, he had made, in reverse, almost the same journey
that they had, and had contrived, after lying low for a few
days, to get in touch at last with Dom Fernando. The news
he received from him was part good, part bad. At last he
knew that he had been right in his instinctive refusal to
believe that Camilla and Chloe had gone willingly with
Charles Boutet. Better still, he knew that they had escaped,
but of the end of their story Dom Fernando himself was
ignorant. He had learned, from his agents, of their near
capture by the French, but at that point his information
failed. They must hope, he said, that, since there was no
further news of them, they had succeeded in making contact
with the frigate and were now safely in England. "I only
hope your son survived the voyage."

"My son?"

"You did not know? Dona Camilla gave birth to a fine boy
while she was staying in my cottage. You have an heir,
senhor." He did not, being a kindly man, add, "I hope."

He hurried, however, to assure Lavenham that his wife
and sister had the best possible guide in the shape of "Mr.
Smith," a British agent of whose daring and ingenuity he had
heard amazing stories. "If anyone could get them home safe,
he would. But now, we must think of you. Lisbon is no place
for you these days. The French tyranny grows worse every
day; they know that a British landing is imminent and are
trying to terrorise us out of joining them. They are wasting
their efforts," he went on proudly. "I can tell you that when
your countrymen land the Portuguese will rise to a man.
There are rumours, which the French strenuously deny, that

169

Oporto is in a state of revolt already, and we only await the opportunity to follow their example. The Spaniards are not the only ones with courage to resist a tyrant. But in the meanwhile, we must think what we can do to hide you. I fear that I am the most dangerous of hosts. Charles Boutet is my sworn enemy and he is all in all with Junot these days—I will not dignify him with his title of Count of Abrantes." Once more, as he had done to Camilla, Dom Fernando explained the maddening impossibility of getting a boat out to the British squadron which still blockaded Lisbon harbour. They were talking in his house which overlooked the harbour and could see the lights of the British ships as they spoke, but, Dom Fernando said, to reach them, in the teeth of the French guard, was impossible. "No, my friend, you must await the English landing."

And so Lavenham spent a month of infuriating inactivity working as a gardener on Dom Fernando's estate in Sintra. He had much to think about. He had a son—or had he? As so often before, he tortured his brain in a hopeless effort to remember what had really happened that night when he rode wounded and exhausted home to Camilla. That obstinately, despite everything, he loved her he now admitted ... Could her story be true then? In that moment of light-headed exhaustion could he really have forgotten his long loathing of women? Surely incredible, if so, not to remember. And yet, if not he, who was the father? Something about Dom Fernando's reception of him had convinced him at least that suspicions in that direction were unjustified—shameful. Apologising, in his heart, to Dom Fernando, he let his circling suspicions range once more, until inevitably, they settled on Charles Boutet. All women were false. Suppose Chloe had been lying all the time to protect Camilla. And yet, all his instincts cried out against this explanation. In the teeth of everything, some instinct in him insisted his wife was innocent. The result, after some days of intolerable thought, was a dreadful hatred of Charles Boutet. Ignorant of his true relationship to Camilla, he came finally to the conclusion that, not content with making love to Chloe, the Frenchman must have seized some unguarded moment to rape Camilla. This explanation, at last, had the ring of possibility about it. It would explain everything except Camilla's lies to him ... If only (here he savagely cut away a whole swathe of baby grapes), if only she had told him the truth: he would have cared for her, protected her . . . He stopped and gazed, for a moment, in astonishment at the drooping vine leaves on the ground. He had come a long way from hating women.

That night one of Dom Fernando's servants rode out with the news that the British had landed at last, north of Lisbon, and been joined already by a Portuguese contingent. Helpless himself in Lisbon, Dom Fernando advised that Lavenham make his way north to join them, and, in the hope that he would succeed in doing so, sent him a packet of reports on the state of the French defences to be delivered to the British commander, Sir Arthur Wellesley. Delighted to have something to do at last, Lavenham set out at once but found the countryside alive with French troops, so that it took all his skill and knowledge of the district to avoid them through a day of arduous hill walking. By evening, he found himself on a little hill commanding a view of the British camp, but saw, to his dismay, a thin line of French outposts strung out between him and it. But there was no time to be cautious. Wellesley must have the papers tonight. He tucked them more securely into the secret pocket he had contrived in his rough peasant's jacket and started to make his way inch by inch down the hillside. He had memorised the positions of the different French pickets as best he could from his point of vantage, but as he worked his way along the winding bed of a little stream he soon found it hard to be sure exactly where he would encounter them. His progress grew slower and slower, with frequent pauses, in the gathering dusk, to look and listen for any clue as to the whereabouts of the enemy.

Just the same, he was almost upon them when a sentry's muttered curse made him shrink back among the bushes that grew along the stream. Watching and listening, he realised that the valley that had seemed so promising had, in fact, brought him directly towards French headquarters. Its sides were too precipitous to be climbed; there was not the slightest chance of going forward; he would have to retrace his steps to the head of the valley. It was dark, now, with only the promise of moonlight later, and it was lucky for him, as he felt his way back up the valley, that the attention of the French was concentrated in the other direction, towards the British lines. Otherwise, they must surely have heard him as he tore and fumbled his way, almost by feel alone, through the thick undergrowth.

Back once more on his hilltop, he had to admit to himself

that the position, for the time being, was hopeless. He would have to wait for first light and make another attempt at crossing the French lines then. Having decided this, he settled himself philosophically for a few hours of uncomfortable sleep. Waking with the first glimmerings of dawn, he was aware of a stirring of activity in the British camp. His hopes flared up at once. If they were preparing an attack, his chance of getting through to them, in the confusion of the fighting, would be enormously improved. Forcing himself to patience, he waited and watched, chewing meditatively on his last dry crust. He must know the direction of the attack before he set out to try and get through to the advancing forces. As the light gradually strengthened, and he was able to get a better view of the British and French positions, he found himself increasingly certain of what must be the direction of the British advance. Inevitably, before they could march towards Lisbon, they must dislodge the French from the little village of Brilos, which commanded the route they must take. If he stayed where he was, he would almost certainly be taken in the course of the day. He decided to stake everything on his interpretation of the British plan and set out for Brilos.

His best route, at first, took him back into the hills, and for a while the going was easy enough, with a thick screen of shrubbery masking him from the nearest French position. Both armies were awake now, and he could hear, in the clear morning air, the echoes of commands from the two camps. These sounds, with their suggestion of the comradeship of a soldier's life, intensified the loneliness and danger of his own position and he found himself, for a moment, near to despair. What was the use of going on? He was merely courting inevitable capture and death. And yet, what had he to live for? Camilla and Chloe were almost certainly dead, through his fault. How could he face England without them? He did not even want to. Strange to realise that Camilla had become the most important thing in his life. If she and her child should, by any miracle, have survived, he would forget everything and acknowledge the boy as his heir. The decision, towards which he had slowly been coming for several days, brought him an immense happiness and in its sudden glow he turned a corner too fast and walked straight into a French picket. Alerted by danger, he began to call furiously for an imaginary mule, pretended belatedly to see the Frenchmen, and demanded in peasant Portuguese whether they had seen an imp of Satan, in the form of a big wall-eyed mule, pass that way. With many curses he described how the beast had escaped him and began to hope, as they showed signs of tiring of his monologue, that they would let him go without question. But one of them, more alert than the others, interrupted him. "That is all very well," he said in French, "but we have orders to take in anyone we find for questioning."

His heart sinking, Lavenham pretended he did not understand, and the man turned impatiently from him to shout to one of his companions. "Here, you, François, you said you were cold. Here's an errand to warm you; take this cretin to Captain Boutet. It was he who wanted to examine all these *canaille* . . . let him have them."

For a moment, Lavenham wondered whether to make a dash for it, but decided his better chance lay in sticking to his character of an ignorant peasant and praying that the English attack would come soon. He knew this countryside pretty well, but not well enough to pose for long as a native. François tied his hands behind him and then drove him ahead of him down the little path that led to headquarters. Stumbling obediently along, Lavenham had much to think about. He was being taken to Captain Boutet. Could this possibly be Chloe's and, as he now thought, Camilla's betrayer? The long bitterness boiled within him and, if he could have escaped, he would not.

The question did not arise. Five minutes' uneventful walk brought them to the little farm that served as the French headquarters. Outside it, a slim figure in captain's uniform was standing drinking a beaker of coffee. Was this the same man he had seen, once, so indistinctly in the garden of the Marvila palace? Infuriatingly, he could not be sure, but stood, inwardly fuming, outwardly a picture of peasant stupidity while François described his capture in rapid, vulgar French.

Boutet listened impassively, then dismissed the man. He stood for a moment gazing thoughtfully at Lavenham, whose hands were still tied behind his back, then, carelessly fingering his pistol, he spoke, in English: "Welcome to our camp, my dear brother-in-law."

Lavenham could not believe his ears. "What?"

Boutet laughed. "So they never told you, the dear girls.

Well, to tell truth I rather wondered whether they would. Yes, my Lord Lavenham, I am your wife's brother, and hope soon to complete our delightful relationship by becoming your sister's husband. In the meanwhile, we must consider what use to make of your not altogether opportune appearance. You are searching, I collect, for my sister—and yours. You will not find them, though I might contrive a meeting once you have given your consent to my marriage to Chloe. It is not, by the way, a matter of the slightest moment to me whether I have it or not, but we French, as you know, treat family ties with a good deal more respect than you British seem to. Chloe will be grateful to marry me on whatever basis, but I for my part would prefer to do everything gracefully and in order. So come in, my dear brother-in-law, and give me your consent in writing." Still lightly touching his pistol, he gestured Lavenham ceremoniously into the main room of the little farmhouse.

Obeying in helpless silence, Lavenham thought he had never known despair before. Ever since he had talked with Dom Fernando, he had hoped against hope that Camilla and Chloe were safe home in England; now it seemed that they were in Boutet's hands, and Chloe dishonoured beyond repair. Anguish for her was mixed with a baffled questioning about Camilla. Boutet was her brother? Scoundrel though he clearly was, it was not possible that he was the father of her child. Tormented with new doubts—could it be Dom Fernando after all?—he hardly listened to what Boutet was saying but watched almost without interest as he produced paper and pen and began rapidly to write. "There," he said at last, "that I think should do it." He held up the paper for Lavenham to read. "We shall have to unbind your hands so that you may sign, but I trust you will not attempt to take advantage of it. My men are within call, and—they do not love the British overmuch." As he spoke, he had quickly untied the rope that held Lavenham's hands behind him, and now laid the paper on the table with his left hand and stood back, covering him with the pistol.

The paper was a brief and comprehensive statement of Lavenham's entire approval of Chloe's marriage with Boutet and a guarantee of his assistance (if such should be needed) in bringing it about.

"It will be best for everyone," said Boutet significantly, "if you sign without delay."

"I must see my, wife and sister first."

"Do you think so? How droll. But, first things first, my lord. I do not believe you would wish to see them as you might if you refused to sign."

The threat was all the worse for being so vague. Lavenham picked up the pen. "But how do I know you have them?" he asked, playing at once for information and for time.

"How do you know? Because I tell you so. Word of a Forêt."

"Oh?" Dryly. "I have had some experience of your father's word."

Boutet turned sallow with rage. "Enough of this. You will sign at once, or—you will regret it."

"Shall I?" Lavenham took up the pen again and shifted the paper a little on the table. If only something would distract Boutet for even a second, he might have a chance now that his hands were free. "How soon shall I see my wife and sister?"

"I said enough of this talk!" Boutet was interrupted by the sound of shots and shouting outside. It was the distraction for which Lavenham had prayed, and in the moment when Boutet's attention shifted, he swung the heavy table in his face, seized a sword from a pile of arms in the corner of the room, and leapt for the door.

Boutet was after him in an instant, with a shout of "Stop him," but, like Lavenham, he was distracted by what he saw. The British attack had begun in good earnest and the little detachment that had been based on the farmhouse were fighting for their lives. For the moment, Boutet's duties as commander outweighed personal thought and he was too busy shouting orders to his hard-pressed followers to spare more than a curse for Lavenham, who threw himself headlong into the thickest of the fray.

It was a risky enough action, since he wore the uniform of neither army, but his furious onslaught on the French rear did much to break their spirit. Imagining themselves surrounded, they broke and fled, leaving only Boutet and a few of his men still fighting furiously against the outnumbering British. Once more, Lavenham threw himself into the little knot of fighting men, his one idea, now, to preserve Boutet's life. He must learn from him where Camilla and Chloe were.

Most of the British had gone on in pursuit of the fleeing

French, but an officer and a few men were still engaged in hand-to-hand combat with Boutet and his followers. The result was a foregone conclusion. The French had never recovered from the first shock of surprise and, even as Lavenham ran up, all but Boutet had fallen or surrendered. The rest of the little English force was busy with the prisoners, while their officer was engaged in a furious sword fight with Boutet. Lavenham, waiting his chance to intervene, could not help admire the Frenchman's cold skill as a swordsman. As he watched, a skilful thrust disarmed the Englishman and another would have finished him, since none of his men was near enough to come to his assistance. But this was the moment Lavenham had been waiting for. His sword flashed out and sent Boutet's flying. "Surrender!" He spoke in English, and, quickly, to the officer, "I am English, though I may not seem so. It is of the greatest importance that this man live."

"Oh?" The English officer calmly retrieved his sword. "I should be inclined to say I did not see the necessity of it, but I owe you something; my life. I rather think; and you are welcome to his—if you want it." He gave a quick succession of orders to those of his men who had come running up. In a moment, Boutet was disarmed and bound. "And now," he held out his hand to Lavenham, "pray tell me to whom I am indebted for this most timely assistance?"

"My name is Lavenham." He was surprised to find his hand being furiously wrung.

"The lost Lord Leominster? My dear sir, this is a happier encounter than I had dreamed. I am Weston, and more at your service than I can say. But come, I am afraid my rascals may run into trouble if they follow the French too far."

"One moment." Lavenham turned to Boutet. If you wish to live," he said, "tell me where my wife and sister are."

Boutet spat. "Why should I?"

The Duke of Weston intervened. "Lady Leominster and Lady Chloe?" he asked. "What has this rascal been telling you of them? It is not long since I had the pleasure of escorting them to England. If his only usefulness lies in a pretended knowledge of their whereabouts, I suggest we dispose of him at once."

"Good God." Lavenham looked at Boutet with loathing. But, "No," he said, "favour me so far. Neither she nor I have much cause to love him, but he seems to be my wife's brother."

Weston whistled. "Lady Leominster's brother? How devilish inconvenient. We really do not want a brother-in-law in the hulks, do we?"

While Lavenham was digesting this startling remark, Weston gave a series of quick orders to his sergeant, and then, "So much for that," he said. "Will you give me the pleasure of your company while we round up these idiots of mine before they get themselves into real trouble?"

Horses were brought up and as they mounted Lavenham asked, "You said, 'We do not want a brother-in-law in the hulks'?"

"Why yes. I have been trying to forget Lady Chloe for the last six weeks, but I begin to think it would be simpler to marry her. With your permission, of course."

CHAPTER 14

In the end, Camilla and Chloe went to Brighton after all. It was much against Camilla's will, for she could not help a superstitious terror that by leaving Haverford Hall she might fail to receive some vital message from her husband. But in the country quiet that was to have refreshed her, Chloe pined so visibly from day to day that at last Camilla had to give in to old Lady Leominster's insistence that what they all needed was a touch of sea air and society. Everyone who was anyone was at Brighton courting the Prince of Wales, for who knew whether his father might not plunge finally into madness and leave him master of the country.

"Not that I care two straws about that," said the old lady robustly to Camilla, "but, frankly, I am anxious about your sister. If you ask me, she is pining for that young scapegrace of a duke, and it seems, unfortunately, as if he has forgotten that she so much as existed. The only cure I ever found for a broken heart was another one, and I suggest we take her to Brighton and see what we can do about it."

Having wrung reluctant agreement from Camilla and a listless acceptance of the plan from Chloe, she gave them no time to change their minds but went to work with a will to find them a suitable house in Brighton. This was no easy matter, since all the most eligible houses had been taken long since, and Camilla had just begun to hope that they would be able to stay at home after all, when Lady Leominster announced triumphantly, one morning, that her agents had secured her a charming house on the cliff above the town and that they were all to set out next day.

It proved indeed a delightful house, and though Lady Leominster's friends muttered gloomy warnings about the chances of being held up and robbed on one's way home at night, Camilla and Chloe liked its position somewhat out of the town, and the extent of grassy hill that stretched away behind it. Nor did they find themselves entirely immune to the delights of Brighton, particularly since they were welcomed even more enthusiastically here than they had been in London. Sir Arthur Wellesley had landed in Portugal by now and society talked of nothing but his position, his chances, and, inevitably, Portugal itself. Camilla and Chloe, who had actually been there, who had seen the country over which many a son and brother must now be marching, found themselves the objects of all attention, the centre of every conversation. So courted, so admired, so listened to, they found it impossible not to enjoy themselves a little. After all, when the Prince of Wales took the trouble to cross the room and talk to them, they must, inevitably, warm to him and to life in general.

Seeing them surrounded with would-be partners for the dance when they visited Brighton's Assembly Rooms, or listened to like oracles at one of the Prince's musical evenings at the Pavilion, Lady Leominster was almost alarmed at the success of the cure she had wrought. A superficial old creature herself, she had not the perception to realise that it was all on the surface. The only time of day when Camilla and Chloe really lived was when the mail came in. Mutually aware of this, they tacitly helped each other in a thousand dodges to ensure that they were always at home at this all-important moment, and as the hot August days wore on they found themselves closer friends than ever in their silent, shared anxiety.

They were at the Pavilion for an afternoon concert when the news of Wellesley's victory at Vimeiro began to be rumoured about. No one knew how the rumour had started, but as usual Camilla and Chloe found themselves the centre of an eager little crowd of enquirers. They had actually been to Vimeiro? What was it like? Would the terrain favour the English forces or the enemy? Were the French soldiers really such raw troops? Would the Portuguese come out strongly on the side of their old allies? Torn with anxieties of their own, the two girls nevertheless did their best to answer these questions, which themselves sprang from the terrors of many a mother and sister.

Presently Camilla looked about her. "But where is the Prince?"

"He retired, hurriedly, this half hour past or more," said one of Chloe's admirers. "Perhaps he has received despatches at last."

The questions continued, but Camilla and Chloe answered at random, their eyes and thoughts fixed on the entrance to the Prince's private apartments. One good lady was surprised to be told that Vimeiro was a thriving city (Camilla was thinking of Lisbon) and another that Lisbon was an insignificant village (Chloe, of course, had Vimeiro in mind). Both their thoughts were taken up with the same, all-important question. If the Prince had indeed retired to read the despatches describing the battle, would Lavenham—or the Duke—be mentioned? In some ways, Camilla's anguish was the greater. After all, Chloe knew that the Duke was in Sir Arthur's army. If he had been killed, it would certainly be reported, so that for her even silence would be good news. But all Camilla knew about Lavenham was that he had been landed north of Lisbon. He might have perished weeks since at the hands of the French. It was when she was thinking this that she told a particularly portentous dowager that the French were gallant allies, and the Portuguese raw troops.

The old lady raised her eyebrows and began an elaborately sardonic query, when Chloe interrupted her unceremoniously.

"Look," she said, "the Prince."

The door of the private apartments had been thrown open and the Prince appeared, his plump person magnificent as usual, with, behind him, two gentlemen in travelling dress. As he paused for a moment, looking about the room, Chloe caught Camilla's hand.

"It is," she said. And then, "Can it be?"

Camilla was chalk white. "Yes."

Followed by the two dusty and unsuitably garbed gentlemen, the Prince crossed the room to where Camilla and Chloe stood, holding hands for courage.

"My dear Lady Leominster, Lady Chloe." The Prince received their curtsies with his usual affable dignity. "I bring you, you see, the best of news. We have won a great victory. These gentlemen have but now brought me the despatches; they are covered with glory, as well as with dust; you will welcome them, I know, for my sake as well as their own."

And then, with the royal act of which he was sometimes capable, he turned away to answer the eager questions of the crowd, leaving Camilla and Chloe face to face with Laven-

ham and the Duke. It was a moment of almost unbearable
tension. Camilla had not seen her husband for almost a year;
Chloe had not seen the Duke since she had been so rude
to him on board the *Indomitable*. To make it worse, they
knew themselves the target of all eyes. Camilla, who had
tormented herself with imagined meetings with Lavenham,
had never conceived of anything so frightful as this.

He was kissing her hand: "At last," he said.

The Duke was kissing Chloe's. "If I dare?" His eyebrows
rose in a grimace reminiscent of Mr. Smith. And then, "My
dear Lady Chloe, allow me to congratulate you on being
once more a blonde."

"Oh, you are impossible," fumed Chloe. "Camilla, everyone is staring: let us go home."

"Yes," said Lavenham. "Let us indeed go home." He urged
the Duke to accompany them, but Weston refused. "You will
have much to say to each other. I will not risk Lady Chloe's
further displeasure by intruding myself on your reunion.
Besides, I intend to ride over, this evening, to visit my mother.
I will give myself the pleasure of calling upon you tomorrow
morning, if I may?"

The remark was addressed equally to Camilla and to
Chloe, but it was Chloe who answered, "Tomorrow morning?
Absurd! The Duchess lives clear at the other side of the
county." Then she coloured, furious with herself at having
betrayed too much knowledge.

He merely bowed, took her hand in farewell, and repeated, "I shall see you, I hope, betimes in the morning.
Though I can hardly hope to find you still sleeping as I did,
once, on our travels."

This reminder of the enforced intimacies of their journey
at once infuriated and silenced Chloe. Colouring up to her
exquisite eyebrows, she retrieved her hand, which he had
somehow managed to keep, and followed Lavenham and
Camilla from the room. Catching up with them, she broke
into angry speech. "I can see my grandmother was right. He
is nothing but an overgrown schoolboy after all. Ride across
country and back in a night, indeed! I have never heard of
anything so ridiculous."

"You would not have thought him ridiculous," said Lavenham mildly, "if you could have seen him on the field of
Vimeiro. He was mentioned in despatches, remember."

"And so were you," said Chloe, "and with more reason, I'll

be bound." She fell silent, gazing steadfastly away towards
the sea to conceal, Camilla suspected, the tears she could not
control. A strange, electric silence fell on the three of them as
they stood there, waiting for their carriage. There was so
much to say, but how to begin? Normally, Chloe might have
been relied on to plunge in with question and exclamation,
but today even she was silent. It was a relief to all of them
when their carriage appeared at last and the little bustle of
installing themselves provided a momentary slackening of the
tension.

As the carriage moved forward, Lavenham and Camilla
both began to speak at once, then fell silent, deferring to each
other. At last, Chloe laughed. "At this rate," she said, "we
shall arrive home without the slightest inkling of each other's
adventures and my grandmother will think us quite absurd.
Come, Lee, you begin: tell us what you have been doing,
racketing about in Portugal, and how you came to fall in
with that braggadocio Duke of Weston."

"Why, if you must know," he told her gravely, "we saved
each other's lives—and from a friend of yours, too, a Monsieur Boutet! . . ." And then, sparing her confusion, he turned
to Camilla. "My dear, why did you not tell me he was your
brother?"

The endearment, the affectionate tone of the question were
almost too much for Camilla. Swallowing tears, "I . . . I did
not dare," she stammered.

"Was I so formidable a husband? Truly, I have much to
answer for, and you much to forgive."

Unable to speak, Camilla was grateful when Chloe burst
in with a question. "You encountered Charles? And saved Weston's life? But, tell me, what did you do to Charles?"

"Why, that was Weston's affair, since he was in command
of the troops that rescued me and took Boutet prisoner."

"A prisoner?" Camilla breathed. "In England?"

"No, no," Lavenham took her hand, "do not distress yourself about him. I do not know exactly what instructions Weston
gave his men. I can only tell you that by the time we reached
the main body of the army, your brother had escaped."

Camilla breathed a heart-felt sigh of relief as Chloe spoke.
"Really, sometimes that duke shows glimmerings of sense."
And then, anxiously, "Lee, you did not tell him about Charles
and me?"

"Why, no. I did not think it my business. I merely told him

what Boutet himself had just told me, that he was my brother-in-law." He smiled to himself as he recollected the Duke's reaction, and Chloe teased him in vain to find out what had amused him.

The carriage had left the town by now and was rolling up the hill towards their house. When Chloe pointed it out, Lavenham pulled the check string and told the coachman to stop. "We have much to talk of, you and I," he said to Camilla. "Can I persuade you to walk the rest of the way with me?"

Panic seized her. She had counted on Lady Leominster's support at this crucial moment. But instinct answered for her, a faint, half-intelligible, "Yes."

The carriage had stopped. Lavenham jumped lightly down, held out his hand for Camilla, and apologised quickly to Chloe for leaving her. Then he gave Camilla his arm and led her away from the road to the grassy path that ran up over the cliff. The carriage rumbled away; they were alone with the voice of the sea below and the larks above. For a little while, these were the only sounds. Lavenham walked on in silence, and her quick, anxious upward glances showed him a little pale, a little forbidding. At last he spoke.

"You have a son," he said.

She stopped short. It was now or never. "*We* have a son."

He looked down at her, surely more kindly than she had expected. "That is your story still? I wish you would tell me the truth. I have tortured myself so, these long months, trying to understand, to believe ... But how can I? Only this I do believe, you were never, purposely, false to me. It is not in your nature— Only tell me what happened, what disaster befell you there, alone—and through my fault—in a strange land, and we'll speak no more if it. The child shall be my heir."

Too much moved for words, Camilla clung, for a moment, silently to his arm, searching vainly, in face of this extraordinary generosity, for the best way to tell him that the child was provably his. But, preoccupied with each other, they had approached the house without noticing, and now saw Lady Leominster and Chloe coming to greet them.

Lady Leominster took them quickly through the first greetings, her bright, observant eyes travelling, as she did so, from Lavenham to Camilla and back. Then, "But why do we linger here? You must be impatient to see your son, Lavenham. He is asleep, but I told the nurse to expect visitors." And, her bright eye fixing his, "He has the Lavenham foot. My poor Camilla was in despair till I explained it to her."

"I was nothing of the kind," said Camilla, maternal feeling conquering every other anxiety. "He is the most beautiful baby . . . " Her voice dwindled and died.

Lavenham had gone chalk white. There was a little silence, while Camilla trembled and Chloe looked, puzzled, from one to the other. At last Lavenham spoke. "If he has his mother's looks, to make up for his father's deformity, I am sure he is. Come, my love, take me to see him." And then, as they climbed the stairs, alone, for a moment, together, "You will forgive me, Camilla? Can you? Why did you not tell me?"

She pressed his hand. "I am glad I did not. I shall never forget your goodness. Thinking as you did, you would have acknowledged him just the same. But come, see—" They were at the nursery door.

Edward was sleeping with an infant's passionate intensity. Bending over him, Lavenham smiled. "I think I should have known him anyway."

"Yes. I have often thought he had something of your look of determination."

"You mean my damnable obstinacy? Well, thank God, with you for a mother, he will have a better upbringing than his father's. Do you know, I heard the other day, quite by chance, that my mother is dead."

"Oh." She did not know what to say.

"You will think it heartless, perhaps, but I cannot tell you what a relief it is to me." And then, in a rush, "Oh, Camilla, give me time, and I may be some kind of a husband to you yet."

"Of course." But little Edward, disturbed by their voices, rolled over and gave something between a yawn and a grunt. "Come," she said, "we shall wake him."

"He sounds just like a pig," said his father.

There was so much to be said, so many stories to be exchanged, that they all sat up till the small hours while Lavenham told of the hardships of the voyage to the Brazils ("But they were as nothing, compared to my anxiety for you."). And Camilla and Chloe, in return, described their rustication in the convent grounds and then their flight with "Mr. Smith."

"He seems devoted to you," ventured Lavenham at last.

"Oh, to Camilla, yes," answered Chloe. "As for me, he found me an unspeakable burden from first to last, and made no secret of it. But, Lee, you look dead—have you the migraine again?—as for me, I intend to be up and riding on the downs before breakfast."

"But the Duke is to call on us," Camilla reminded her, and then, forgetting the Duke at sight of Lavenham's pale and furrowed face, "Chloe is right; you have the migraine, Lavenham. I can see it."

"Yes, but at last, I have my wife, too, to soothe it away with her clever hands."

It was the signal for the party to break up. Conducting Lavenham to his room, Camilla paused for a moment at the door. "Do you really wish me to try and soothe away your headache?"

"If you are not too tired." There was something chilling about the formal phrase, and as she followed him into the room Camilla felt, with something like despair, that after all nothing had changed. They had slipped back, fatally, into the old intolerable position. She was still, after all that had passed, a figure in a farce, a wife and not a wife.

Lavenham closed the door behind her, removed his jacket, and lay down with a sigh of relief on the wide bed. Her thoughts in a rebellious turmoil, she began the familiar task of soothing away his pain. He lay quiet for a while, yielding himself to her ministration, then, suddenly, turned over and grasped her wrists.

"Is it possible that you can still love me? After all I have done to you?"

Too late, now, for pride and pretence. "How can I help it?" she said simply.

Slowly, tenderly, his hands were travelling up her arms to her bare shoulders. "You should have let the girl undress you," he said. "You will find me but an awkward lady's maid, but, oh, my love, if you can truly forgive me, I mean to be a good husband." His hands had found the fastenings of her dress now, but were indeed making but a bungled job of it.

"Let me." As their hands touched, her impatience matched his. There was the sound of tearing cloth, a little sigh of satisfaction (from him? from her?) as her dress fell, an empty shell on the floor, and he pulled her down on the bed beside him. His lips moved hungrily across her shoulder. "To think I could have forgotten," then, as she opened her mouth to speak, he closed it with his burning lips on hers.

The morning was gay with larks as Chloe rode up the downs behind the house, with only a groom in attendance. Her grandmother always breakfasted in bed and neither Camilla nor Lavenham had come down in time to prevent her escape. Now, taking great breaths of cool, salt-flavoured air, she set her horse to a gallop, congratulating herself on having got clean away from them all. It had been easy enough to see, last night, that Camilla and Lavenham were set for a reconciliation and domestic bliss, but how could she endure to share it? They treated her as a child—and all of them had apparently forgotten that today was her eighteenth birthday. They should be congratulating her on being grown up at last, but they were too much occupied with their own affairs. And why not? she asked herself bitterly. All she had done with her life so far was make a fool of herself, first over the music master, then over Charles Boutet. It was no wonder her family had little patience or thought for her . . . And now . . . But she would not let herself think of her newest folly, the madness of loving the Duke, who cared more for his old mother than for her. She put her horse once more to the gallop, leaving her grumbling groom far behind.

Drawing up at last, breathless, on the hilltop, she found herself looking down on the house from which she had come, and saw the figure of a horseman ride out of the gate and turn up the long slope towards her. At once she turned her horse's head away and started at a steady canter down the further slope of the hill. Absurd to imagine that the solitary rider might be the Duke, but intolerable, if it should happen to be, that he should think she had expected him to follow her. She urged on her horse with foot and voice, but it was tiring now and responded only sluggishly to her encouragement. And suddenly, illogically, she was sure that the lone horseman was indeed the Duke come in search of her, having discovered at last to what an extent she had been compromised by that journey across Portugal. She was a romantic heroine—no doubt about that—but one, it had been gradually borne in upon her, not in the very best of taste. Camilla, overwrought with anxiety on Lavenham's account, had failed to notice the faint, delicate overtones with which society had contrived to indicate that while it was one thing for a married lady and her infant son to escape, glamorously, across Portugal with an eligible Duke, it was quite something else again for an unmarried girl about whose name some faint grey hint of scandal already clung.

Camilla had missed those slight, almost imperceptible withdrawings of rustling skirts, but Chloe had felt every one of them. Her heart sore already because of the Duke's disappearance first to Ireland and then to Portugal, she had been a helpless target for the gentlest, the subtlest and most intolerable of persecutions. The very admiration of her courage expressed by the ladies she met had contrived to carry in it a hint of shock, the suggestion, always implied, never outspoken, that they were glad it had not happened to them, or, worse still, to their daughters; the attentions of the young men who thronged around her had had a hint of freedom about them that she had found equally detestable and difficult to handle. This had been bad enough, but the thought that the Duke might become aware of it and feel himself in honour bound to offer her his hand was much worse. She looked back. The solitary horseman had reached the crest of the hill and caught up with her loitering groom. She saw them talk for a moment, then the groom, apparently dismissed, turned his horse back the way he had come, while the other figure, black and unrecognisable against the light, began to descend the hill towards her.

With a desperate kick of her heels, she contrived to urge her horse into an unwilling canter and then, at last, a gallop. No use; an occasional surreptitious glance over her shoulder showed her the figure behind steadily gaining and becoming, as he drew nearer, more and more unmistakably the Duke. Absurdly, illogically, she panicked, and her horse, sensing it, wheeled suddenly and started hell-for-leather for home. Its reins were caught in a grip of iron. "Good morning, Lady Chloe," said the Duke politely.

Short of breath, helpless, and furiously panting, she was aware that her hat had slipped to the back of her head, her cheeks were flushed, her hair, no doubt, all to pieces. His hands still held her horse's reins; helpless, she faced him. "Good morning, Your Grace."

"My Grace?" He raised his eyebrows. "We are very formal all of a sudden. You did not treat Mr. Smith with such courtesy."

"Nor did he me."

He laughed. *"Touché.* Will you ever forgive me, I wonder, for that journey? So long as we live, I believe you will be twitting me with the fact that when we first met you were a reluctant brunette."

"I cannot believe that it is a matter that will concern you greatly."

"No? Not to have my wife forever out of charity with me. You give me credit for greater fortitude than I possess."

"What did you say?"

He laughed. "At last I have contrived to startle you out of that society calm of yours. I said, 'my wife.' Surely you must know that we are beyond the social pale, you and I, if we do not marry? It is a regrettable truth, but if you do not make an honest man of me, I do not know how I am to face my devoted family—who have, by the by, been praying this age that I would die gloriously on the field of battle."

"I wish you had," she said furiously.

"Do you?" Very leisurely, he reached into the deep pocket of his riding coat, produced a piece of paper, and handed it to her. Her eyes huge with amazed indignation, she saw that it was a special licence for the marriage of His Grace the Duke of Weston with Lady Chloe Beatrice Sophronisba Lavenham, Spinster.

"You take things, surely, somewhat for granted," she managed. And then, "How did you know about the Sophronisba."

"Your guilty secret? Your brother told me, of course, when he consented to the match."

"Lavenham? Consented? I do not understand you, sir. My brother has said nothing to me of this."

"Naturally, since I asked him not to. I prefer to do my own wooing. Besides, he has had his own affairs to think of. We settled it all when we first met, in Portugal, and, being men, have not spoken of it since."

"In Portugal? You knew already what would be said?"

"I knew at last that I could not live without you. My good Chloe, why do you think I went away but to try and forget you, and why have I come back, but because I can't do it? Marriage has always been the thing of all others I meant to avoid. Do you seriously think that a little gossip would drive me into it? I shall be a deplorable husband: I shall drink and ride to hounds and probably beat you, but, I flatter myself, you will be as bad a wife. Do you not think we might make a fine cat and dog affair of it, you and I, and snap our fingers at society?"

She had sat, so far, frozen in her saddle, but now she could not help laughing. "It is a most moving proposal, sir, and I am grateful to you for your efforts to spare me the knowledge of its real motives. But it is no use. I know as well as you do that only consideration for my brother drives you to it. Well, rest easy, and tear up your licence, for I'd not have you if the gossip were ten times as loud."

"No?" He took the licence readily enough, but tucked it carefully back into his pocket, from which he produced a small leather box. "Then your birthday present is sadly wasted. Unless you wish to use it for your wedding with Charles Boutet."

He handed her the box and she could not help opening it and looking for one heart-wrung moment at the two rings that nestled there side by side, one a magnificent ruby, the other a plain gold band. She looked up at him. "I . . . I do not understand."

"You thought me a monster, did you not, to ride off so callously yesterday, but I had to fetch these. No Duke of Weston has been married without the ruby since the Conquest—or before, for all I know—and I look on marrying you as a desperate enough venture without risking a family curse."

She could not help laughing. "Your proposal, sir, is grossly flattering!"

"Is it not? Shall we not have a fine quarrelsome life of it, you and I?" He took her hand. "But it is your birthday. Let me give you joy." He slid the ruby ring on to her engagement finger. "If you call it joy to be engaged to a bully, which I know all too well is what you think me."

She looked up at him. "I . . . I do not know what to say. Are you *sure*?"

"Sure that I love you? Having fled you, from London to Ireland, and from Ireland to Portugal? I am back, my love, and you only lose time arguing, for I mean to have you." Suddenly, his arms were round her, his lips found hers. For a long time, peacefully, their horses grazed, heads down to the close turf.

"Well," he said at last, "am I still to destroy the licence and make my cousins happy?"

She turned her flushed face up to his. "I should be sorry to waste your trouble."

"Well, thank the Lord for that," was his surprising reply. "In that case, we must hurry. Mr. Fisher will have given us up long since."

"Mr. Fisher?"

"The Reverend Mr. Fisher, vicar of Hove, who has been waiting our coming this two hours past."

"You cannot be serious?" But she knew he was.

"Never more so. Why should society have the chance to whisper at our wedding? And why should I have to wait longer for you? Besides, I might change my mind, or you yours. The risk is too great." And he kissed her again to underline the remark.

Rising late, with the lethargy of pure happiness, Camilla was surprised to learn that Chloe had been out riding for more than two hours, and that the Duke of Weston had called and had ridden after her. When she reported this to Lavenham, he merely smiled. "They will return, no doubt, in their own good time."

Lady Leominster, however, when she came down, every hair and patch of rouge in place, was anxious and angry. "That child will shame us yet," she said, "mark my words but she will. To have run off again, and on her birthday, too."

"Her birthday?" Camilla exclaimed. "Oh, why did you not tell me?"

"I had other things to think about," said her husband.

At that point, their first caller was announced, and for the next hour they came in droves, full of congratulations, fuller still of questions. In the face of Camilla's and Lavenham's obvious happiness, questions were hardly in order, but Chloe's absence produced a plentiful crop. "Dear Lady Chloe ... such a romantic story ... such a pity the dear Duke is ... well ... you know ..."

Smiling, listening, answering, Camilla began, with growing horror, to realise what Chloe must have been going through. Anxiety gnawed at her. She looked to Lavenham for reassurance, but he, too, was deep in a babble of question and compliment which seemed to grow more and more strident as time passed and still Chloe did not appear. Camilla had been through despair and back again, had found Chloe's lifeless body at the foot of the cliff, or drifting with the tide, when a red-faced footman opened the doors of the room, cleared his throat to ensure silence, and announced, in stentorian tones, "Their Graces, the Duke and Duchess of Weston."

FAWCETT CREST BESTSELLERS

IN THE BEGINNING *Chaim Potok*	2-2980-7	$1.95
THE ASSASSINS *Joyce Carol Oates*	2-3000-7	$2.25
LORD OF THE FAR ISLAND *Victoria Holt*	2-2874-6	$1.95
REBEL HEIRESS *Jane Aiken Hodge*	2-2960-2	$1.75
CIRCUS *Alistair MacLean*	2-2875-4	$1.95
CSARDAS *Diane Pearson*	2-2885-1	$1.95
TARRINGTON CHASE *Sylvia Thorpe*	Q2843	$1.50
AMERICAN MADE *Shylah Boyd*	C2861	$1.95
THE GOLDEN MISTRESS *Basil Beyea*	C2862	$1.95
WHITTON'S FOLLY *Pamela Hill*	X2863	$1.75
WINNING THROUGH INTIMIDATION *Robert J. Ringer*	C2836	$1.95
THE HOUSE ON HAY HILL *Dorothy Eden*	X2839	$1.75
THE WITCH FROM THE SEA *Philippa Carr*	C2837	$1.95
THE MASSACRE AT FALL CREEK *Jessamyn West*	C2771	$1.95
EDEN *Julie Ellis*	X2772	$1.75
SPINDRIFT *Phyllis A. Whitney*	C2746	$1.95
HOPSCOTCH *Brian Garfield*	X2747	$1.75
THE ROMANCE OF ATLANTIS *Taylor Caldwell with Jess Stearn*	X2748	$1.75
A MONTH OF SUNDAYS *John Updike*	C2701	$1.95
CENTENNIAL *James A. Michener*	V2639	$2.75
LADY *Thomas Tryon*	C2592	$1.95